About the Author

Alan Frost is an experienced IT professional being a Fellow of the British Computer Society and a Chartered Engineer. He has spent his life moving technology forwards from punch cards to AI, but always knowing that the key constituent in any system is the liveware, the users.

Other books by Alan Frost:

Admiral Mustard Series
1. Beware The Brakendeth
2. Beware The Nothemy
3. Beware The Humans
4. Beware The Future
5. Beware The Empire
6. Beware The Past

Merlin Series
1. The Battles of Malvern
2. The Struggles of Malvern

Other
- Blind to the Consequences

The Struggles of Malvern

Book Two in the Merlin Series

Alan Frost

The Struggles of Malvern

Olympia Publishers
London

www.olympiapublishers.com
OLYMPIA PAPERBACK EDITION

A CIP catalogue record for this title is
available from the British Library.

ISBN: 978-1-80074-592-6

This is a work of fiction.
Names, characters, places and incidents originate from the writer's imagination.
Any resemblance to actual persons, living or dead, is purely coincidental.

First Published in 2023

Olympia Publishers
Tallis House
2 Tallis Street
London
EC4Y 0AB

Printed in Great Britain

Dedication

I dedicate this book to Vanessa, Peter and Sophia.

1
The Homecoming

Lady Malander rushed to meet Thomas, or should we call him Merlin? She hugged and kissed him as if they were close relatives who hadn't met in many years.

Thomas, 'Good Morning, my lady. So you remember?'

Lady Malander, 'Of course, all of the magicians remember everything. The good, the bad and the seriously unpleasant. The ones that died are still suffering from trauma.'

Thomas, 'But they must be pleased to be alive?'

Lady Malander, 'I'm not so sure. Some had moved on to a happier place and weren't so keen to come back. And time anomalies are very hard to get your head around. Lord Malander says he believes me regarding the Slimies and Galattermous, but there is no actual evidence to support what happened. And as far as everyone is concerned, it didn't happen.'

Thomas, 'But we know it did.'

Lady Malander, 'Did it? We know we had those experiences, but they have been wiped clean. They never happened.'

Thomas, 'They might be true for everyone else, but those experiences have shaped and changed us. I was a poor butcher boy with few cares in the world. Now I'm an experienced magician. I'm different.'

Lady Malander, 'You certainly are, but to the outside world, you are still a butcher boy, and Lord Malander, who treated you like a son, doesn't know you now.'

Thomas, 'I assumed that would be the case. That saddens me as I value both his friendship and his trust in me. He made me feel wanted and needed.'

Lady Malander, 'That's because you were, and his lordship does have the ability to generate loyalty amongst his colleagues and subordinates.'

Thomas, 'Will he see me?'

Lady Malander, 'Of course, but don't expect to see much friendship.

You are once again a complete stranger.'

Thomas, 'Does he want to know what happened?'

Lady Malander, 'Not really. I've told him what I know, but to him, it just doesn't seem real.'

Thomas, 'I can understand that.'

Lady Malander, 'Can I ask you a favour?'

Thomas, 'Of course, my Lady.'

Lady Malander, 'There are a couple of things that I want to be kept quiet. The first one is the pig incident. I don't want him to know that I was fucked by half the pigs in Malvern, and secondly, I haven't mentioned my pregnancy. Anyway, I think I was going to die during labour, so you probably saved my life.'

Thomas, 'Your secrets are safe with me, my lady. I'm not sure if you know, but I saw your body inside the pig. That's when I first met his lordship when I alerted him to your dilemma.'

Lady Malander, 'And then you saved me.'

Thomas, 'Yes, my Lady.'

Lady Malander, 'We were very lucky to find you. The whole world was lucky.'

Thomas, 'Thank you, my lady.'

Lady Malander, 'Now let's go and see his lordship.'

Thomas, 'Yes, my Lady. I must admit that I'm a bit nervous about seeing him.'

Lady Malander, 'You can't be after everything you have seen and done. By the way, he knows you as Thomas.' They walked up the stairs to his lordship's antechamber.

In the Manor House was a note:

> *The learned one is back,*
> *Never again a simple slack.*
> *But more an ace or a jack,*
> *Magic spells for him to crack.*

2
Lord Malander

Lady Malander, 'Can I introduce you to Thomas.'

Lord Malander, 'I understand that we know each other?'

Thomas, 'I certainly know you, my Lord, but as far as you are concerned, I'm just a butcher's boy.'

Lord Malander, 'I understand that you are not a butcher's boy any more?'

Thomas, 'I certainly was, my Lord, but circumstances have changed me.'

Lady Malander, 'It's more likely that necessity unleashed your hidden talents and those of your sister.'

Lord Malander, 'Show me one of your magical tricks.'

Lady Malander, 'That's unfair. Magic is not a game.'

Lord Malander, 'If he is as magical as you tell me he is, then let him show me.'

Thomas, 'What would you like me to do?'

Lord Malander, 'You choose.'

Thomas displayed a vision of the First Battle of Malvern, concentrating on the Gathering at Ledbury and the fighting at British Camp and the Wyche Cutting. It was the first time that his lordship had seen a Slimie.

Lord Malander, 'Show me more.'

Thomas displayed the epic battles near Cirencester and Gloucester and the flight of the remaining Slimies into the South Downs near Brighton.

Lord Malander, 'I had no idea.' He turned to his wife and said, 'I'm so sorry for not believing you fully. It's hard to accept that we have been through all that together, and I don't remember any of it.'

Lady Malander, 'I do understand, Alan. It's not your fault. But it's sad in a way because you were a hero. You were Commander-in-Chief of all the human forces. You were effectively King.'

Thomas, 'And a naturally gifted leader, my Lordship.'

Lord Malander, 'Thank you for saying that.'

Thomas, 'Never was a truer word spoken, my Lord.' Thomas displayed images of Lord Malander in action and also several examples of them working together. He wanted to avoid the fact that Lord Malander was killed in the final engagement against Galattermous.

Lord Malander, 'Thank you for those images, Thomas. It's hard to believe that it was me. And it clearly shows that we worked closely together. Lady Malander wants to appoint you as our Master Magician, and I now have no objections to that although you are still quite young.'

Thomas, 'Thank you, my Lord.'

Lady Malander, 'In that role, you will help me build an Academy of Mystic Arts, and get paid fair recompense.'

Thomas, 'Again?'

Lady Malander, 'Yes, Thomas.'

Thomas, 'Thank you, my Lady.'

Lord Malander, 'Before you go, is there any chance of showing me what the Citadel looked like.'

Thomas, 'Of course, my Lord.'

He displayed the magnificent towering Citadel, the local professional regiments marching, cannons in action, muskets, and daily life in Malvern.

Lord Malander, 'So many marvels. Perhaps we should put some of them into action?'

Hiding on the Lord's table was a note:

On Malvern Hills resides our Lord,
More than able with pen and sword,
The master of planning and the chessboard,
He bravely fought off the enemy horde.

3
Academy of Mystic Arts

Lady Malander walked Thomas across to the Academy building that he knew well to find his old friends— Lorrimore of Lendle, Lionel Wildheart and The Enchantress of Evermore. It was strange meeting people he had previously grieved for, but he didn't mention their deaths in case it was too distressing.

He had always fancied the Enchantress, but that was probably true of most men. There was something about her that was uniquely attractive. And that was it; she was attractive but not beautiful. She was tall and slender, elf-like, and utterly charming. Her smile could melt butter, her eyes twinkled, and her legs seemed to go on forever.

Thomas still felt that her name was totally inappropriate. As far as he was concerned, she wasn't a Betty. She was something else, something ethereal, something mystical and enchanting. He remembered that she offered to cure him of his virginity as if it was a disease. Well, Rachel had cured him of that disability. Tracking Rachel down was on his list of planned activities, although he knew that deep down, he was reluctant to see her again.

The Enchantress rushed to hug him. Through her flimsy gown, he could feel the curve of her hips and her unfettered breasts gently pushing against him. He swore that he could feel her nipples harden as they hugged.

The Enchantress of Evermore, 'Merlin, it is so good to see you.'

Thomas, 'I'm not sure if I'm Merlin in this world.'

The Enchantress of Evermore, 'You reek of Merlin now. You have more magical energy than anyone or anything I've ever come across.'

Thomas, 'And you are as lovely as ever.'

The Enchantress of Evermore, 'It looks like you don't need to be cured any more.'

Thomas, 'How do you know that I'm not a virgin?'

The Enchantress of Evermore, 'Your magic has changed from that of a child to a fully-fledged man. It's a shame, really, as I was looking forward to taking your virginity.'

Thomas, 'I never had the courage to make that visit.'

The Enchantress of Evermore, 'You were worried that you wouldn't measure up and whether you would get an erection or not.'

Thomas, 'How did you know?'

The Enchantress of Evermore, 'All men have those fears, especially when confronted with a sexually active older woman.'

Thomas, 'Well, I don't have those fears nowadays.'

The Enchantress of Evermore, 'Well, come around and let's see what you can do.'

Thomas, 'I will. I don't think you will be disappointed.'

The Enchantress of Evermore, 'We will see.' Betty had the ability to be a right sex-pot and totally terrifying at the same time.

Thomas hugged Lorrimore and Lionel with great enthusiasm, but he had no plans to have sex with them.

Lady Malander, 'Thomas, we need to track down your mystical friends, the ones that joined us before the time-reversal.'

Thomas, 'They are all making their way here now of their own accord.'

On the back of the academy door was a note:

Merlin goes back to school,
Always the jester, never the fool,
Our history used the ducking stool,
Now the mystic master of them all.

4

Lord Eleonar

Lord Eleonar of the High Order's command structure studied the map covering his division to see the full extent of the River Severn. His area of responsibility was Worcestershire. He had commanded a backwater for some time, but it looked like things were changing as the Severn was becoming hot news. The river entered the county just north of Tewkesbury and left near Kidderminster.

It appeared that ships were sailing up the Severn, landing at small towns, stealing anything valuable, murdering the men and kidnapping the women and children. The elders had instructed him to investigate.

He had forces at Malvern, Worcester, Pershore, Evesham and Kidderminster, although the bulk of the forces were at Malvern under Lord Malander's command. He had never had much time for Malander, partly because he was ambitious and partly because he had controversial views regarding military tactics and strategy. He would have replaced him years ago, but he was the son of the third elder.

But Lord Eleonar had to play the game. The elders held power and had organised the defence of Grand Britannica on a county basis. It had been designed to avoid the accumulation of too much power in one person. The elders feared the rise of a warlord that would challenge them, not that there had been an attempt at that for hundreds of years.

Lord Eleonar's position depended on the patronage of the elders. Therefore, Malander kept his command, but many would argue that he deserved it. He had introduced the concept of cavalry and mounted archers. He supported the use of regimental structures, detailed training of the troopers and full pay for professional soldiers.

Lord Eleonar sent a courier ordering Malander to investigate the situation regarding these invaders, but it was not to operate outside of Worcestershire. Strict county restrictions had to be adhered to.

5
Rachel

Thomas started his campaign to track Rachel down. He visited her parents, but they denied any knowledge of her. He could tell that they were telling the truth, but he could detect her essence, the spirit of her past. But it was faint, very faint.

He recalled their innocent love-making. Two virgins who knew nothing but had a shared lust. They practised on each other's bodies and swore eternal love. An eternal love that rapidly petered out when she partnered with the evil Galattermous. Thomas never saw it coming and even now found it difficult to believe. He loved her and 'knew' that she loved him, but that was clearly wrong.

Thomas's love for her turned to hatred, but as the days went by, it mellowed into anger and then into disinterest. Now he just wanted to track her down and bring her to justice, but technically she was now innocent of any crime.

Rachel was a naturally powerful wizard, almost as powerful as him and in certain aspects of the mystic arts even more powerful. She had either voluntarily turned to the dark side or was somehow forced to turn. No one knew and perhaps would never know, but the fact was that she was dangerous. It was important to both know her whereabouts and to determine what she was up to.

But she had disappeared and covered her tracks well. She didn't want to be found. Thomas had the whole academy scanning for her whereabouts, but there was no sign of her, but they could tell that she was there and that she was resisting their searches. In fact, anyone who searched was sent images of impending doom and despair. The more they searched, the worse the images. The weaker magicians were almost suicidal.

Little progress was being made, but Thomas wasn't going to give in.

But there was a note somewhere:

Tommy boy was back from hell,
From times too hard to foretell,
Did he hear his heart's death knell?
And to his love, he said farewell.

6
Elderberry Whine

The twelve elders were effectively the rulers of the land. They were the High Order which had been in place for more than forever because nobody was too sure how long forever was. Some would say that they had been effective as the land was at peace. Prosperity had improved, and reasonably just laws were in place.

However, others would say that Grand Britannica was in a state of inertia. Nothing had changed for centuries. The rich were still rich, and the poor were still very poor. But not poor enough to be destitute or starving. Everyone knew their place, and if they weren't sure, they would be told, and that was how the elders liked it.

There was little enforced sexism. Women were not the property of men. They could lead their own lives, and follow their own careers, and many actively fought in the Army, but generally, they didn't, and generally, they were home-makers. Over the centuries, women had become more and more subservient. The elders argued that it was the natural order of things, and that was how they liked it.

Government and defence were managed at the county level. Each county had a Lord Protector and then a military and civil head. They were given free rein to manage their jurisdiction within the constraints of the law. This effectively meant that each county was governed differently. The only way for the elders to issue a country-wide instruction was to change the law, and that was a complex and long-drawn process, and that was how the elders liked it.

In fact, no one could remember the last law change. So inertia led to more inertia, and that was how the elders liked it.

Despite everything, the elders were concerned about the increasing number of warlike incursions down the Eastern coast of Grand Britannica and also along the major river networks. The county structure made it difficult to get a clear national picture.

They had been discussing it for some months, but no action was taken. Given time it might go away, and once again, inertia ruled the day.

On a tree near the elders' residence was a note:

So the elders kept the law,
Another piece in the jigsaw,
Once they were held in awe,
Now they were the country's flaw.

7
Enchanting Times

The Enchantress of Evermore, 'I wondered when you would call.'

Thomas, 'You sound confident that I would.'

The Enchantress of Evermore, 'It's not every day you are offered fanny on a plate.'

Thomas, 'I'm assuming that it is a plate with consequences.'

The Enchantress of Evermore, 'There are always consequences.'

Thomas, 'And what would they be?'

The Enchantress of Evermore, 'I'm not called an enchantress for nothing.' Betty removed her gown to reveal her nudity. She was totally at home with it. She sat on a chair, parted her labia, and started pleasuring herself with her fingers.

Thomas, 'Is that part of your enchantment?'

The Enchantress of Evermore, 'No, this is just me getting ready for you to fuck me. Is it turning you on?' She knew it was because his body made no secret of his desire.

Thomas, 'You know that it is.'

The Enchantress of Evermore, 'Men are so easy to excite. How do you want me?'

Thomas, 'I will let you choose.'

The Enchantress of Evermore, 'I quite like the doggie or duck position. It gives you the opportunity to give me a good old thrusting.'

Thomas, 'Is that what you want?'

The Enchantress of Evermore, 'I like the man to be a man. He should fuck a woman as if his life depended on it.' Betty rested against the arms of the chair and bent over. Her breasts hung low, ready for attention. She wiggled her arse and presented her pussy in such a way that few men could resist.

And Thomas couldn't resist. He removed his tights, and his aching cock sprung free, rigid in its desire. He lined his penis up against Betty's vagina and entered her. He was conscious that he was following a path trodden by many before him.

But this wasn't real, or was it? His mind was in her mind. He suddenly knew Betty like he had never known anyone else before. He saw her beauty, her charm and the love that was in her heart for all of humanity. He could feel his cock thrusting away, but it was the mental aspect that was totally exhilarating.

His magic was mixing with hers. His soul was mixing with hers. Her love of life was awe-inspiring. He could see her entire life, everything; nothing was hidden. He could see her conception and her death. There were no words to explain the immensity of the experience. It was like a sun exploding in your head. It was like every sunset that had ever happened all at once. He knew that his cock was nearing orgasm, and he could see hers.

He didn't want an orgasm; he wanted this, whatever it was called to last forever. His orgasm was getting near, but she stopped it. And the fucking continued. The mental fireworks continued, and they flew through the sky and into space. They visited every star and every planet and every moon and every molecule. They lived forever and died a thousand times. And the fucking went on. He was now desperate to reach a climax, but she stopped it.

Then she was about to come, but Thomas stopped it. No one had ever done that before. It was her job to control him. He increased his thrusts to the point that her cunt could take no more. She shook with anticipation, and now she knew that he was playing with her. They danced and hugged and kissed, and the sensitivity of their bodies reached an all-time high, and he let them both come.

It was the mother of all orgasms. They were lucky to survive as the human body wasn't designed to handle that much concentrated pleasure. They both collapsed into a sweat-drenched heap of sleeping bodies and mental exhaustion.
The whole experience took but a few seconds, but they slept for hours.

There was always a note somewhere to be found:

Was it good or bad luck,
To be enchanted by a duck,
Or mentally moonstruck,
By a dammed good fuck?

8
Protecting the Severn

Lord Malander called a meeting of his archery captains. He had two squadrons of mounted archers who still saw themselves as infantry rather than cavalry. Most dismounted to fire their long-bows, but a few could do it on horse-back.

Lord Malander, 'Lord Eleonar has ordered us to investigate the attacks on the riverside villages along the Severn. Apparently, the villages have been robbed, the men were slaughtered, and the women and children have been kidnapped.'

Captain Mainstay, 'Do we know who did it?'

Lord Malander, 'No, it's all a bit sketchy. It appears that they sailed up the river. The village is then encircled, and every inhabitant is processed.'

Captain Mainstay, 'Sorry, my Lord, what do you been by processed?'

Lord Malander, 'The men are ritually murdered and then burnt on large stacks of hay. The women are raped and then kidnapped along with their children.'

Captain Bandolier, 'How do you know that the women were raped if there are no witnesses.'

Lord Malander, 'I've no idea. That is what was said on Lord Eleonar's note.'

Captain Mainstay, 'How many attacks have there been?'

Lord Malander, 'Again, I'm not sure, but the last place that was attacked was Tewkesbury.'

Captain Mainstay, 'Should we start our investigation there?'

Lord Malander, 'I've been categorically told not to leave Worcestershire, but we could easily cross the boundary by mistake, couldn't we?'

Captain Mainstay, 'It's very easily done.'

Lord Malander, 'My orders are as follows:

- Captain Mainstay to stray as suggested
- Captain Bandolier to check out Upton-Upon-Severn.'

Both captains replied, 'Yes, Sir.'

Lord Malander, 'You may engage the enemy unless you are seriously outnumbered.'

A note was found on an archer:

With their bow and quiver,
They would defend the mighty river,
From an evil foe, they would deliver,
And their enemies would cower and shiver.

9
Tewkesbury

Captain Mainstay had always liked Tewkesbury. It was a classic riverside town with the Cotswolds on one side and the Malverns on the other. It was fairly low-lying and suffered serious floods almost every year as it was sited where the River Avon joins the Severn. In fact, the floods added a beautiful, graceful ambience to the town.

The regular flooding had made the surrounding countryside exceptionally fertile. Tewkesbury had developed as a trading post and market town and had its own mop fairs. The merchants grew rich on the backs of the poor farmers, but they were the rules of the game.

Tewkesbury was not looking its best with mounds of still burning human flesh along the High Street. The Avon River was blood red from the slaughter of both humans and livestock. A good third of the houses had burnt down, and most windows and doors had been smashed open.

No one was found alive. There were a few dead men and women in the houses who had obviously put up a fight, and the invaders were too lazy to drag them outside. There were no enemy bodies and no sign of their vessels.

There wasn't much that Captain Mainstay could do, and he was conscious that he was in Gloucestershire, which was clearly outside of his jurisdiction. He decided to follow the river north and join up with Captain Bandolier at Upton. Some of his troopers were teary-eyed as they had never seen death before.

On a tree on the way into Tewkesbury was a note:

> *In Tewkesbury, there was no one alive,*
> *Not a single person did survive,*
> *The enemy killed all and did deprive,*
> *A market town of its hive.*

10
The Upton Blues

Captain Bandolier wasn't expecting a battle. He had never been in a battle before, but his training kicked in. He entered Upton from the north, following the river along to the High Street. It wasn't a big settlement having about a hundred houses.

It had a small riverside port used to transport agricultural produce up and down the river to Worcester and Gloucester. But strapped to the port's side were thirty-odd boats the like of which he had never seen before. They were low in the water with curved ends and a single large sail.

They had arrived too late to save the men who were already a burning heap of dead bodies, but they might be just in time to save the women who were being gang-raped.

Bandolier's men crept into position and started firing their arrows. Their accuracy was pretty good, but it was difficult as a lot of the women were in their way. The enemy quickly used the women as shields and slowly walked backwards to their ships. They then used other prisoners already in the boats as additional shields.

Whilst this was going on, Mainstay's squadron was following the path of the river. He was astounded to see an armada of ships coming his way. He had never seen anything like it. Black ships with large multi-coloured sails decorated with a variety of images. On-board were fierce-looking warriors in furs and horned helmets abusing numerous semi-naked women. Shields of many colours were arranged along each side of the ships.

Mainstay was considering sending a barrage of arrows at them, but the women would probably suffer the most, and arrows were far too valuable to waste.

11
Updating the Boss

Captains Mainstay and Bandolier returned to Malvern to update Lord Malander.

Lord Malander, 'Firstly, I would like to introduce you to Thomas the Merlin. He is our new Head of Mystical Arts. He knows both of you quite well.' Both the captains looked quite mystified, as this was the first time they had seen a Merlin, whatever that was.

Captain Mainstay, 'You have me at a loss.'

Lord Malander, 'It's a long and difficult story, but I'm hoping that Thomas will show you a vision.'

Thomas, 'Gentlemen, you were like brothers to me. We fought the Slimenest together, and then the whole world reverted back to a previous time.'

Captain Bandolier, 'That all sounds like humbug to me.'

Thomas, 'Let me show you.' He showed a vision of Major Bandolier fighting the Slimies near Cirencester and then another image of his archers using tanylip.

He then showed a vision of Mainstay during the Battle of Malvern, followed by another image of Mainstay offering his sword to his lordship and another where he was Governor-General of Wales.

Captain Bandolier, 'And you are saying that this actually happened. It's not just one of your magic tricks.'

Lord Malander, 'My wife and the other magicians can all verify the truth. They don't lose their memory during time anomalies like mere mortals.'

Captain Mainstay, 'So what is a time anomaly?'

Lord Malander, 'I suggest that you have a few drinks with Thomas later, and he will explain everything or nothing depending on your desire. Anyway, enough of that, update me.'

Captain Mainstay, 'I went to Tewkesbury to find that the town had been ransacked and depopulated. There were heaps of burning corpses but no women or children. I then proceeded northwards to join up with Captain Bandolier but then saw a fleet of aggressive-looking vessels travelling south. I have never seen ships like it before.'

Lord Malander, 'Can you draw one for us please.' He did, but still, no one recognised them.

Captain Bandolier, 'I had a similar experience. When I got to Upton, the men had already been killed, and the women were gang-raped.'

Lord Malander, 'Bastards. Did you manage to stop them?'

Captain Bandolier, 'No, my Lord. The invaders managed to retire to their ships with their captives. We couldn't fire all our arrows because of the risk of killing the women, and it wasn't long before we were low on arrows.'

Lord Malander, 'What is the arrow problem?'

Captain Bandolier, 'The men have to make their own arrows or pay someone else to make them. It is an expensive and time-consuming process making arrows.'

Lord Malander, 'Nonsense, they are only sticks with sharp points and some bird feathers. It can't be that difficult?'

Captain Bandolier, 'I think you will find that our archers would disagree.'

Lord Malander, 'Thank you, Captains, for the updates. I would like you to organise some regular patrols and place sentries along the Severn at strategic points. Perhaps have some warning fires linked to the guards on the hills. You are dismissed.'

Thomas, 'My Lord, I have a few ideas regarding arrows.'

Lord Malander, 'Tell me more.'

12
Further Enchantment

Thomas had to leave Betty fast asleep as he had a meeting with Lord Malander. When he got back, she was still fast asleep, and there was no sign of her waking. Thomas was getting worried and decided to wake her. But it is very hard to wake up a dead person.

Thomas was shocked to the bottom of his soul. What had he done? He left Betty as she was and walked to the manor to get Lady Malander. When he arrived, he was distraught and sobbing madly.

Lady Malander tried to calm him down, but it was almost impossible. She was frightened that he would have a seizure. Slowly he managed to regain control of his body and was at last in a position to explain.

Lady Malander was still cuddling him when she said, 'Tell me what happened?'

Thomas was almost too shy to say that they had sex as if Lady Malander had never encountered it before.

Lady Malander, 'Are you trying to tell me that you and Betty had sex?'

Thomas, 'Yes, and I feel terrible about it.'

Lady Malander, 'I'm surprised that you feel that way.'

Thomas, 'No, the sex was fabulous but did I kill her?'

Lady Malander, 'Sex doesn't usually kill people.'

Thomas, 'Sex with Betty was like a mystic experience. It was truly amazing.'

Lady Malander, 'I know I've made love to Betty many times.'

Thomas, 'But I thought you were happily married to your husband.'

Lady Malander, 'I am. This was years ago.'

Thomas, 'You don't seem surprised or even upset over her death.'

Lady Malander, 'I'm not. She was keen to move on, and as you know, she had once and was dragged back.'

Thomas, 'Are you suggesting that she committed suicide.'

Lady Malander, 'In a way, I am.'

Thomas, 'I don't understand.'

Lady Malander, 'None of us ever do.'

Thomas, 'So what killed her?'

Lady Malander, 'Your love. Your love allowed her to move on, but she will always be part of us.'

Thomas, 'I'm still confused.'

Lady Malander, 'One day, you will understand nirvana. It was her time. It was actually past her time. And she is sorry that you were the vessel that freed her.'

Thomas, 'So it was a good thing.'

Lady Malander, 'Yes, Thomas, it was a good thing.'

Thomas, 'But she was so young.'

Lady Malander, 'Was she?'

Thomas, 'What do you mean?'

Lady Malander, 'I've known her for six hundred years.'

Thomas, 'Can I ask how old you are?'

Lady Malander, 'A lady never divulges her age, but you can expect to live a long, long time.'

Near where she died, there was a note:

She was a wizard to adore,
A friendly smile, perhaps a whore,
Always a teacher and a mentor,
She will always be the Enchantress of Evermore.

13
Arrows

Lord Malander, 'So tell me about arrows.'

Thomas, 'To be honest, I don't know much about them.'

Lord Malander, 'But I thought that you had some ideas?'

Thomas, 'I do. I would like to suggest that we set-up a factory.'

Lord Malander, 'What on Earth is a factory?'

Thomas, 'It's a building where you manufacture items.'

Lord Malander, 'Why do we need a building?'

Thomas, 'Let me show you a vision of your gunpowder factory.' And he did.

Lord Malander, 'What is gunpowder?'

Thomas, 'It's a powder that is used to make explosions. I can show you later when we have the factory established.'

Lord Malander, 'So what is your plan?'

Thomas, 'That's put me on the spot. I would suggest the following:

- Build the factory
- Find some fletchers to take us through the arrow-making process
- Find a source of shafts
- Find a source of arrowheads
- Find a source of feathers
- Investigate possible production processes
- Test the manufactured arrows
- Go into production.'

Lord Malander, 'Can I leave the project to you?'

Thomas, 'I'm happy to help, but I would track down Clutterbuck or Staniforth. They were both experts.'

Lord Malander, 'I know Lindsey Clutterbuck. He is an ideal choice. I will get in touch with him. But we will still need your assistance.'

Thomas, 'Certainly my Lord. It is a start. The factory will also be used for other developments.'

Lord Malander, 'I'm pretty sure that Captain Bandolier will know quite a few fletchers. Thank you, Thomas.'

A fletcher found the following note:

The factory would be a new construction,
Leading to the fletcher's destruction,
Men will be taught and given instruction,
And the gods of production will be their seduction.

14
The Invasion

Lord Malander was having lunch with his father, who was the third elder and also the Duke of Mercia. He had never had a close relationship with his father, which was something he regretted. They were too similar, both men of action with little chit-chat.

However, Lord Malander had noticed that his father was showing him more respect. He wasn't sure if he deserved it or not, but it was welcomed.

Lord Malander, 'So how is my favourite father?' They laughed, and the duke poured out a glass of brandy for his only son.

Elder Three, 'Worried, angry, desperate, frustrated.'

Lord Malander, 'So much the same as usual then?'

Elder Three, 'Yes, but even more so. I need to update you.'

Lord Malander, 'Go on.'

Elder Three, 'We have been experiencing Viking attacks for two years now.'

Lord Malander, 'Vikings?'

Elder Three, 'Men from the north. Some people call them Norsemen. They are barbaric pirates that have raped and pillaged their way throughout Europe. Now it is our turn.'

Lord Malander, 'We have had some local attacks. We just didn't have a name for them.'

Elder Three, 'What do you mean local attacks?'

Lord Malander, 'Both Tewkesbury and Upton have been attacked. All of the men were slaughtered, and the women were raped and kidnapped.'

Elder Three, 'No one told me. That's just a few miles away.'

Lord Malander, 'I have men patrolling the Severn as we speak.'

Elder Three, 'This is far worse than I expected.'

Lord Malander, 'As I was requested by Lord Eleonar to investigate, I assumed that the elders knew.'

Elder Three, 'The Chief Elder might have known, but he keeps most of us in the dark.'

Lord Malander, 'So how bad is it?'

Elder Three, 'It's bad. At first, there were just raiding parties, which were mostly ignored. Then the size of the raids grew.'

Lord Malander, 'What did the Chief Elder do?'

Elder Three, 'He sent people to investigate. Then did nothing. There have been unfounded rumours that he is receiving some form of payment from the Norsemen.'

Lord Malander, 'What is he doing now?'

Elder Three, 'Very little, even though it looks like the Vikings have settled in parts of Yorkshire and are building up their forces.'

Lord Malander, 'That sounds like war.'

Elder Three, 'You are right. You need to prepare for it.'

Lord Malander, 'I don't have the funds.'

Elder Three, 'Take it from me. Don't worry about that. Start building a fighting force but don't shout about it.'

Lord Malander, 'I understand, Father. What do you plan to do?'

Elder Three, 'Stage a coup.'

Lord Malander, 'Please be careful.'

Elder Three, 'Of course.' Which clearly meant he wasn't going to.

A note was found in Malvern Link:

Who will stop the Viking horde?
With bow and arrow and trusty sword,
Who will take our armies forward?
Will it be our Malvern Lord?

15
War Council

Lord Malander called his first-ever War Council. The attendees were as follows:

- Captain Mainstay, Mounted Archers (On assignment from Worcester)
- Captain Bandolier, Mounted Archers
- Lieutenant Clutterbuck, Engineering
- Lord Hogsflesh, Scout
- Lieutenant Lambskin, Infantry
- Lieutenant Dragondale, Archers
- Thomas Merlin, Mystical Arts
- Lady Malander, Mystical Arts

Lord Malander, 'Welcome to our first War Council, although I understand that they were quite common in a previous life.' By now, most of the delegates knew of the far-fetched Slimie encounters.

Lord Malander, 'We now have a new threat: the Vikings. These are aggressive warriors from tribes in Scandinavia.'

Lieutenant Lambskin, 'Apologies, my Lord, but I've never heard of Scandavium.'

Lord Malander, 'They are from up north where the sun never shines in the winter, and the land is covered in ice.'

Lord Hogsflesh, 'That doesn't give them the right to come here and steal our women.'

Lieutenant Dragondale, 'I thought you had enough of your own.'

Lord Malander, 'Order, there are some important issues to discuss. Firstly, they have been raiding the Eastern coast of Grand Britannica for two years.'

Captain Mainstay, 'What action did the elders take?'

Lord Malander, 'Very little.'

Captain Mainstay, 'But that is just inviting further attacks.'

Lord Malander, 'That was clearly the case as the raiding parties have got steadily larger, and now it would appear that they have settled in parts of Yorkshire.

'My father believes that they are building up an Army. Consequently, he has ordered me to establish an effective fighting force as soon as possible. Funding will not be an issue.'

Captain Mainstay, 'Has he got approval for us to create an Army?'

Lord Malander, 'Probably not, but you know what my father is like. Anyway, I propose the following:

- Captains Mainstay and Bandolier will form regiments of Mounted Archers of at least a thousand men or women
- Lieutenant Dragondale, you are now a captain, and you will create a regiment of one thousand unmounted archers
- Lieutenant Lambskin, you are also now a captain, and you will create five infantry regiments of one thousand men and women
- Lieutenant Clutterbuck, you are also now a captain. Your factory must be brought on-line as soon as possible
- Lord Hogsflesh, please recruit as many spies and scouts as you need
- Thomas Merlin now is the time to build up your mystical arts team.

'Any questions?'

Captain Bandolier, 'Are you saying that these will be full-time, paid positions?'

Lord Malander, 'Yes, that is the case.'

Lord Hogsflesh, 'I thought that the elders were totally opposed to a standing Army.'

Lord Malander, 'They are but needs must. We are up against a formidable foe. I think that there is every chance that we have lost a large part of the country already, and we are not safe here.

'I also plan to build a strong, defensive citadel here.'

There was a lot of enthusiasm in the room.

Lord Malander, 'One last thing. It's going to be difficult to hide, but we need to keep this undercover for a while.'

It was supposed to be undercover, but there was a note:

Lord Malander creates his team,
Full of talent and self-esteem,
Bravery and courage were a theme,
Professional soldiers, now mainstream.

16
Making Shafts

Lord Malander, Captain Clutterbuck, Captain Bandolier, and Thomas watched three fletchers make arrows in their new empty factory. Each fletcher made their arrows using different techniques and different material, which wasn't that surprising as it was an art form. The factory approach would effectively de-skill it.

They identified that the following raw materials were needed:

- Straight shafts of varying lengths
- Arrowheads made from flint, metal, bone etc
- Feathers
- Gluing agent
- String
- Fire-making material

Some of the fletchers favoured bone arrowheads as they were cheaper, but metal heads were the most successful.

The first challenge was to find a source of shafts. There was general agreement that thin straight saplings or recently coppiced shoots made the best arrows. One of the fletchers was very keen on ash coppices and made it known to the others. It soon got into a bit of a brawl, but this was partly due to the solitary lives that most fletchers live. Typically, they exist deep in the forest where conversational skills were not in high demand.

Lord Malander, 'So what do you look for in a shaft?'

Fletcher one, 'Straightness, that is the most important factor.'

Fletcher two, 'I couldn't agree more. They have to be straight.'

Fletcher three, 'You don't want bends in them.'

Fletcher two, 'Bends are not good. Nor insect damage.'

Fletcher one, 'I always check for insect damage first.'

Fletcher three, 'If it had insect damage, but it was straight, I wouldn't pick it.'

Fletcher one, 'I always check the grain.'

Fletcher two, 'I've always said that a shaft should be straight, insect-free and have the grain in the right direction.'

Fletcher three, 'I've always said that as well.'

Fletcher one, 'Well, I'm not keen on knots or twists.'

Fletcher two, 'I've always said…'

Lord Malander, 'I think we got the gist. How thick should the shaft be?'

The fletchers all started making strange hand signals demonstrating sizes with their fingers. Well, the long and short of it seemed to be a quarter of an inch. Any smaller and an arrow would be too weak, and any larger, the arrow would be too heavy. But the fletchers kept making the point that arrows have to be designed for a specific bow, and a bow had to be designed for a specific person.

It was all a very skilled task. Thomas had to remind Lord Malander on a few occasions that it could and had to be de-skilled. A lot of arrows were going to be needed. Thomas also pointed out that they could grow trees specifically for shaft-making.

Lord Malander, 'What happens next?'

Fletcher one, 'Weathering.'

Fletcher two, 'Warming. '

Fletcher three, 'De-moisturising.'

Lord Malander, 'Well, that's all very clear.' It turned out that the shafts need some time to dry out. The actual time required varied on the time of the year, the type of wood selected and the art of the fletcher.

Captain Clutterbuck, 'We are going to need a drying shed. Gentlemen, what do you do next?'

Fletcher three, 'I call it trimming.'

Fletcher two, 'Do you mean de-knobbing?'

Fletcher one, 'I take the shaft and carefully cut off any offshoots and nubs to make it as smooth as I can. I then remove any bark. I might have to trim some of the rougher areas.'

Fletcher three, 'That's what I do.'

Fletcher two, 'And me.'

Lord Malander, 'Is that it?'

Fletcher one, 'No, no, no.'

Fletcher three, 'No, laddie, it certainly is not.'

Lord Malander, 'So what is next?'

Fletcher one, 'Most arrows are not straight, so we have to gently heat them and then press them straight.'

Fletcher two, 'A very skilled job.'

Fletcher three, 'Very skilled indeed.'

Lord Malander, 'I think I will call that a day for now. We will need to think about shaft management.'

Captain Clutterbuck, 'I've got quite a few ideas that I need to work on, but we are going to need someone to manage our stocks.'

Thomas, 'I would like to suggest Fay Mellondrop.'

Lord Malander, 'Why is that? Don't answer. I know what you are going to say.'

Captain Clutterbuck, 'Fay would be a good choice.'

The New factory had a note on the door:

The arrow needs to be straight,
But fletchers tended to stagnate,
Ahead lie plans to automate,
Because they failed to abdicate,
To the one that calls checkmate.

17
The Chief Elder Shafts us all

The High Order or the Council of Twelve Elders was a pure formality. It was really a vehicle for Chief Elder to do whatever he wanted. And what he wanted was for nothing to change, but then he had inadvertently initiated change because of his greed.

And what was worse was that he had no need for the gold bullion provided by the Vikings. It was supposed to help him ignore the odd coastal attack. But the attacks kept coming, and so did the bullion. Typically, he was getting twenty per cent of the take. He was finding it more and more difficult to hide his booty.

He just wished that he could find a way of escaping from the nightmare. The other councillors were getting more and more vocal. The Duke of Mercia was becoming a serious problem. And to be honest, you couldn't blame him as his land was threatened. He had to act; otherwise, his position would become untenable.

If he acted, then the Vikings would expose him. In fact, he was surprised that some of his assistants hadn't exposed him already. But as his wealth grew, so did theirs. His servants were now seriously rich men. He had to laugh the other day as some of the booty actually came from a property he owned in Tewkesbury. He had effectively robbed himself.

The Chief Elder knew that it couldn't carry on. His days were numbered. His options were limited: death by a Viking sword, a state execution, death by intrigue or suicide. There was the option of simply fleeing, but where would he go? He had lived a very long time, and he had no desire for it to end like this. His name and his family honour would be ruined for all eternity.

And to make it worse, there was a Council Meeting tomorrow. Normally they would be drab, tedious affairs where nothing was ever achieved. Just how he liked them, but the duke wouldn't have it any more. He would be stamping on the table demanding action. Perhaps eliminating the duke was the best way forward?

Perhaps eliminating the duke and his own servants was the best way forward? Perhaps exposing the duke as a traitor would work but would the Vikings go along with it? They might in order to get their way. But their way would eventually be the death of him. Even now, they didn't really need him any more.

His policy of doing nothing had always worked quite well, so he would see what tomorrow brought. Whatever happened, might force him down a particular route.

He didn't sleep very well. But then he hadn't slept very well for the last two hundred years.

Hidden in the treasure, there was a note:

It was an amazing sight to behold,
The tons of stolen Viking gold,
In exchange for a token foothold,
The country was no longer a stronghold.

Yorkshire was now the home of the cold,
Those Vikings, barbaric but so very bold,
The Elder welcomed them with a blindfold,
Is it too late, or is it a stranglehold?

18
The Magicians Meet

Slowly the magicians that had fought the Slimenest arrived at Malvern. They still remembered. They were all a bit pissed off that they had to repeat all of the work that they had done before: the building of the school for mystical arts, the laying down of ley lines and the creation of protective amulets.

Thomas was excited about seeing Robin, his sister. She had walked nearly sixty miles to get there. It was particularly tough on Herbert, her cat. They hugged each other, and she said, 'I'm sorry about Rachel and Betty.'

Thomas, 'How did you know about Betty?'

Robin, 'I was there with you.'

Thomas, 'You were there when I was fucking her?'

Robin, 'It was a lot more than a fuck. Sometimes men are so thick. It was her swansong, and you made it marvellous for her. How could you not know? Anyway, I'm so proud of you.'

Thomas had no idea what she was talking about. Robin had always been a lot smarter and more sensitive than him.

Robin, 'And what are you planning to do about Rachel?'

Thomas, 'What is there to do? I've no idea where she is.'

Robin, 'I know where she is. I broke her spell of concealment.'

Thomas, 'Where is she?'

Robin, 'Where would you least expect to find her?'

Thomas, 'Here?'

Robin, 'Good answer, try again.'

Thomas, 'I have no idea.'

Robin, 'Devil's Dyke.'

Thomas, 'Where the Slimenest fled?'

Robin, 'That very Devil's Dyke.'

Thomas, 'What is she doing there?'

Robin, 'I've no idea, but it won't be good news. If we don't eliminate her, she will grow into your ultimate nemesis.'

Thomas, 'We can't just kill her.'

Robin, 'Why not?'

Thomas, 'It's not what we do.'

Robin, 'It's not what you do, but she needs to be punished for her crimes.'

Thomas, 'But they didn't happen.'

Robin, 'Don't be naive. I have every intention of killing her. And it's not just me. Lots of the other magicians feel the same.'

Thomas, 'How do you know that?'

Robin, 'You are possibly the greatest wizard the world has ever known or will ever know, and you don't use your powers. Your colleagues are constantly talking to each other telepathically, but your mind is closed.'

Thomas, 'I like it that way.'

Found on Herbert's head, a note:

She's certainly a miss and not a mister,
That's my beautiful little sister,
She arrives in a storm, almost a twister,
But already, my tongue has a blister.

19
More Production News

Captain Clutterbuck, 'Good morning, gentlemen, and your lordship.' The three fletchers responded, but it was clear that they were nervous about what they were doing.

Lord Malander, 'Morning, Captain.'

Thomas, 'Morning, Lindsey.'

Captain Clutterbuck, 'Can I introduce you all to Fay.' The appropriate greetings were made.

Lord Malander, 'How are we doing on the shaft front?'

Captain Clutterbuck, 'Good progress is being made. Fay has found multiple sources of material, and we have got an elementary production line going.'

Lord Malander, 'Let's move on with the arrow-making process.'

Fletcher one, 'We need to add a head and a fletching.'

Lord Malander, 'What's a fletching?'

Fletcher one, 'It's the feathers.'

Lord Malander, 'Please continue.'

Fletcher one, 'In terms of the head, it could be just sharpened wood.'

Fletcher two, 'That's just about good enough for killing rabbits.'

Lord Malander, 'So obviously we need something more effective.'

Fletcher one, 'Absolutely, bone, flint or metal are the only options.'

Captain Clutterbuck, 'What's the norm?'

Fletcher two, 'It depends on price. You get what you pay for.'

Captain Clutterbuck, 'What's the most effective?'

Fletcher two, 'In terms of piercing ability, then the metal head is the best option.'

Captain Clutterbuck, 'How do you make the metal arrowheads?'

Fletcher two, 'We don't. We buy them in.'

Fay Mellondrop, 'I will need the contact details.'

Fletcher two, 'I can get you those.'

Fay Mellondrop, 'Thank you.'

Captain Clutterbuck, 'How Do you connect the head to the arrow?'

Fletcher two, 'I use sinew and some pine pitch resin. I make the resin by heating the pine sap and mixing it with small amounts of charcoal. I then attach the head to the shaft and wrap sinew around it to keep it in place.'

Fletcher one, 'I always chew the sinew to moisten it and make it sticky.'

Fletcher three, 'It's a bit of an art getting the head firmly attached to the shaft.'

Captain Clutterbuck, 'I think we need to investigate better ways of fitting metal heads to the shaft. Let's work on that for now. Later we can look at the fletching process.'

And then another note appeared:

Arrows will be made, I vow,
By hook or crook, but somehow,
Advanced production will endow,
If the Lord Malander does allow.

20
Deceit Detected

The meeting of the twelve elders was about to start when the Chief Elder stood up and said, 'There are some pressing matters that need my attention, so I have decided to postpone this meeting.'

Elder Three (Duke of Mercia), 'Fellow Elders, I don't see any reason why we can't continue in the absence of the Chief Elder.'

Chief Elder, 'But that is unprecedented.'

Elder Three, 'Does that matter?'

Chief Elder, 'But who will chair the meeting?'

Elder Three, 'I'm happy to volunteer my services.'

Chief Elder, 'But that is unprecedented.'

Elder Three, 'Does that matter?'

Chief Elder, 'But what if a resolution is made?'

Elder Three, 'Then it is made.'

Chief Elder, 'But that is unprecedented.'

Elder Three, 'Does that matter? We can't carry on with this conversation. I can't see any reason not to continue. It is absolutely critical that we discuss the Viking situation.'

Chief Elder, 'It's all in hand.'

Elder Three, 'In what way?'

Chief Elder, 'I can't discuss it now as I have pressing business.'

Elder Three, 'What can be more pressing than the Viking invasion?'

Elder Four, 'I agree. What are we doing about the Vikings?'

Elder Two, 'If the Chief Elder says that he has pressing business, then he has pressing business.'

Elder Three, 'That's fine, let him go and press his business. The rest of us need to discuss the Viking invasion.'

Chief Elder, 'It's not an invasion.'

Elder Three, 'What is it then?'

Chief Elder, 'They are just raids.'

Elder Three, 'What are we doing about the raids, and why is York under Viking control?'

Chief Elder, 'Who told you that?'

Elder Three, 'The Lord Protector of Yorkshire. He is outside. Shall I invite him in?'

Chief Elder, 'That won't be necessary.'

Elder Three, 'I think it is.' He sent his aide to request the Lord Protector's attendance.

Chief Elder, 'I object to this.'

Elder Three, 'I thought you were going due to pressing business.'

Lord Protector, 'Morning, honoured elders.'

Elder Three, 'Can you update us with the position in Yorkshire, please?'

Chief Elder, 'I forbid you to talk.'

Elder Three, 'Why would you do that?'

Chief Elder, 'Because it is unprecedented. He is not an elder.'

Elder Two, 'I have to agree with the Chief Elder.'

Elder Three, 'Would this have a bearing on the matter?'

Two guards dragged in one of the Chief Elder's servants. He had clearly been tortured.

Elder Three, 'What have you got to say?'

Servant, 'What do you want me to say?'

Elder Three, 'The truth.'

The servant stuttered and then blurted out, 'My Lord has been taking bribes from the Vikings.'

Elder Three, 'What proof do you have of this?'

Servant, 'I can take you to his treasury.'

Elder Three, 'Fellow elders, let's follow the servant and see what we find.' And they did. And what a horde they found.

Elder Three, 'Chief Elder, how do you explain this?'

Chief Elder, 'No comment.'

Elder Three, 'I demand an impeachment. I will accept a show of hands.'

It was ten to two. This had never happened before, and as there was no precedent, they weren't sure what to do.

21

The Lord Protector

The Chief Elder was taken away and incarcerated, and the Lord Protector of Yorkshire was asked to address the Council of Elders.

Elder Three, 'My apologies Lord Protector for that unfortunate interlude.'

Lord Protector, 'No problem, my Lord. That explains a lot.'

Elder Three, 'Please describe your current position.'

Lord Protector, 'Certainly my Lord. About two years ago, there were a series of coastal attacks by, at that time, an unknown foe. Whitby, Scarborough, Bridlington, Hull, and Middlesbrough were specific targets. Typically, the men were slaughtered in their thousands and burnt in large heaps, with some of the men still being alive. Quite often, their ears had been cut off.

'The women were kidnapped after being despicably abused. They were literally dragged onto brightly coloured longships and taken out to sea with whatever treasure the Vikings managed to extract. We had forces available to defend those towns, but we had strict instructions from the Chief Elder not to intervene.

'About a year ago, we noticed that some of the denuded coastal towns were being permanently inhabited by the Vikings, and they had even taken over some of the local farms. Once again, the Chief Elder expressly refused us permission to intervene. It just didn't make any sense to us. Our people were being murdered, and the Vikings were effectively invading our lands. The lack of any defensive counter-measures simply encouraged them to take what they wanted, and they did.

'Some of the locals attempted to mount a defence, but the barbarians crushed them, and the survivors were then hideously tortured. Their remains were left hanging from large poles. The women and children were then stripped and impaled. Along one road, there must have been three hundred victims stuck on stakes pushed through their rectums. They had

48

long, agonising deaths. And still, we were refused permission to intervene.

'Yorkshire is blessed or cursed with several substantial rivers, including the Ouse, Don, Humber, Derwent, and Tees. The Vikings have been using this river network to move inland. Nowhere is now safe in Yorkshire, and when York itself fell, then that was effectively the end of the county.'

Elder Three, 'How many Vikings are there in Yorkshire?'

Lord Protector, 'Without men on the ground, it is hard to be accurate, especially as reinforcements have been arriving on an almost daily basis. But I venture a figure of fifty thousand.'

Elder Three, 'That's not possible.'

Lord Protector, 'I'm afraid that it is my Lord. But there are several other invasion points.'

Elder Three, 'Where?'

Lord Protector, 'All along the Eastern Coast. I think you will find that even London has been threatened.'

Elder Three, 'What's the position of your troops?'

Lord Protector, 'Many were sent home as the Chief Elder banned their use, and I fear that they have been murdered. The core of my force is now in Lincolnshire, but the Lord Protector there has the same problem as me.'

Elder Three, 'You have my permission to defend Lincolnshire with the best of your abilities. Please inform your colleagues accordingly. In the meantime, we will formulate a new policy. Mark my words, we will not stand by and let murderous thugs take over our country.'

Lord Protector, 'That's excellent news, my Lord.'

A note was found in the Lord Protector's pocket:

Run, it is the Viking spectre,
Come to steal our women and nectar,
We can't defend due to the Elder defector,
Despite the wishes of the Lord Protector.

22
The Severn in Crisis

Lord Malander, 'Calm Down.'

Courier, 'Sorry, my Lord.'

Lord Malander, 'What is your message?'

Courier, 'The Vikings are attacking.'

Lord Malander, 'Whereabouts, are they?'

Courier, 'There are thousands, my Lord.'

Lord Malander, 'Calm Down, I beg you.'

Courier, 'Sorry again, my Lord, but they are coming. We have to flee.'

Lord Malander, 'Sit down, take a few deep breaths and slowly update me.'

He did as he was told.

Courier, 'Viking boats are in the Severn Estuary.'

Lord Malander, 'Are they coming upriver?'

Courier, 'Not yet, my Lord.'

Lord Malander, 'How many boats are there?'

Courier, 'About seven hundred, my Lord.'

Lord Malander, 'And do the Bristol and Gloucester garrisons know about them?'

Courier, 'Yes, my Lord.'

Lord Malander, 'Any idea how many individual Vikings we are talking about?'

Courier, 'There are forty to sixty men on each boat.'

Lord Malander, 'So a worst-case scenario would be forty-two thousand men.'

Courier, 'If you say so, my Lord. There is also a possibility that there were some Vikings already along the Severn.'

Lord Malander, 'When you say possibility, are you just guessing?'

Courier, 'Sorry, my Lord. There is a settlement of a few thousand.'

Lord Malander, 'That means that there is an infrastructure to support them. The invasion has already started.'

On the estuary was a note:

Once it was the Viking raider,
Now the longships have turned invader,
What we need is a British crusader,
To rescue us from our nadir.

23
A Military Quandary

The Duke of Mercia wandered into Lord Malander's study for a chat, which wasn't good timing as he was studying a rather poor map of the Severn Estuary.

Lord Malander, 'Morning, Father, how are you on this chilly but sunny day?'

Duke of Mercia, 'Not feeling that sunny, to be honest. In fact, I feel quite sick.'

Lord Malander, 'Can I get you something?'

Duke of Mercia, 'I don't mean that kind of sick. I mean the sort where a trusted friend and someone I had respected for a very long time does the dirty on you.'

Lord Malander, 'I did hear some rumours. Is it serious?'

Duke of Mercia, 'Serious? It's a fucking disaster.'

Lord Malander, 'Well, we can add another one to that. Tell me your problems, and then I will update you on mine.'

Duke of Mercia, 'Yorkshire has been lost to the Vikings because the Chief Elder was accepting bribes.'

Lord Malander, 'Never.'

Duke of Mercia, 'He fucking was. I've seen the horde of gold. Some of it is being returned to its rightful owners, but most will be given to you to fund your Army.'

Lord Malander, 'Can we not counter-attack?'

Duke of Mercia, 'With what? They have at least fifty thousand troops in Yorkshire, and they are settling.'

Lord Malander, 'What about the county forces?'

Duke of Mercia, 'It's going to take a while to get them organised. I wondered if you could help?'

Lord Malander, 'Not after I tell you about my problem.'

Duke of Mercia, 'Go on.'

Lord Malander, 'A messenger told me this morning that there is a fleet of seven hundred Viking ships in the Severn Estuary, plus some settlements nearby.'

Duke of Mercia, 'My God.'

Lord Malander, 'That is probably a force of forty-two thousand men. I doubt if I could rustle up twelve thousand from here. I need to find out what the Gloucestershire and Somerset forces can do.'

Duke of Mercia, 'If we are not careful, we will be surrounded.'

Lord Malander, 'I'm more than happy to help up north at a later date, but this fleet needs to be crushed. And crushed quickly.'

Duke of Mercia, 'In the meantime, can I borrow old hogsface?'

Lord Malander, 'Of course, my Lord.'

The duke found a note in his pocket:

> *Troubles for both father and son,*
> *Yorkshire has been over-run,*
> *The Severn's fight has just begun,*
> *What will happen in the long run?*

24
A Pig in a Blanket

The Duke of Mercia and Lord Hogsflesh decided to visit the Chief Elder in his cell.

Duke of Mercia, 'Morning Lord Manchester.'

Lord Manchester, 'Please address me as Chief Elder.'

Duke of Mercia, 'You are no longer Chief Elder.'

Lord Manchester, 'You have no right to do that.'

Duke of Mercia, 'I know, there is no precedent.'

Lord Manchester, 'You may laugh, but you will suffer later.'

Duke of Mercia, 'I doubt it as we are here to organise your heart attack.'

Lord Manchester, 'But I feel fine.'

Duke of Mercia, 'You won't with a dagger in your heart.'

Lord Manchester, 'You wouldn't dare.'

Duke of Mercia, 'We are here to revenge all those you have killed.'

Lord Manchester, 'I've not killed anyone.'

Duke of Mercia, 'You have killed hundreds of thousands by your inaction and your deceit and possibly lost us the country.'

Lord Manchester, 'You have no legal right.'

Duke of Mercia, 'You are right, but no one can predict a heart attack, especially at your age.'

Lord Manchester, 'I deserve a trial.'

Duke of Mercia, 'That may be the case.' The cell door was unlocked, and the two men entered. The Chief Elder cowered in the corner. Lord Hogsflesh had his dagger ready. He then poured raw alcohol onto the straw-covered floor.'

Duke of Mercia, 'I order you not to stab me.'

Lord Manchester, 'Fair enough, and the two men walked out, locking the door behind them.'

Lord Hogsflesh threw his dagger at the lit candle on the wall.

Unfortunately, it fell onto the alcohol-drenched straw, and unfortunately, it caught fire. And even more, unfortunately, the Chief Elder suffered an agonising death.

Lord Hogsflesh, 'That was all rather unfortunate.'

Duke of Mercia, 'You did everything you could to save him.'

Lord Hogsflesh, 'So I did.'

A note survived the fire:

The poor Elder was found in a fire,
There was not much left to admire,
It was a truly terrible way to expire,
Burnt alive in a funeral pyre.

25
Another War Council

Lord Malander called his second War Council. The attendees were as follows:

- Captain Mainstay, Mounted Archers
- Captain Bandolier, Mounted Archers
- Captain Clutterbuck, Engineering
- Lord Hogsflesh, Scout
- Captain Lambskin, Infantry
- Captain Dragondale, Archers
- Thomas Merlin, Mystical Arts
- Lady Malander, Mystical Arts

Lord Malander, 'Welcome to our second War Council. Since the last one, there have been a lot of developments.

'Firstly, the Chief Elder died a terrible death in a prison cell. But before you show any sympathy, you need to know that he had been caught taking bribes from the Vikings. He had deliberately stopped our forces confronting the enemy. Thousands, even hundreds of thousands, have died because of his greed.

'Secondly, my father is now Chief Elder, and extensive sums have been made available to support the development of the Malvern Army. It is go, go, go!

'And now for some seriously bad news. York has fallen to the Norsemen.'

Captain Mainstay, 'But that is effectively the capital of the north. Where was the defence?'

Lord Malander, 'Suppressed by the Chief Elder. They were ordered not to fight. They just watched their people being murdered and raped.'

Captain Mainstay, 'I wouldn't have stood by.'

Lord Malander, 'And nor would I. Anyway, York has fallen, and it is estimated that there are fifty thousand Vikings in Yorkshire. And they are settling.'

Captain Bandolier, 'We must march to the north's aid.'

Lord Malander, 'That would make sense except that there are forty-two thousand Vikings on the Severn Estuary.'

Captain Lambskin, 'That can't be true.'

Lord Malander, 'I'm afraid it is. There are seven hundred longships, and apparently, there are also some Viking settlements. We have no choice but to ignore the North at the moment. My father is going to focus on them.'

Captain Dragondale, 'So what is the plan?'

Lord Malander, 'My orders are as follows:

• Captains Mainstay and Bandolier will accelerate the formation of their regiments of Mounted Archers

• Captain Dragondale will accelerate the creation of a regiment of one thousand unmounted archers

• Captain Lambskin will accelerate the creation of five infantry regiments

• Captain Clutterbuck will bring the arrow-making factory on-board as soon as possible

• Lord Hogsflesh will talk to the Lord Protectors of Somerset and Gloucestershire to determine their situation. You must tell them the situation regarding the Chief Elder

• Thomas the Merlin will determine if the Vikings have any magical capabilities

• Captain Clutterbuck will build a castle at Upton-Upon-Severn

• Captain Clutterbuck will escalate the building of a citadel at Malvern

• Lord Hogsflesh will discuss the defence of Worcester with Lord Eleonar

• Captains Mainstay and Bandolier to increase the number of patrols

• All of you will prepare for war

'I will go through your reports at the next meeting.'

As usual, a note was found:

> *The team are keen to fight,*
> *The dreaded Viking blight,*
> *Lead by their valiant knight,*
> *On to glory in the limelight.*

26
Production Continues

Captain Clutterbuck, 'Good morning, gentlemen, and your lordship. This is probably our final meeting.'

Once again, the three fletchers, Thomas, Fay Mellondrop and Lord Malander, were with Captain Clutterbuck.

Captain Clutterbuck, 'Today we are going to cover the fletching process.'

Lord Malander, 'Before we start, how are things progressing?'

Captain Clutterbuck, 'Ignoring this last process, we are very confident that we can increase arrow production by at least four hundred per cent.'

Lord Malander, 'That's excellent news.'

Fletcher one, 'But what about our jobs?'

Lord Malander, 'There will be plenty of work for you here.'

Fletcher one, 'We like working in the open. We are not shed workers.'

Fletcher two, 'We want daylight and sunshine.'

Lord Malander, 'That might be the case, but we desperately need larger and more regular supplies of arrows.'

Fletcher one, 'But what you are doing ain't natural.'

Fletcher two, 'We won't show you the fletching process.'

Lord Malander, 'Then you can spend some time in jail, and you won't get your fee. I'm not joking.'

Fletcher one, 'Take some feathers and split them down the middle vein so that you have three or four similarly sized feather pieces. Then use some sinew to stick them in place. Once again, I chew the sinew to make it nice and sticky.

Fletcher two, 'I wrap the sinew around the base of each feather between ten and twenty times. Push some of the sinews through the feathers to get a tight fit.'

Fletcher three, 'Then you need a few nocks in the tail so that it can rest on your bowstring.'

Captain Clutterbuck, 'Now show us how you do it.'

The demonstration took place, and then the fletchers were off with money in their pockets.

Lord Malander, 'What do you think?'

Captain Clutterbuck, 'It's a very simple, archaic process. It's hard to believe that we didn't automate it before.'

Fay Mellondrop, 'My Lord, we will have the arrows you want, I guarantee it.' And his lordship believed her.

And strangely, from that day onwards, no one ever talked about a shortage of arrows.

They looked for the note and found it:

> *The factory-made arrow,*
> *Would be straight and narrow,*
> *It would hit the poor little sparrow,*
> *As if it was just like a wheelbarrow.*

Along with two more esoteric notes:

> *From our land built on straw,*
> *We laid in stone our practised law,*
> *Now we have finished the jigsaw,*
> *But along comes Danelaw.*

> *So on life's grand seesaw.*
> *Some march forward, others withdraw,*
> *What says the Dragon's claw?*
> *Are we once more the outlaw?*

27
Somerset

Lord Hogsflesh, 'Your lordship, I've met with the Lord Protectors of Somerset and Gloucestershire. Both are fully aware of the situation. In Somerset, they have troops along the riverside in case of any incursions. They are somewhat over-awed by the sheer size of the fleet. Because of the Severn's width in their county, they can't reach the enemy armada with arrows.

'The Severn narrows as it gets near Gloucester, and they have both sides of the river manned with longbowmen, but they are concerned about a possible attack on the city itself. The only good news is that the fleet is so large that they would have to stagger their journey up the Severn.'

Lord Malander, 'Have they got any plans for placing defensive boats on the river?'

Lord Hogsflesh, 'There has not been any mention of that.'

Lord Malander, 'Can you investigate how many boats there are between Gloucester and Worcester?'

Lord Hogsflesh, 'Of course, my Lord.'

Lord Malander, 'I'm thinking about fireships.'

Lord Hogsflesh, 'That's an excellent idea.'

Lord Malander, 'Take whoever you need and get it organised.'

Lord Hogsflesh, 'Yes, my Lord.'

Lord Malander, 'Have a chat with Captain Clutterbuck about having defences across the river. Could we use chains? Ask him if he could build temporary forts at strategic river points to house bowmen? Let's think riverine defence.'

Lord Hogsflesh, 'Yes, my Lord.'

Lord Malander, 'Sorry I've changed my mind. You do the fireship project, and I will talk to Lindsey.'

Lord Hogsflesh, 'Certainly, my Lord.'

Lord Malander sent an aide to track Captain Clutterbuck down. It wasn't long before the captain was with his lordship.

Lord Malander, 'Sorry to drag you away from your work.'

Captain Clutterbuck, 'It's not a problem, my Lord. I was at the factory. To be honest, Fay is doing most of the hard work. She is brilliant, naturally creative and a workaholic. I can't keep up with her. Her attention to detail is just extraordinary.'

Lord Malander, 'That's excellent news. It should free you up for another project.'

Captain Clutterbuck, 'That sounds interesting.'

Lord Malander, 'One can only assume that the Viking fleet will sail up the Severn.'

Captain Clutterbuck, 'It's a tricky river in that it has an enormously strong tidal flow and some deadly sands. A few times a year, it has a tidal wave called the Severn bore.'

Lord Malander, 'I've met a few bores in my life-time.'

Captain Clutterbuck, 'Me too.'

Lord Malander, 'Anyway, we need to find ways of stopping them. Lord Hogsflesh is investigating the use of fireships.'

Captain Clutterbuck, 'Excellent idea. I could certainly help him with that.'

Lord Malander, 'I have some other ideas that I would like you to consider.'

Captain Clutterbuck, 'Go on.'

Lord Malander, 'Firstly, could we put a chain across the river?'

Captain Clutterbuck, 'No reason why not. We would need secure fastenings at both ends.'

Lord Malander, 'Can you do it?'

Captain Clutterbuck, 'Yes, but we would have to ban all of our riverine travel.'

Captain Clutterbuck, 'Please go ahead.'

Lord Malander, 'I would also like to build a series of forts from which archers could fire into the river.'

Captain Clutterbuck, 'No problem, I can organise that. The only challenge is selecting the sites.'

Lord Malander, 'Lord Hogsflesh could assist you with that. Any other ideas?'

Captain Clutterbuck, 'That's probably enough for now. I'm going to need some more engineers.'

Lord Malander, 'Hire some more. Thomas recommended someone called Staniforth.'

Lord Malander found a note on the floor:

So is it good or bad luck?
To have a name like Clutterbuck,
For some, it's just a ruck in the muck,
While others feel quite awestruck.

28
Vikings on the Move

Lord Hogsflesh, 'My Lord, my men on British Camp have spotted the warning fires along the river. The Vikings are on their way?'

Lord Malander, 'Are the fireships ready?'

Lord Hogsflesh, 'Yes, my Lord. There are about four hundred of them full of combustible materials stored in Upton. The plan is that each one will be rowed until it is not safe to continue. Hopefully, the current will do the rest.'

Lord Malander, 'How do we decide when to release them?'

Lord Hogsflesh, 'We think that we should release two hundred at Tewkesbury, which should surprise the Vikings and hopefully confuse them and with some luck destroy some of their ships.

'We don't believe that it will put them off. Once they cross the border into Worcestershire, we plan to let the Vikings pass and then install the first chain to stop them from retreating. We will then release the second armada of fireships. Once that is done, we will install the second chain, effectively trapping them.

'Our forts are along that part of the river. They will pour flaming arrows into the boats. Then our troops will line up each side of the river to stop them disembarking.'

Lord Malander, 'It's quite a detailed plan.'

Lord Hogsflesh, 'Do I have your permission to go ahead?'

Lord Malander, 'You do, but I would like to discuss some aspects of the plan with Captains Mainstay, Bandolier and Lambskin.'

Lord Hogsflesh, 'I will go and get them.'

Lord Malander, 'Get Thomas as well.'

Lord Hogsflesh, 'Yes, my Lord.'

It wasn't long before all four arrived.

Lord Malander, 'Captain Mainstay, tell me what you plan to do.'

Captain Mainstay, 'We will ride to Upton, cross the bridge and guard the agreed eastern side of the River Severn. My archers and Captain Lambskin's infantry will attempt to stop any Vikings disembarking. We will use both conventional and flaming arrows.'

Lord Malander, 'What is your plan if they do manage to disembark? There are a lot of them, and they are experts at this.'

Captain Mainstay, 'I hadn't given that any thought, my Lord.'

Lord Malander, 'Captain Bandolier, what are your plans?'

Captain Bandolier, 'Much the same as Captain Mainstay except we will defend the western bank.'

Lord Malander, 'And what are your plans if the Vikings managed to disembark? They will outnumber you at least thirty to one.'

Captain Bandolier, 'We will run to the hills.'

Lord Malander, 'At least you have a plan. Captain Lambskin. What are your plans?'

Captain Lambskin, 'I will provide troops to support the archers on both sides of the river. And if the Vikings do disembark, then we will fight.'

Lord Malander, 'Then you will be massacred. They will have at least forty thousand brutal killers. If they manage to disembark in numbers, then you should flee. Obviously, the mounted archers have an advantage. They need to take at least one infantryman with them if a retreat is required.

'The retreating troops need a meeting point where they can reform. We need to consider evacuating the locals onto the hills. I assume that Captain Dragondale's troops will be defending Malvern?'

Lord Hogsflesh, 'That is right, my Lord.'

Lord Malander, 'We should also request support from Gloucestershire and Worcester. Thomas, what can you do to assist?'

Thomas, 'I could create a series of illusions.'

Lord Hogsflesh, 'What sort of illusions?'

Thomas, 'Almost anything you want. How about lightning. They might see that as a curse from Thor.'

Captain Lambskin, 'Who is Thor?'

Thomas, 'The leader of their gods is called Odin and Odin's son is the God of War. He fires lightning bolts.'

Lord Hogsflesh, 'They might see that as a good omen. I would prefer a wall of flames.'

Thomas, 'Then a wall of flames it will be.'

Lord Malander, 'In that case my orders are as follows:

- Lord Hogsflesh to manage the fireships and release them as per the plan
- Captain Mainstay to guard the west bank of the Severn
- Captain Bandolier to guard the east bank of the Severn
- Captain Lambskin to guard both banks
- Lord Hogsflesh to raise the chains
- Captain Dragondale to guard Malvern
- Lady Malander to organise the evacuation of the locals and the elders
- Thomas the Merlin to create flaming illusions
- If the Vikings disembark, then all forces will head towards the hills
- Mounted archers will take an infantryman with them
- Mounted archers will man the forts
- Lord Hogsflesh will issue the meeting point.'

They all confirmed their acceptance of the orders. Everyone got into position, and Lord Malander went to bed. He knew the benefits of a good night's sleep.

A note was waiting for them on the bank:

The plans were crafted for the prank,
Archers would guard the Severn bank,
We will kill them where the Viking fleet sank,
Great flames will terrify that are blank.

29
Up North

The Duke of Mercia had been voted in as the Chief Elder. There was no other choice; the duke made sure of that.

He moved his headquarters to Litchfield and called a meeting of the Lord Protectors. A plan was needed to defend the North and recapture lost lands, but as they met, the Vikings were on the march.

Lord Protector Lincolnshire, 'I believe that Lincoln is their next target.'

Lord Protector Durham, 'There are also forces marching on Durham.'

Lord Protector Northumbria, 'I have similar concerns.'

Duke of Mercia, 'Gentlemen, I've called this meeting to agree on the best way forward. The first thing we need to know is what resources we have at our disposal. I've put the following chart on the wall:

County	No of Troops
Cheshire	
County Durham	
Cumberland	
Derbyshire	
Lancashire	
Leicestershire	
Lincolnshire	
Northumberland	
Nottinghamshire	
Rutland	
Staffordshire	
Suffolk	
Westmorland	
Yorkshire	

'I would like each of you to take turns and fill it in. I need to know how many fighting troops that each county can muster. You need to be honest in your assessment as this is, without doubt, a life and death exercise. You will still maintain your position, but the above troops will be used to a create a professional Army under the command of a single general.'

Lord Protector Staffordshire, 'Can we ask who that will be?'

Duke of Mercia, 'Yes, his name is Earl Winterdom. He is preparing to take over command of all northern land forces in the next few weeks. In the meantime, please complete the chart.'

They took their time as it wasn't an easy question to answer. Each county had a mixture of full-time professionals and militia. There were also mercenaries, civil guards, police, gentlemen officers, private regiments, and every possible combination in between. They also knew that whatever figure they put down would be the figure they would be expected to provide.

The chart was completed:

County	No of Troops
Cheshire	9,900
County Durham	12,500
Cumberland	13,900
Derbyshire	22,400
Lancashire	27,900
Leicestershire	24,700
Lincolnshire	18,800
Northumberland	16,750
Nottinghamshire	19,000
Rutland	900
Staffordshire	25,800
Suffolk	22,000
Westmorland	11,800
Yorkshire	4,000
Total	230,350

Duke of Mercia, 'That is quite a considerable force. I would suggest that you have all underestimated your true county strength and the total figure is nearer three hundred thousand. What is hard to judge is the quality of these men, but we will find out.

'Please return to your counties and declare a "State of War". You will receive instructions shortly from General Winterdom regarding dispositions. Collect arms and provisions for a forthcoming battle.

'Please report all Viking troop movements to me as soon as possible. If you have to engage the enemy, you have my authority to do so but don't look for a fight until we have got our act together.'

A note was found stuck to the chart:

The duke tried to inspire,
Both loyal county and shire,
But poor Yorkshire was in the mire,
Destroyed by the Viking hellfire.

30
The Enchantress of Nomore

Thomas was still feeling guilty as they buried Betty, The Enchantress of Evermore. He thought that really it should be Nomore! He had accepted Lady Malander's view that Betty wanted to go, but that was not what Betty's soul was telling him.

They gently placed her body on the funeral pyre and lit it. Then the ear-piercing screams started, but they weren't coming from the body. They were coming from Thomas. He was more surprised than anyone. He even looked around to see who was making the noise and then realised that it was his mouth that was causing the screams.

Thomas had no control over his mouth. The screams just got louder and louder. It was terrifying. Clearly, someone was suffering unbelievable agony. And then it died down as the flames fully consumed the body.

Lady Malander, 'What have we done?'

Thomas, 'What do you mean?'

Lady Malander, 'We have killed Betty.'

Thomas, 'But she was already dead.'

Lady Malander, 'No, I see it now, but it's too late.'

Thomas, 'See what?'

Lady Malander, 'When you copulated, you captured her spirit in your body.'

Thomas, 'Where is it now?'

Lady Malander, 'Still inside you.'

Thomas, 'I can't sense her at all.'

Lady Malander, 'Gradually, you will.'

Thomas, 'So now her body has been burnt she can't go back?'

Lady Malander, 'That's correct and what is worse is that she felt her body burning. That's what the screams were about. She must have been in agony.'

Thomas, 'So what do we do now?'

Lady Malander, 'I think you are stuck with her until you can find a suitable body for her to transfer to.'

Thomas, 'That doesn't sound too likely.'

Lady Malander, 'I agree, and I guess that there is no point in carrying on with the memorial service.'

Thomas, 'I see what you mean.'

Lady Malander, 'I'm sorry that this happened, but no one knew.'

Thomas, 'So is it a curse or a blessing?'

Lady Malander, 'Probably a bit of both.'

Thomas, 'Thank you.'

On the charred remains, they found a note:

Merlin never planned to host,
His lover's bright eternal ghost,
Now it was stored innermost,
Like a constant mystical signpost.

31
Fireboats

They looked very pretty with the flames reflecting in the water. Lord Hogsflesh let the first two hundred fireships loose as the Vikings were approaching Tewksbury. They had already experienced a fairly tough time from the Gloucestershire forces.

Arrows had poured down on them for the last ten miles. The raiders were already complaining about aches and pains from holding their shields over their heads to protect themselves. Dead and seriously wounded Vikings were simply being thrown over-board. They weren't used to any resistance, especially from the cowardly Brits. They had been promised no resistance. This just wasn't playing the game.

And then things got worse for them. They had never experienced fireships before. The men who had been rowing and steering the ships jumped overboard and let the current take the fireships towards the longships. There were so many Viking boats that the fireships just couldn't miss.

The highly flammable materials onboard the fireships soon got the longships ablaze, and, as the Vikings tried to put the fires out, they were hit by volley after volley of arrows. And these were mostly from the Gloucestershire forces who had been following the Viking armada along the riverside.

A good third of the Viking fleet was soon ablaze, and the crews had to abandon the ship and wade ashore. Most were either hit by arrows or had their throats slashed as they clambered up the riverbank. Eventually, enough Vikings got ashore to engage the Gloucestershire forces in serious hand-to-hand combat. It was a fairly even match, but the Vikings didn't seem to be in the mood for an all-out fight and fled the field.

The surviving Viking longships, about four hundred in total, continued on their journey. They got more strung out as the river narrowed, which was perfect for the Worcestershire forces. Once the Viking fleet passed a point along the river about two miles from Ryall, the chain was pulled across. The second batch of fireships were released, and a second chain was stretched across the river nearer to Ryall.

Now it was the turn of the Worcestershire archers to inflict as much damage as possible. The Vikings had never seen mounted archers before. Nor had the Gloucestershire archers who were still pursuing the barbaric raiders.

The fireships effectively blockaded the river. The Viking boats that were brave enough to push their way through the inferno caught fire. The Worcestershire archers then fired flaming arrows at the rear of the Viking fleet, causing them to move forward. The front ships then hit the chain.

The Viking rowers' forward pressure caused the chain to act like a saw ripping the woodwork and the human crews to shreds. They tried to reverse row, but the upcoming ships just caused one collision after another.

Then it was Thomas's turn. There was an almighty loud cracking sound, and a wall of illusionary flame covered the entire river. It was quite terrifying for both sides, but those on the boats felt terribly vulnerable. The Viking ships that could go downstream did so, but they then hit the second chain, leading to a huge loss of ships and men.

Eventually, Captain Mainstay ordered Lord Hogsflesh to release the first chain so that the Vikings could escape. If the survivors all managed to clamber on shore, there would be far too many for the Worcestershire forces to handle. Obviously, the Vikings didn't know that and did the right thing and fled.

It was an outstanding victory of military planning and cunning. The Viking fleet had been effectively destroyed. There were large gangs of Vikings wandering around the countryside that had to be dealt with. Here the mounted archers were particularly effective as they could attack and then withdraw and then repeat the process.

Lord Malander couldn't believe how successful the operation had been. He knew that the Vikings wouldn't be such easy prey next time.

In the wreckage, there was a note:

The Viking fleet hit the chain,
For them, it was a great pain,
And many good men were slain,
But it wasn't the time to be humane.

32
More Vikings

Lord Hogsflesh, 'My Lord, I have some bad news.'

Lord Malander, 'But we have just had an outstanding victory.'

Lord Hogsflesh, 'Apparently that was a Viking settlement fleet. Half of the men onboard were farmers. There is another fleet in the estuary full of mean killers wanting revenge.'

Lord Malander, 'How many ships?'

Lord Hogsflesh, 'About two hundred.'

Lord Malander, 'That's still about fourteen thousand men.'

Lord Hogsflesh, 'You mean vicious killers bent on revenge.'

Lord Malander, 'What do you think their strategy will be?'

Lord Hogsflesh, 'Clearly, they will be a lot more cautious. I suspect they will sail up the Severn until they are within arrow distance, disembark and attack us cross-country.'

Lord Malander, 'Who will they attack?'

Lord Hogsflesh, 'Difficult one. They probably see us as the same enemy. Effectively they see us as one force.'

Lord Malander, 'That doesn't help much.'

Lord Hogsflesh, 'There is every chance that Ryall will be their target.'

Lord Malander, 'There's nothing much there, so they will probably go for Upton-Upon-Severn.'

Lord Hogsflesh, 'Regardless, we need a plan.'

Lord Malander, 'In that case, we will probably need another council meeting. Any news from up north?'

Lord Hogsflesh, 'It would appear that Winterdom is knocking the Army into shape.'

Lord Malander, 'He is a good man. A bit obvious in terms of tactics but solid. He lacks imagination, which you need with this type of enemy, but nevertheless very solid.'

33
More Power

Lord Malander didn't fancy the journey to Litchfield. He always ended up with a massive arse and backache, but he needed more power.

Lord Malander, 'Evening, Father, how is it going?'

Duke of Mercia, 'It's not easy trying to create one unified force. For centuries we elders had maintained a county structure, and I guess that it kept the peace. Power was decentralised, but it also meant that each county did things their own way. Now there is a lot of in-fighting and internal power struggles, but I'm knocking heads together and winning.'

Lord Malander, 'Well, you are good at head-knocking.'

Duke of Mercia, 'Anyway, I believe that congratulations are in order. You managed to defeat a Viking Army considerably larger than yours. That has given everyone a lot of hope. Please send my best wishes to your team.'

Lord Malander, 'They probably weren't the strongest Viking Army.'

Duke of Mercia, 'Nonsense, I don't want to hear any more. It was a brilliant tactical victory over a barbarian horde. It was a stunning victory.'

Lord Malander, 'If you say so.'

Duke of Mercia, 'And I want you to say it and believe it. It has been a great morale booster. Anyway, why have you come here? It wasn't just to get a pat on your back from your old dad.'

Lord Malander, 'You will never be old. I swear that you are getting younger every day.'

Duke of Mercia, 'I haven't got all day. Spill the beans.'

Lord Malander, 'OK, I want more power.'

Duke of Mercia, 'Brilliant, tell me what counties you want.'

Lord Malander, 'I thought you would resist that.'

Duke of Mercia, 'That was my original plan. I wanted you to build up a force that we could use as a professional Army while we were fighting up north. But the Vikings have brought the war to you. Do you mind if I get old Winterdom involved in this discussion?'

Lord Malander, 'Of course not.' The Duke of Mercia sent an aide to go and get him.

Duke of Mercia, 'And how's your wife?'

Lord Malander, 'Doing fine, my Lord.'

Duke of Mercia, 'I never really understood what you saw in that old witch, apart from a nice arse and a fine pair of tits.'

Lord Malander, 'Let's not go down that road.'

Duke of Mercia, 'You are probably right.'

Earl Winterdom arrived, and the two lords shook hands warmly.

Duke of Mercia, 'Well, Henry, the boy wants more power.'

Earl Winterdom, 'You said, that he would. It certainly fits into our thinking. So, Alan, what counties do you want?'

Lord Malander, 'I was thinking of the following:

- Cornwall
- Devon
- Dorset
- Gloucestershire
- Hampshire
- Herefordshire
- Isle of Wight
- Oxfordshire
- Shropshire
- Somerset
- Warwickshire
- West Midlands
- Wiltshire

Duke of Mercia, 'That looks all right to me.'

Earl Winterdom, 'I will draw it on our map.'

Duke of Mercia, 'It still looks all right to me.'

Earl Winterdom, 'I would include Wales.'

Duke of Mercia, 'In that case, it is a done deal. Who should he report to?'

Earl Winterdom, 'I think it should be you, my Lord. I have enough on my plate.'

Duke of Mercia, 'So we still need someone to look after the south-east.

Any suggestions?'

Earl Winterdom, 'No, my Lord.'

Duke of Mercia, 'What about you, Alan?'

Lord Malander, 'No, my Lord.' Neither commander wanted to lose a key member of their team.

Duke of Mercia, 'Are you happy with that, Alan?'

Lord Malander, 'Yes, my Lord. Will you be writing to them?'

Duke of Mercia, 'There is no need. The letters went out last week announcing your promotion.'

Lord Malander, 'How did you know?'

Duke of Mercia, 'I'm very long in the tooth, and I know my boy.'

Earl Winterdom, 'Congratulations. You will be my boss one day.'

Lord Malander, 'I've got a lot to learn, my Lord. On that note, I will say my goodbyes.'

A note was found on a soldier's tent:

For the want of great power,
His lordship's father did empower,
So that the Vikings he could devour,
Like a well-cooked cauliflower.

34
Magical Congratulations

Lady Malander, 'Thomas, everyone is saying what a great contribution you made to our victory.'

Thomas, 'Thank you, my Lady.'

Lady Malander, 'Your performance has certainly helped the magical cause. Even my husband is starting to believe. So well done.'

Thomas, 'Thank you again, my Lady.'

Lady Malander, 'How are you coping with the Betty situation?'

Thomas, 'OK, it's a bit like having a wiser person in your head questioning your judgements. She keeps urging me to find a good woman to fuck. I would like that, but you can't just approach any pretty girl, can you?'

Lady Malander, 'I wouldn't know, for many, life is too short, and even for the long-lived, it is often too short. Enjoy your randiness while you have it.'

Thomas, 'But Betty keeps saying that one over there looks nice. I'm sure that she would like a good rutting.'

Lady Malander, 'Betty was always a free spirit verging on being a slut.'

Thomas, 'Careful she can hear you.'

Lady Malander, 'Don't worry, I've called her far worse than that over the years. Anyway, I'm picking up some concerns and worries. I assumed that it was Betty-related, but it's not, is it?'

Thomas, 'No, you are right. I'm not sure how to put it, but I think that I'm under attack.'

Lady Malander, 'From Rachel?'

Thomas, 'I thought that at first, but there are quite a few of them.'

Lady Malander, 'Who then?'

Thomas, 'The witches of Pershore.'

Lady Malander, 'But witches don't have our power of remembrance.'

Thomas, 'Exactly. So they probably aren't the ones that originally attacked the citadel.'

Lady Malander, 'You mean the ones wiped out by his lordship.'

Thomas, 'I will never forget the horrors inflicted on Pershore. We assumed that the Witches of Pershore came from Pershore, but it turned out that their nest was focussed on Bredon Hill and especially Elmley Castle. We murdered many innocent men, women and children.'

Lady Malander, 'It took his lordship a long time to get over it. And in the end, it never happened.'

Thomas, 'That's the downside of our gift. We remember.'

Lady Malander, 'So what are your plans?'

Thomas, 'I was hoping that you would have a few ideas.'

Lady Malander, 'We either meet with them and discuss our future together or we eradicate them.'

Thomas, 'I think I prefer the second option, but I guess that we should try the other first option.'

Lady Malander, 'I will set a meeting up, but you will have to protect yourself from their witchery.'

Thomas, 'What will they do?'

Lady Malander, 'They will use your randiness against you.'

Thomas, 'I'm far too strong for that.'

Lady Malander, 'Well, let us see, shall we?'

Two notes were found in the Centre for Mystical Arts:

What goes into a witches brew?
Dead frogs and slugs and the seeds of the yew,
Just to make a tasty stew,
That will make Merlin want to screw.

Is it magic, or is it voodoo?
That rots a man's brain to subdue,
To revenge the witches barbeque,
And to get what we are due.

35

The Battle

General Winterdom lined his forces up in the traditional way with stakes in the ground, pikemen, and archers. Behind this row were thousands of men at arms. There were forests protecting both of his flanks. He had some mounted archers but very few as it wasn't the traditional British way of fighting. They had the advantage of securing the higher ground.

The General felt quite confident in his dispositions, especially as the enemy was just a mass of barbaric thugs. There didn't appear to be any structure. In fact, their lack of structure made it difficult to assess their likely tactics.

There were two types of general. Those who initiated action and went for it. And those who waited for the enemy to attack and then react. The latter was easier as it didn't require an immediate decision, and it was always the tactic adopted by General Winterdom.

It also appeared to be the tactic adopted by Snorri, the Viking leader who came from Iceland. Both leaders had a good view of the battleground. An hour went by with both sides just jeering at each other and throwing insults back and forwards, although the linguistic differences tempered the slurs somewhat.

General Winterdom was getting quite frustrated, as there wasn't much he could do. He had adopted a defensive position behind stakes. Besides, he didn't want to lose the advantage of his hilly location. It was looking like a stalemate. Then half of the Vikings marched to the left towards the forest.

Traditionally the British had never fought in forests. It was not an accepted practice. It was not following the rules. General Winterdom sent scouts into the woods to check on the enemy's intentions, but they were never seen again.

General Winterdom now had three options:

1. Re-structure the defence to cover the forest
2. Retire from the Field

3. Attack the forces in front of them.

The restructuring was a difficult manoeuvre and made them vulnerable to attack. It was also difficult to tell how far the outflanking would go. They could be faced with forces directly behind them and even an encirclement.

Retirement was not something that he could contemplate.

So the General ordered a full-frontal attack with everything he had. He wasn't a subtle commander. He believed in a good old melee. The Vikings were outnumbered two to one and had the difficulty of fighting off an enemy that had the momentum of running down a hill. Even getting your weapons in position to defend against that sort of attack was difficult.

Then it was cold steel against cold steel. The pikemen simply skewered hundreds of the Vikings. The archers picked their targets well. The Vikings were on the run. Every now and then, the Vikings turned to fight, but the British weren't having any of it. Their pent-up hatred of the Vikings made them merciless. Many of the Norseman were slaughtered as they tried to fight their way through bramble bushes. Surrender was not an option.

General Winterdom sounded the recall. He was surprised how well they responded as it was clear that their blood-lust was up. But many of them were exhausted from the downhill run and the adrenaline rush.

The General now found himself in the opposite position. Snorri and the remaining half of the Viking Army were now nicely positioned behind the British stakes, and the British were down the bottom of the hill. But the Vikings were now heavily outnumbered, but they held the hill.

For the second time, both armies stared at each other. The Vikings wanted revenge for their lost brothers. The British gloried in their victory but wondered what the General was going to do next. He contemplated a flanking manoeuvre of his own, but they had no experience of forest fighting. So he decided to retire from the field, collecting Viking souvenirs as they went.

A note was found on the battleground:

What is a victory without skill?
As the Brits rushed down the hill,
And Viking blood they did spill,
A happy day for those with a kill.

36
Bolts from the Blue

General Winterdom was quite pleased with himself. He had destroyed half of the Viking Army with practically no losses. But on the way back to base, disaster struck. From nowhere came thousands of bolts of lightning. Whole columns of men where simply electrocuted and burnt alive.

The smell of burnt flesh was sickening. There was no obvious source. There were simply huge claps of thunder and then death from lightning. There wasn't even a storm and certainly no sign of rain. What was worse was the ball lightning as this hit the troops horizontally.

General Winterdom ordered his men to scatter, but they could hardly hear his commands with all of the noise going on. Then it just suddenly stopped. The devastation caused was horrific and occasionally comical. Groups of men were fused together, forming semi-live montages. Other men had been burnt-out from the inside. One man had been pushed inside a tree to create a merged entity.

Hundreds of men became vegetables with frazzled brains. Others had horrific burn marks where the lightning had entered their mouth and came out elsewhere. The men were terrified and had every reason to be. It took some time for the sergeants to restore order partly because they were so frightened themselves.

The dead were buried, and the horrifically injured were given a welcome release. General Winterdom ordered the survivors to return to base in battalion order to minimise the potential target. What had started as a good day turned into a calamity. There were not going to be any victory celebrations now, not that anyone could be blamed.

He wasn't sure what the duke was going to say as there was no rational answer to this development.

37
Magical Meetings

Thomas was not looking forward to meeting the witches. The venue was on top of Bredon Hill. The name always made him laugh as 'Bre' means hill, 'Don' means hill, and surprisingly 'Hill' means hill. So they were meeting at Hill, Hill, Hill.

It was a tough climb, but the views made it all worthwhile. You could see his beloved Malvern range. Nine miles of undulating peaks. Before the climb, the six wizards cast a full range of protective spells. It was well-known that the followers of the black arts could not be trusted, and they had previous experiences of that.

At the top of the hill, they were met by Endora, the Altar of the Circle, effectively the Coven leader. She was stunningly attractive in her black robe. Thomas could already feel his pecker taking some interest. He could also hear Betty in his mind's eye, egging him on.

Sitting in a circle were eleven naked women, all of child-bearing age. There was not one old crone among them. Betty warned him that they were probably not what they seemed as they might be using a glamour spell. Nevertheless, the proximity of so many naked pussies was intoxicating, and that was probably their intent. Endora removed her gown and displayed her nudity to the world. Thomas was mesmerised by her figure and her fully erect nipples. Well, it was quite chilly.

The magicians were herded to sit in the middle of the circle, possibly not the best position, but there were no obvious threats.

Endora, 'I assume that you have come to apologise for the attack on Pershore.'

Lady Malander, 'Firstly, I would like to thank you for agreeing to this meeting.'

Endora, 'Cut the crap, let's get down to the detail.'

Lady Malander, 'There is nothing to apologise for.'

Endora, 'You know that in your heart that is not true.'

Lady Malander, 'But witches don't have the power of remembrance.'

Endora, 'But I do. My father was a wizard.'

Lady Malander, 'So you want us to apologise for something that didn't happen?'

Endora, 'Yes. I want you to apologise for your Army destroying most of Pershore and murdering men, women, children, and young babies. Why would your soldiers stab a suckling baby? What did it achieve?'

Lady Malander, 'If my husband were here, I'm sure that he would happily apologise for a gross mistake. Blood lust took over, but it was in revenge for the actions of the witches.'

Endora, 'Don't try and push the blame onto us.'

Lady Malander, 'But your coven attacked Malvern and killed thousands of soldiers and civilians.'

Endora, 'But that was war.'

Lady Malander, 'It was an unprovoked attack.'

Endora, 'We were following the orders of our paymaster.'

Lady Malander, 'Now you are trying to blame someone else.'

Endora, 'But that is our nature.'

Lady Malander, 'You attacked us and therefore, retribution was justified. Anyway, the events that we are discussing never happened.'

Endora, 'They did happen.'

Lady Malander, 'And then they unhappened. Let's accept that and move on.'

Endora, 'So why are you here?'

Lady Malander, 'We are now fighting the Vikings. We need to know where you stand.'

Thomas was struggling to keep his manhood under control as most of the naked witches were fondling themselves, quite outrageously.

Endora, 'We stand where we stand.'

Lady Malander, 'What does that mean?'

Endora, 'Whatever I want it to mean.'

Lady Malander, 'And why are your witches currently carrying out lewd acts?'

Endora, 'We are trying to entrap the mighty one.'

Lady Malander, 'You mean Thomas?'

Endora, 'Yes, the one with one inside him.'

Lady Malander, 'Why would you do that?'

Endora, 'He has so much power that we could use, and the whore inside of him has weakened him. He is desperate to fornicate, and we are here for him. It is only a matter of time before he gives in.'

Lady Malander cast a reality spell, and the damsels became what they were: ugly old crones. In fact, they became the epitome of witchery: large noses, wrinkles, spots, boils, straggly hair, curved spine, rotten teeth etc. Thomas felt ill thinking about his earlier desires.

Lady Malander, 'You are either an ally or an enemy. What is it going to be?'

Endora, 'Enemy.' And the attack began.

On a fence on Bredon Hill, a note was found:

It was time to ring the alarm bell,
It was wizard against the infidel,
Their evil comes directly from hell,
Whereas wizardry is a good spell.

38
The King is Dead

When General Winterdom returned to Litchfield, he found both the town and the military headquarters destroyed by lightning. There was hardly a building standing, just charred remains. Parts of the town were still on fire. Some of the locals had fled, but most had been frazzled where they stood.

The Army camp was in a worse state. It had been systematically destroyed. The garrison buildings, the stores and the HQ were no more; just burning wrecks surrounded by the dead. But worst of all, he found the duke headless. It looked like he had been tortured by a series of small lightning bolts. The fear in the eyes of his decapitated head was palpable.

General Winterdom wondered what to do as he had no defence against this sort of weapon. In the end, he decided to march half of his Army to Malvern and leave the other half encamped throughout Staffordshire so that they could be easily recalled when required. He decided to take half his forces to Malvern in case they had encountered a similar attack.

Then he had the awful job of telling Lord Malander that his father had been killed in action. He would, of course, be returning the body.

He sent scouts ahead to warn the Malvern HQ of his return and to assess the situation there. He just hoped that there wasn't going to be another lightning attack.

They found a note near their dead leader's body:

It was a massive lightning bolt,
That caused the locals to revolt,
It was a really shocking jolt,
That killed them with a very high volt.

39
The Magical Battle

The top of Bredon Hill was ablaze with unadulterated magic. It was a classic fight between witches and wizards, black and white magic, and good versus evil. There were no rules.

It was Lionel Wildheart, Tinton of Taverton, Thomas, Robin, Lady Malander and two other wizards against a coven of twelve. The main advantage the wizards had was that a squadron of mounted archers was on the way to assist them. They had seen the signal requesting their assistance.

Thomas had loads of power but often lacked direction. He was never sure what to do. Betty suggested that he should take out Endora with an End Spell which he did. Endora simply ceased to exist. The other witches were shocked, especially as one by one he repeated the spell. The last six witches made a run for it. To be honest, it was more of a hobble. The mounted archers tracked them down and slit their throats.

The remains of the witches who hadn't disappeared were collected to form a funeral pyre. Thomas was not happy about his actions. He hated the idea of killing anything but needs must. And was nullifying them actually killing them? Lady Malander said that it was. She realised that Thomas needed toughening up.

Lionel Wildheart and Tinton of Taverton were given the job of tracking down any other members of the witch infestation. They were ordered to find both practising witches and those who had latent powers.

Lady Malander was going to update her husband regarding their action when she learnt about the death of his father, and whilst they were engaged, another coven attacked Malvern.

Thomas found a note on the hill:

Death visited the Hill of Bredon,
The evil coven is now long-gone,
The wizards are a paragon,
That fought this strange phenomenon.

40
Things are not Good

General Winterdom marched into Malvern with his thirty thousand troops just in time to be attacked by multiple witch covens. His men scattered as sixty-odd flying witches fired energy bolts at them from high in the sky. Captain Dragondale's archers returned fire, but few of the witches were in range.

It was hard to see what the witches were trying to achieve, but one of their targets was the Academy of Mystical Arts. It looked like they were trying to eliminate as many magicians as possible. But the magicians in training managed to put a protective bubble around their school. They soon extended this to include Lord Malander's residence and some of the outbuildings.

The magicians were very inexperienced, but they remembered what the Enchantress of Evermore taught them. When confronted by multiple enemies, it is often a good idea to focus on just one. Six of them got together and blasted a single witch, causing her to explode, which shocked the other witches. The witches got nearer to the bubble protecting the school in an effort to break it down, but this meant that they were within the range of the archers.

Captain Dragondale saw this as her chance, and volley after volley targeted the flying fiends. The magicians were steadily knocking out one witch after another, but it was a slow and exhausting process, especially as magic was a very limited resource.

Most of the witches were still targeting General Winterdom's Army. The men were suffering a huge variety of surreal and unpleasant deaths. Some were literally petrified. Others were turned into jelly. Some simply dissolved. A whole squadron of troops from Rutland were turned into frogs, quite large ones.

The troops sought refuge in buildings, but these proved nearly as fatal as they were blasted apart. Sonic booms burst ear-drums. Water was turned into acid. These were skilful witches with a variety of different tactics, but they were subject to the same magical laws. Their power was being trained away.

Slowly the combined efforts of the magicians and the archers were getting the upper hand, and the surviving witches fled. It was a shocking waste of human life. No one should have been subjected to the awful deaths that were on display.

General Winterdom surveyed the horrors and did his best to encourage his troops. Most of them had been through enough with lightning bolts and witchery. But they had no choice but to continue. Captain Mainstay did his best to find lodgings and refreshments, but they had never expected an Army of that size to descend on them. At least they had some more hands to help with the clean-up.

General Winterdom had got to the point that he was dreading. He had to go and tell Lord Malander about his father's death.

Lord Malander, 'Good to see you, General.'

General Winterdom, 'I'm afraid that I'm the bringer of bad news.'

Lord Malander, 'It's my father, isn't it?'

General Winterdom, 'Yes, we have brought his body back with us.'

Lord Malander, 'I was a bit surprised that you brought a whole Army with you.'

General Winterdom, 'I wasn't sure what I was going to find after what we have been through.'

Lord Malander, 'Go on.'

General Winterdom, 'We had a pitched battle against the Vikings which we won. We destroyed at least half of their Army before retiring. On the way back to Litchfield, we were attacked by lightning bolts.'

Lord Malander, 'Lightning bolts?'

General Winterdom, 'Both your classical vertical ones and horizontal fireballs. We lost a lot of good men. When we got to Litchfield, we found the town and the military camp destroyed. And, sadly, we found the dead body of your father.

'As I said earlier, I brought half of the Army here as I thought you might have suffered the same fate.'

Lord Malander, 'Thank you for bringing my father's body back and thinking of us.'

General Winterdom, 'I don't want to go into the gory details, but it looks like your father was tortured and then decapitated.'

Lord Malander, 'The bastards.'

General Winterdom, 'You are right there. And when we got here, we found that you are being attacked by witches.'

Lord Malander, 'Yes, it hasn't been normal recently.'

General Winterdom, 'Changing the subject, on the way here we saw a lot of activity on Bredon Hill.'

Lord Malander, 'Oh God, my wife is there.' He called for an aide to go and check out the hill, but then his wife turned up. Lord Malander ran over to hug his wife.

Lady Malander, 'What happened here?'

Lord Malander, 'We had a bit of bother from some witches.'

Lady Malander, 'That can't be a coincidence as we were fighting them as well on Bredon Hill.'

General Winterdom, 'It looks like it was a coordinated attack.'

Lord Malander, 'Let's have a good night's sleep and have a war council meeting in the morning.'

General Winterdom, 'One last point. This means that you are Chief Elder now.'

That was just what Lord Malander needed.

41
A Private Conversation

Lady Malander asked to see Thomas for a private conversation. Before the meeting, she swore him to secrecy.

Thomas, 'If you are that concerned, why don't you zap me with a silence spell?'

Lady Malander, 'I don't need to as I trust you. I probably trust you more than anyone else in the world.'

Thomas, 'That's not the issue. Someone might force it out of me. Who knows what scrapes we will get into in the future?'

Lady Malander, 'Are you sure that you don't mind?'

Thomas, 'I would welcome it. And you should include Betty in the spell.' He could hear Betty complaining, but it was for the best.

Lady Malander prepared the 'Everlasting Silence' spell, and the two wizards that were sharing the same body were silenced, although they could not detect any difference.

Thomas, 'Now that's done, you can share anything and everything with me.'

Lady Malander, 'It's very simple, really. I urgently need to get pregnant.'

Thomas, 'I'm sure that his lordship could help you with that.'

Lady Malander, 'That's the problem, he has been helping me an awful lot. Sometimes two or three times a night. He always has been a randy bugger, but it's not working. In ten years, I have not got pregnant.'

Thomas, 'So do you know which of you is the problem?'

Lady Malander, 'We have always assumed that it was me, partly my age and partly my magical abilities. That and a typical man's ego. Therefore, it must be me, but we know that it is not the case.'

Thomas, 'How do we know that?'

Lady Malander, 'Don't you remember I got pregnant when I was a pig?'

Thomas, 'Of course, you were fucked by practically every boar on the farm.'

Lady Malander, 'You don't have to put it that way.'

Thomas, 'Well, you certainly put it around a bit.'

Lady Malander, 'There was a sort of innocence. Fucking was just a normal everyday experience. There was no pretence, just good hard fucking.'

Thomas, 'I think Lord Hogsflesh was a particular fan.'

Lady Malander, 'I have my suspicions that he was the father.'

Thomas, 'So you are saying that the problem is not you but his Lordship.'

Lady Malander, 'Probably, but it is hard to tell. Anyway, things have got critical. With his father's death, he will become the Duke of Mercia, Head of the Military and Chief Elder. He needs an heir to maintain stability. I need to deliver a son urgently.

'I wondered if you would oblige? You got Rachel pregnant.'

Thomas, 'I don't think, in fact, I know that I wasn't the father. I suspect that I'm infertile like most male magicians.'

Lady Malander, 'Are you willing to have a go?'

She started to unwrap her shawl.

Thomas, 'I don't think I could. It would seem like a betrayal of his Lordship's trust.'

She took her blouse off, exposing two beautiful breasts.

Lady Malander, 'Don't you find me attractive?'

Thomas, 'You are gorgeous, my Lady. A stunning beauty and I would love to fuck you.'

Her skirt fell to the ground, and she looked radiant in her nakedness.

Lady Malander, 'My pussy is aching for your seed.'

Lady Malander bent over, exposing her arse to him.

Lady Malander, 'Take me, no one will know.'

Then Thomas got a whisper from Betty, which confirmed his thinking.

Thomas hit her with a spell of 'Disenchantment', followed by a spell of 'Exposure'. This was a witch in front of him trying to capture his seed. Thomas then froze her and called the guard.

They were a bit surprised to see a naked Lady Malander, but she gradually reverted to the old crone she was.

Thomas was going to tell Lady Malander about the witchery trickery, but he found that he couldn't. That damn spell!

A note was found on the library door:

> *It was another cunning, devious witch,*
> *That stood there without a stitch,*
> *For Lady Malander did she switch,*
> *To capture Merlin's seed, the sly bitch.*

42
Greatness imposed upon them

Lord and Lady Malander laid in bed, talking for a change.

Lord Malander, 'It's all a bit soon.'

Lady Malander, 'I know my love. Your father died before his time.'

Lord Malander, 'All I wanted was a couple more years, and I would be ready.'

Lady Malander, 'But fate intervened.'

Lord Malander, 'Can I rely on you to organise the funeral?'

Lady Malander, 'Of course, my love. It will be a funeral to honour the best of the best.'

Lord Malander, 'Thank you.'

Lady Malander, 'Do you plan to take the duke's title? I quite fancy being a duchess.'

Lord Malander, 'I will, but I would still like the men to refer to me as Lord Malander. Anyway, if we are not careful, there won't be much of Mercia left.'

Lady Malander, 'I need to be honest with you. During the Slimenest war, which didn't happen, I got pregnant.'

Lord Malander, 'Never.'

Lady Malander, 'It's true. The baby was due just after the time-reversal.'

Lord Malander, 'So, I can sire children.'

Lady Malander, 'Possibly not.'

Lord Malander, 'You never had an affair?'

Lady Malander, 'Yes and no.' She could tell that his lordship was starting to get angry.

Lord Malander, 'What do you mean by yes and no?'

Lady Malander, 'The witches turned a few of us into pigs, including hoggy. Because of my rather poor toiletry habits, I was placed in a field with the other pigs, including my fellow human conversions. I'm sorry to

93

say that as a pig, I was fucked quite a few times.'

Lord Malander, 'How many times?'

Lady Malander, 'About a dozen.' It was nearer to thirty.

Lord Malander, 'You have committed adultery a dozen times. Lord Malander's anger now was clearly visible.'

Lady Malander, 'I'm not sure if it counts as adultery as I had no choice.'

Lord Malander, 'Are you saying that it was rape?'

Lady Malander, 'Not really as I was a willing participant. I was living the life of a pig.'

Lord Malander, 'Who transformed you back into human form?'

Lady Malander, 'Thomas.'

Lord Malander, 'Did he fuck you?'

Lady Malander, 'No. Anyway, your alter-ego forgave me in his excitement that I was pregnant. We agreed never to mention actual parenthood again.'

Lord Malander, 'So what you are saying is that I'm firing blanks.'

Lady Malander, 'I'm afraid so.'

Lord Malander, 'So if I want an heir, we will have to be a bit creative.'

Lady Malander, 'I think so.'

Lord Malander, 'I will give it some thought.'

Lady Malander, 'I know you will.'

On the bedpost, there was a note:

The things people do for a child,
The patter of small feet for the defiled,
The father is not known but soon reconciled,
Should the raped mother be exiled?

43
A National War Council

Lord Malander called his third War Council, but this time he was in charge of the entire country. The attendees were as follows:

- Captain Mainstay, Mounted Archers
- Captain Bandolier, Mounted Archers
- Captain Clutterbuck, Engineering
- Lord Hogsflesh, Scout
- Captain Lambskin, Infantry
- Captain Dragondale, Archers
- Thomas Merlin, Mystical Arts
- Lady Malander, Mystical Arts
- General Winterdom, Northern Army.

Lord Malander, 'Welcome to our third War Council. A lot has happened since the last one.

'Firstly, I would like two minutes of silence for my father who died a horrible death doing his duty. He will be remembered.'

There was a two-minute silence.

Lord Malander, 'Just to clarify the position, I'm now the Duke of Mercia. I'm also the Chief Elder and leader of the military forces of Grand Britannica. I still wish to be called Lord Malander.'

Everyone in the room spontaneously clapped, including his wife.

Lord Malander, 'Here is an update:

- The production of arrows has improved dramatically. My thanks to Captain Clutterbuck and his team. I believe that Fay also deserves a mention
- A Viking fleet was seen in the Severn Estuary, and a plan using fireboats and chains was put into action. This was remarkably

95

successful, and as almost everyone here was in action, then you all need to be complimented. I understand that Thomas's wall of flames was a great success

- General Winterdom took over the Northern Command and totally reorganised them
- He then beat a Viking Army in the field. A most impressive achievement
- On his return, he was attacked by both vertical and horizontal lightning bolts, which killed a lot of good men
- On reaching Litchfield, he found that both the town and the military camp had been destroyed by lightning bolts. He also found the dead body of my father
- General Winterdom then marched half his Army to Malvern, fearing that we had been attacked
- Lady Malander, Thomas and other magicians fought a coven on Bredon Hill
- While that was going on, a large number of witches attacked Malvern.

'That's a quick summary of what has happened.

'There is a lot to do, but these are the main challenges:
- Recapturing the northern lands
- Establishing an effective military command structure
- Finding a solution to the lightning problem
- The eradication of the witches
- Development of new war technology.

'Before we address those issues, I would like your updates. Captain Mainstay, can I have your update, please.'

Captain Mainstay, 'My target has been achieved. There is no difficulty in recruiting troops at the moment, but the training is quite challenging. We have got to teach them to ride a horse and fire an arrow.'

Captain Bandolier, 'I've experienced exactly the same issue.'

Lord Malander, 'This is now a continuous process. We need more and more troops. Expand the training facilities. Captain Bandolier, I want you to take over control of all the mounted archers.'

That shocked Captain Mainstay.

Lord Malander, 'Captain Mainstay, I want you to assume command of the south-east forces.' That shocked Captain Mainstay even more.

Lord Malander, 'Captain Dragondale, how has your recruitment campaign gone?'

Captain Dragondale, 'Again, it has been very successful. Men and women are queuing up to fight. My job is easier than the other two as I only have to train them to fire arrows.'

Lord Malander, 'I understand that you nearly have ten regiments, twice the target.'

Captain Lambskin, 'That is correct, my Lord.'

Lord Malander, 'Well done, and how is your factory going, Captain Clutterbuck?'

Captain Clutterbuck, 'Brilliant. It has been a revelation. I now need some new projects.'

Thomas, 'I have some ideas.'

Lord Malander, 'We will come back to that later.'

Thomas, 'Sorry, my Lord.'

Lord Malander, 'Any updates, Lord Hogsflesh?'

Lord Hogsflesh, 'I believe that the Vikings are consolidating their position in Yorkshire. And I can't see Lincolnshire standing. In the short term, I think they will attack the eastern counties and probably target London. Should I set-up a national intelligence service?'

Lord Malander, 'Yes, Lord Hogsflesh, please proceed immediately.'

Lord Malander, 'Thomas, do the Vikings have any magical powers? I guess that the lightning attacks prove that they have.'

Thomas, 'That's a tricky question to answer. I've not detected any magic as we would define it, but they do have supernatural powers.'

Lord Malander, 'What can we do about the lightning?'

Thomas, 'I'm at a loss.'

Captain Clutterbuck, 'I have a potential solution.'

Lord Malander, 'Go on.'

Captain Clutterbuck, 'It's called a lightning disrupter. It's a metal pole that you put on tall buildings to attract the lightning away from the building. We could adapt it for battlefield conditions.'

Lord Malander, 'Let's start work on it immediately. How is the castle at Upton going?'

Captain Clutterbuck, 'It's on schedule, my Lord.'

Lord Malander, 'And the building of the Citadel?'

Captain Clutterbuck, 'It's behind schedule partly due to a lack of labour. They are all joining the Army.'

Lord Malander, 'Please let me know what you need to escalate it.'

Captain Clutterbuck, 'Yes, my Lord.'

Lord Malander, 'What is your assessment, General Winterdom.'

General Winterdom, 'I need to put the Army back into the field. I'm only going to do that if the lightning contraption works.'

Captain Clutterbuck, 'It will work.'

Lord Malander, 'Let's stop for lunch, then carry on.'

The customary note was on the council room door:

It was just another meeting,
Where the Brits took a beating,
Those Vikings did the cheating,
But that won't stop them from bleating.

44
The Meeting Continues

Lord Malander, 'Now let's address the main issues:

- Recapturing the northern lands
- Establishing an effective military command structure
- Finding a solution to the lightning problem
- The eradication of the witches
- Development of new war technology.

'We have addressed the lightning issues. When can we see a working model?'

Captain Clutterbuck, 'I can have the lightning disrupter ready for next week, but without lightning, I can't demonstrate its effectiveness.'

Lord Malander, 'Go ahead with the development. I guess that we will just have to wait for the right conditions.'

General Winterdom, 'It must be mobile so that we can use it on the battlefield.'

Captain Clutterbuck, 'I will give that some thought.'

Lord Malander, 'Excellent, let's think about the command structure. The country is effectively divided into three areas:

- North — General Winterdom
- Midlands and South-West — Major Lambskin
- East and South-East — Major Mainstay.'

Both Lambskin and Mainstay thanked Lord Malander for their promotions.

Lord Malander, 'I will act as Commander-in-Chief, and we will continue with the War Council meetings.'

General Winterdom, 'I would like some mounted archers.'

Lord Malander, 'Major Bandolier, can you organise that please?'

Major Bandolier, 'Yes, my Lord. I will get onto that after the meeting.'

General Winterdom, 'You will need to contact every Lord Protector to determine what resources they have. Don't expect too much cooperation or the truth.'

Major Mainstay, 'Excellent idea.'

Lord Malander, 'So how do we throw the Vikings out of the north?'

General Winterdom, 'If we get our act together, we can put an Army in the field that will seriously outnumber them. We need two or three decisive battles, and then we can drive them off the land back to wherever they came from.'

Lord Hogsflesh, 'I agree with that, but we probably need better information on their dispositions. I will get my men working on it.'

Lord Malander, 'But they could land additional troops anywhere they wanted. We have no navy to protect our shores.'

Lady Malander, 'What ships do we have?'

No one seemed to know.

Lady Malander, 'Shouldn't that be a priority?'

Lord Malander, 'Lord Hogsflesh, could you find a good naval man who could advise us?'

Lord Hogsflesh, 'Of course, my Lord.'

Lord Malander, 'What are we doing about the witches?'

Lady Malander, 'We are hunting them down.'

Lord Malander, 'How many are there?'

Lady Malander, 'Locally or in the entire county?'

Lord Malander, 'The latter.'

Lady Malander, 'About thirty thousand.'

Lord Malander, 'What?'

Lady Malander, 'Some are harmless but could be turned.'

Lord Malander, 'You must give their eradication priority.'

Lady Malander, 'I will, my love.'

Lord Malander, 'Thomas, you had some new ideas regarding new developments.'

Thomas, 'I have quite a few ideas that I need to discuss with Captain Clutterbuck. These include muskets, cannons, pencils, cross-bows, and carts. I won't go into the detail here, but they will make a significant difference.'

Lord Malander, 'I look forward to seeing them.

'These are my orders:

- Major Bandolier will continue with the recruitment drive
- Major Bandolier will take over the command of all the mounted archers
- Major Mainstay will take command of the South-East region
- Major Dragondale will continue to increase the number of infantry regiments
- Lord Hogsflesh will set-up a national intelligence centre
- Captain Clutterbuck to build a mobile lightning disrupter as soon as possible
- Captain Clutterbuck to work on the citadel
- Lord Hogsflesh to scout the Viking incursions
- General Winterdom to prepare for another battle against the Vikings
- Major Lambskin to take over command of the Midlands and South-West region
- Major Bandolier to release some mounted archers to General Winterdom
- Major Mainstay to meet with every Lord Protector in the Eastern and South-East regions
- Major Lambskin to meet with every Lord Protector in the Midlands and South-West regions
- Lord Hogsflesh to find a naval contact
- Lady Malander to eradicate the witches
- Thomas to work with Captain Clutterbuck on the new developments.

'That should keep you all busy for a while.'

A note was found in the lavatory:

The lightning had been a great fright,
It robbed men of their birth right,
But due to Clutterbuck's foresight,
We will sleep better under the twilight.

45
The Thing (Meeting)

Berg, 'I'm Berg of Clan Volsung. I've been appointed by Thor to conquer these lands. They will become part of a vast Norse empire stretching to the Russia's. Our performance is unacceptable, and men will die for this. There will be a cleansing, do you understand?'

The warriors in the audience nodded.

Berg, 'Firstly, our settlement fleet on the Severn was wrecked by cowardly defensive measures. The British pig-dogs will suffer for their impudence. We have another fleet in the Severn estuary awaiting my orders.

'Secondly, our Army in Yorkshire only just won. Lord Thor came to our aid with lightning bolts. It should have been a decisive victory where we wiped the pig-dogs off the face of the Earth. Why didn't we succeed?

'Some of our initial plans have floundered. I believe that the Chief Elder has probably been disposed of, and our alliance with the witches has not proved particularly successful.

'The British scum are being more effectively led even though we decapitated their leader. I was hoping that his beheading would cause the Government to fail, but the opposite seems to be the case.

'If you look at the map, you will see the British pig-dogs have strong forces in Staffordshire and Worcestershire. But we also know that they are collecting their forces together to create new armies. We need to strike before they get too strong.'

Hedin, Clan Laxdale, 'Are we expecting further reinforcements?'

Berg, 'We are expecting settlement fleets, but not warriors.'

Hedin, 'Then they will have to become warriors.'

Berg, 'I agree, but what should be the target of our next attack.'

Ketill, Clan Njal, 'We are Vikings. Let's take the fight to them. Let's go to their headquarters and annihilate them.'

Berg, 'Do we all agree?'

There was an outburst of shouting and swearing. They were off to war.

Berg, 'We need to carry out the cleansing. The Daughters of Thor are here with their daggers. Line your men up.'

The Army was called to attention in rows. Every fifty-sixth man was selected and dragged to the front. This equated to nearly a thousand men. It took some time, but every one of them was ritually castrated by the Daughters of Thor. The pile of amputated penises and testicles was a sight to see. They weren't wasted as they were fed to the dogs.

Some of the victims bled to death; some committed suicide, and the rest became slaves. Some were used as comfort men. They weren't allowed to carry weapons, but they could die in a battle as a shield. Castration for most Vikings was far worse than death.

Berg, 'The Gods are satisfied, prepare for battle.'

A note was found attached to a testicle:
Was it a penis or a testicle?
In a plié, one has to be sceptical,
Whatever, it made quite a spectacle,
No more oats for the aesthetical.

46
Severn Worries

Lord Malander, 'Have we heard any more about the Viking fleet in the Severn Estuary?'

Lord Hogsflesh, 'My scouts tell me that they are still there. They have camped near Cardiff, but there are no signs of any movement.'

Lord Malander, 'That's a bit strange.'

Lord Hogsflesh, 'It's as if they are waiting for something.'

Lord Malander, 'If you were the leader of the Vikings, what would you do?'

Lord Hogsflesh, 'That's a good question. We know that their main force is in Yorkshire, but they have a substantial fleet in Cardiff. They are naturally aggressive and prefer to attack. I think that there are two obvious targets: London or Malvern.

'Because their fleet is in Cardiff, I would suggest that they are going to attack Malvern.'

Lord Malander, 'I better stop General Winterdom from returning back north.'

Lord Hogsflesh, 'I will check with my agents in Yorkshire to see if there are any signs of movement.'

Lord Malander, 'Please get back to me as soon as possible as we have quite a lot of planning to do.'

Lord Malander asked his aide to contact Majors Bandolier, Lambskin and Dragondale and General Winterdom and request their attendance at a meeting. The aide was also ordered to warn Captain Clutterbuck and Thomas that their services might be required.

47
New Wonders

Captain Clutterbuck, 'So what wonders are you going to suggest.'

Thomas, 'The first thing I want to talk about is a pencil.'

Captain Clutterbuck, 'What is it?'

Thomas, 'It's a quill that doesn't need ink.'

Captain Clutterbuck, 'That sounds miraculous.'

Thomas, 'It's a hollow piece of wood with a graphite core.'

Captain Clutterbuck, 'So you hollow out a twig and put carbon in it, and so what?'

Thomas, 'You sharpen the end, and you have a writing implement. Having a simple writing device will make everything much easier. It would be great for writing orders. You will wonder how you survived without them.'

Captain Clutterbuck, 'I can see that.'

Thomas, 'The core is a mixture of graphite, clay and water. There's not much more that I can tell you. The next thing on my list is much more serious. Did you get the saltpetre, charcoal, and sulphur?'

Captain Clutterbuck, 'And I mixed it up as you requested, taking a lot of care.'

Thomas, 'Let's take it outside. We need a long piece of material to act as a fuse.'

The bowl of gunpowder was placed in a field, and the fuse was lit. Then they ran back. Captain Clutterbuck wasn't sure why they were running, but he would soon find out.

The explosion was deafening and window shattering. Captain Clutterbuck was beyond being staggered. He wasn't sure how but he knew that human history would never be the same again.

Captain Clutterbuck, 'How do we use this new wonder?'

Thomas, 'You place it in a tube with a ball and set fire to it. The ball flies out with tremendous force, and its energy causes devastation.'

Captain Clutterbuck, 'How big are these tubes?''

Thomas, 'The small ones are called muskets, and the large ones are called cannons. I will draw you some pictures. You are going to need a lot of iron.

'These armaments will make all the difference to our military.'

Captain Clutterbuck, 'The challenge is going to be the engineering of the weapons. We are not well-blessed with metal-working skills.'

Thomas, 'Where can we get them from?'

Captain Clutterbuck, 'Hoggy will have a few ideas.'

Thomas, 'The last item is very simple: a horse-drawn cart using four wheels.' Thomas drew it.

Captain Clutterbuck, 'Why haven't we thought of that before?'

Thomas, 'It's hard to say.'

Captain Clutterbuck, 'Do you have any other ideas?'

Thomas, 'Lots, but we need to focus.'

There was a note on the factory wall:
It was quite some bang,
That made Clutterbuck harangue,
This will give the Brits more fang,
And sing the songs they sang.

48
More Tactics

Lord Malander, 'We think that the Vikings are going to target Malvern. I will hand over to Lord Hogsflesh to update you.'

Lord Hogsflesh, 'My agents in Yorkshire, suggest that the Vikings have left. They must have departed during the night.'

Lord Malander, 'Do we know in what direction they went?'

Lord Hogsflesh, 'They seem to have split into two groups, possibly more. That's partly because they feed off the land.

'And to make things worse, the Vikings in Cardiff are planning to embark.'

Lord Malander, 'So it looks like a two-pronged attack.'

General Winterdom, 'We need intelligence on the route or routes that the Northern Vikings will take. Shall I get the other half of the Northern Army marching south?'

Lord Malander, 'The answer is yes, but we need intelligence on the enemy routes to work out the best positioning for us.'

General Winterdom, 'I will get them moving but instruct them to wait for final orders later.'

Lord Malander, 'In terms of tactics, it is worth getting the fireships and the chains ready, although they will be expecting that.'

Lord Malander, 'Looking at the map, the enemy could attack from several different directions. We will definitely need the use of your scouts, Lord Hogsflesh, to provide ongoing intelligence.'

General Winterdom, 'I would recommend staking out likely battlefield sites.'

Lord Malander, 'Can I leave that to you, Major Lambskin?'

Major Lambskin, 'You can, my Lord.'

General Winterdom, 'Your mounted archers give you a great advantage. They give you far greater mobility, and you could consider hit and run raids.'

Lord Malander, 'Major Bandolier, please give that some thought.'

Major Bandolier, 'I will, my Lord.'

Lord Hogsflesh, 'I need some more men to act as lookouts.'

Lord Malander, 'Where do you want them?'

Lord Hogsflesh, 'Bredon, Suckley, the Cotswold Hills, the Mendips, the Brecon Beacons, Lickey and Clen, and I've probably forgotten a few.'

Lord Malander, 'Major Lambskin, can you assist?'

Major Lambskin, 'I can, my Lord.'

Lord Malander, 'My orders:

- Lord Hogsflesh to provide increased intelligence
- General Winterdom to move his Northern Army southwards
- Captain Clutterbuck to organise fireships and chains
- Major Lambskin to stake our likely battlefield sites
- Major Bandolier to consider hit and run raids
- Major Lambskin to provide look-outs
- Captain Clutterbuck to organise lightning disrupters throughout the area
- General Winterdom to formulate his dispositions
- Major Lambskin to formulate his dispositions
- Magical team to provide support.'

They looked everywhere for a note but couldn't find one.

49

Cannons

Captain Clutterbuck, 'Do you want to see my first attempt at a cannon?'

Thomas, 'I'm on my way over.'

When he arrived, Captain Clutterbuck took him out to the nearby field. The cannon was basically a thick metal tube stuck in the ground, with gunpowder and a metal ball in it.

Thomas, 'Have you been practising?'

Captain Clutterbuck, 'I have. Watch this.' The fuse was lit, and the cannonball was flung into the air, just missing the target.

Captain Clutterbuck, 'That's annoying. I hit it the last two times.'

Thomas, 'You have done it, my man. Now we need the cannons on wheels and a lot more of them.'

Captain Clutterbuck, 'Well, the good news is that Fay has tracked down some metalworkers. We should get a tube production line underway.'

Thomas, 'You are a marvel.'

Captain Clutterbuck, 'If you come inside, I will show you my first carriage.'

Thomas, 'That's impressive as well.'

Captain Clutterbuck, 'But I've failed miserably on the pencil front. I'm getting there, but it is the lead mix that is a challenge.'

Thomas, 'Back to the cannon, when you have made a few more, we need to organise a demonstration.'

Captain Clutterbuck, 'I'm at least two weeks away from that.'

Thomas, 'In that case, I will organise a date with his lordship.'

50
Where are the Witches?

Lady Malander, Thomas, Robin, Lionel, and Tinton were sitting around the table, knocking back some mead and eating some fruit cake. It was a bit different from the formal war council meetings, but then they were magicians.

Lady Malander, 'We have been instructed to hunt down and eradicate the witches. Of course, this is not as easy as it sounds.'

Tinton, 'I don't like the term "eradicate". We are not killers.'

Lady Malander, 'But they have repeatedly attacked us and killed many innocent people.'

Tinton, 'But that was battle. That is different from genocide.'

Lady Malander, 'But they attacked us without any warning.'

Lionel, 'I agree with Tinton. It seems wrong. Why don't we just capture them?'

Lady Malander, 'What would we do with them? They would be far too dangerous in a cell. What do you think, Thomas?'

Thomas, 'How do we decide who is a witch?'

Lady Malander, 'As I've mentioned on previous occasions, there are practising witches, non-practising witches and potential witches. And some of the practising witches are not our enemies.'

Thomas, 'So who are we targeting?'

Lady Malander, 'I guess just the first category.'

Thomas, 'Would you feel happy about killing them?'

Tinton, 'I'm not sure if I could kill anyone in cold blood.'

Lady Malander, 'What if we took soldiers with us to do the killing?'

Tinton, 'I would still see that as murder.'

Lady Malander, 'In that case, Tinton, I excuse you from this meeting.'

Lionel, 'I don't want to be a party to this either.'

Lady Malander, 'So it is just us three. Are you willing?'

Both Thomas and Robin nodded their heads.

Lady Malander, 'How many of the younger magicians will support us?'

Thomas, 'Most will if I ask them.'

Lady Malander, 'I've got the detection spell underway. We might as well start.'

A note was found in Tinton's pocket:

Some magicians refused to kill,
They just won't follow the drill,
No blood do they want to spill,
They left with a righteous thrill.

So it's a challenge uphill,
Our war leaders demand a kill,
Because witches caused such ill,
And the fear of them does chill.

51
Plans Afoot

The plan had been agreed upon, and the actions were being implemented. Malvern was full of hustle and bustle. As an outsider, it wasn't clear if the chaos was planned or not. But for those who knew, then it was an impressive reaction to the call for war.

Captain Clutterbuck was well organised:

- The fireships were in position
- Three chains were in position to stop traffic on the Severn
- Ten cannons were already installed on mobile carriages
- Stocks of gunpowder were in position
- Over a hundred carriages were made available to speed up transport
- Pencils were issued to all commanders
- The stock of arrows was huge and well-distributed
- The fort at Upton was complete and operational
- A system of warning fires was established.

General Winterdom was equally well organised:

- Detailed disbursement plans had been issued
- The forty thousand northern troops were marching south and would quarter in Worcester
- The thirty thousand northern troops based in Malvern were positioned on and around Bredon Hill
- His mounted archers were based in Pershore. Major Bandolier was pretty well-organised as well:
- Half of his mounted archers were based in the Forest of Dean
- The other half was based at Upton-Upon-Severn
- Every regiment in the entire Army was given some mounted archers to aid communication.

Major Lambskin was another great organiser:

- Detailed disbursement plans had been issued with troops based in Gloucester, Upton, and Malvern
- Every Lord Protector was sending troops to Worcester, Gloucester, Hereford, Birmingham, and Oxford, where they were being co-ordinated into regiments
- There was a regiment based on top of the Malvern Hills
- Look-outs were based on the major hills in the area.

Major Dragondale could hold his head up on the organisation front:

- Detailed disbursement plans had been issued
- A third of her archers were based in forts along the Severn
- The rest were defending Malvern.

Major Mainstay was well-organised:

- Every Lord Protector was sending troops to London, Oxford, Lincoln, Nottingham, Reading and Bath, where they were being co-ordinated into regiments.

Lord Hogsflesh was well organised:

- A spread of agents covered all of the northern, eastern, and southern approaches to Malvern
- A network of couriers on horseback was established
- The agent network had been established to cover the whole of Grand Britannica.

Lady Malander was well-organised:

- The witch hunt was underway
- Thomas was kept back to wait for where he could be best used.

All in all, things were pretty well organised, but like most plans, the enemy had different ideas.

The note was found in the mud and nearly lost:

A plan is just a plan,
A man is just a man,
To the end, we defend our kinsman,
As if we were a superman.

52
Something's Wrong

The Viking fleet was being tracked as it sailed up the Severn. To the untrained eye, it looked perfectly normal, if you can call a large Viking raiding fleet normal. Then it anchored when it got dark at Newport. Hundreds of campfires twinkled in the evening sky.

Whilst that was going on, the northern Vikings moved south. They could travel at twice the speed of British troops, and that was at night. They were a silent horde that moved silently and swiftly. Bridgnorth didn't expect to be ransacked. And the women certainly didn't expect to be raped. They hardly knew that a war was going on.

Then Bromyard played host to the murdering, raping, pillagers. It was not a great experience.

Newport and Monmouth suffered the same experience as the southern Vikings moved north. It was a mixture of luck and cunning, but no one spotted them on their journey to Ledbury. It was amazing what could be achieved under the cover of darkness. The Vikings were ready to pounce on a totally unsuspecting Malvern.

Lord Malander, 'It all seems too quiet.'

Lord Hogsflesh, 'Well, we haven't managed to track the Vikings from York. They seem to have literally disappeared. And the fleet is still anchored at Newport.'

Lord Malander, 'I'm starting to get a bad feeling.'

Lord Hogsflesh, 'What are we missing?'

Lord Malander, 'We are ignoring their natural cunning. They know what a potent weapon surprise can be.'

Lord Hogsflesh, 'If we are not careful, we will find out soon.'

There was a note in Ledbury:

Something was more than wrong,

Was someone singing their swan song?
Or was someone just stringing them along?
The tension just went on and on.

53
Over the Hill and Far Away

No one expected the Vikings to climb over the eastern side of the hills, least of all the scattered sentries who were more asleep than awake. The hillside regiment was quickly eliminated, but at least they managed to sound the alarm.

But it was too late; fifty thousand frenzied Vikings rushed down the hills into Great Malvern, which was quite a feat in itself as the hills are pretty steep. Most of the buildings were soon overrun. The factory was captured, although they had no idea what it was. The Academy of Mystical Arts was captured. The half-made citadel was captured, and worst of all, Lady Malander was captured.

Fortunately, Lord Malander was out inspecting his troops, and Thomas and Captain Clutterbuck were preparing the cannons, which were now facing in completely the wrong direction. As was the entire British Army.

The Vikings cared little whether the person in front of them was an armed man or a civilian; they were simply slaughtered. Blood poured down the narrow Malvern streets. Some of the Vikings were drug-induced berserkers who even killed fellow Vikings if they got in the way. It was a massacre of the innocents, but not of the military.

The British troops were urgently trying to reverse the direction of their stakes. The bowmen quickly moved their stocks of arrows. The cannons were moved around with some difficulty, and with some sheer hard work, the cannonballs and gunpowder were moved. The artillery had to be lifted on to logs as they were now required to fire uphill. It had been a massive exercise by Thomas and Captain Clutterbuck, but they were ready just in time.

General Winterdom ordered his troops in Worcester to march to Malvern as soon as possible. Ten thousand of them were to use the hill route to get the advantage of height. Major Bandolier ordered most of his mounted archers in the Forest of Dean to return to Malvern. Some were sent to Newport to see if they could destroy the Viking fleet. The mounted archers in Upton were already engaging the Vikings.

General Winterdom then ordered twenty thousand of the troops on Bredon Hill to march in support of Major Lambskin's regiments. It was going to be a close-run thing. Major Lambskin recalled the troops from Gloucester

Lord Malander ordered some of the mounted archers to protect Thomas and Captain Clutterbuck. If there was any risk to life, they were to be removed from danger. They were assets that his lordship could not afford to lose.

Archers from Major Dargondale's regiments and the mounted troops were soon firing thousands of arrows into Malvern. The Vikings became easy targets as they were being funnelled down specific roads, and there were so many of them. The dead and the dying Vikings were soon impeding the progress of the rest. And those that could still move were finding the blood-splattered, cobbled streets and the growing collection of gore far too much to maintain their stability.

Eventually, the Vikings came onto more open land at Barnard's Green, where they lined up to confront the wall of British archers and men at arms awaiting them. The traditional Viking screaming and jeering started as they began their downhill charge. The last thing they expected was five cannons firing at them along with a few thousand arrows.

The cannon fire shocked most of the Vikings, who simply stopped in their tracks, making them an easy target for the second volley. Men were quickly re-loading the cannons, ready for further volleys, when mounted archers appeared on the Vikings right flank, causing further devastation. It was a serious slaughter. The Vikings were falling in their thousands. So much for clever tactics.

All ten cannons fired again, and although outnumbered, Major Lambskin's infantry marched forward to confront a disorientated and dispirited Viking horde. The Vikings had the difficult task of retreating uphill. Every now and then, the Vikings made mini-charges at the British, but they were too disciplined to give way.

General Winterdom's Northern Army was just entering Malvern when the exhausted Vikings clambered back into Great Malvern. It was not what they expected and the last thing they needed, but then they received some good news. The Viking force had moved from Ledbury to British Camp on the Malvern Hills. These were the cream of the Viking fighting men.

Then the lightning started, which surprised both sides. The Vikings were even more surprised when they saw the lightning being re-directed to tall poles stuck on buildings. They had never seen that before. It looked like their god had been shackled.

The Ledbury Vikings marched past British Camp onto Malvern Wells, where they collided with the mounted archers returning from the Forest of Dean. Initially, the archers were thrashed, but they did what mounted archers do, retreat, reform, and attack. They got within a safe distance, fired a volley of arrows, caused chaos, and retreated and then repeated the process over and over again.

The Ledbury Vikings still managed to make progress along the main road to Great Malvern, although the archers were steadily thinning them out. It wasn't long before they came into contact with General Winterdom's Northern Army coming the other way who were already fighting the exhausted Vikings fleeing from the cannons.

Then the ten thousand troops that used the hill route descended on the Vikings from the west. They ran down the hill and crashed into the Vikings that were now defending from three different directions. The lightning bolts increased in number and intensity, but the lightning disrupters were holding up. Anyway, they were of little value as the two armies were so intermingled.

It was now a slogging match. Normally the Vikings would win that sort of battle. General Winterdom had an additional twenty thousand troops from Bredon heading to Malvern, plus two of Major Lambskin's infantry regiments were marching from Gloucester. You could see the reinforcements from the top of the Malvern Hills.

Now Thor appeared himself with a couple of hundred Valkyries. No one expected this, but apparently, he often appeared at the vital moment when a battle was won or lost.

54
Thor

Thor had no mercy. Thor loved battle. Thor admired the British tactics, but they had to be punished. He couldn't understand why his lightning bolts were being redirected. He suspected sorcery which was clearly unfair.

It was the crunch point, the battle was in the balance, and Thor was determined to push it the Viking way. The Valkyries cut and slashed at every British head they could find. Some of the men were simply turned to dust by their touch. Thor threw his hammer, the mighty Mjolnir, killing dozens of brave archers in one go before returning to his hand. Anyway, Thor's presence terrified the horses causing them to flee, which probably saved the riders' lives.

General Winterdom tried to rouse his men, but the arrival of supernatural entities was just too much for them. Everywhere they were steadily retreating and trying to regroup, but then the hammer would cut a swathe through them. Once men knew that their chances of survival were minimal, then the desire to flee became overriding.

It wasn't long before the British ran down the same narrow cobbled streets that the Vikings had run down earlier. Again, it was difficult to maintain your balance due to the human flotsam. They were being chased by the remnants of the Viking Army, Thor and a century of spear-carrying flying nuns dressed in black gowns and furry, horned helmets.

Captain Clutterbuck and Thomas were waiting for them. The British troops fell in behind the cannons, grateful for a breather. The cannoneers timed their moment perfectly. All ten cannons blasted away. It had a similar effect to before, and then the archers fired their final volley before they fled.

Hundreds, if not thousands, of the Vikings were killed or injured. Thor was furious as his chariot had been scratched, and quite a few of the Valkyries had been wounded. This, unfortunately, only made them angrier. Thor tried to blast the little thunder boxes, but his lightning bolts were simply redirected as usual. This made him even angrier. Angrier than he thought possible.

The bodyguards assigned to Thomas and Captain Clutterbuck did their duty and more or less kidnapped them, which was just in time as Thor disembarked from his chariot and started smashing the cannons to pieces with his hammer.

It would be nice to say that the British carried out a tactical retreat, but it wasn't the case. It was sheer unadulterated panic. The once-formidable fighting force just fled. The troops coming from Bredon and Gloucester wondered what caused it. And then wondered if they should join the flight.

Then they saw the cause of so much panic, and they broke ranks and fled. Thor liked the chase and murdered hundreds just for the joy of doing it. Many brave men died pointlessly. The Vikings had won, or had they?

55
Beasts of Great Monstrosity

Lord Malander looked around at what appeared to be a hopeless cause. Great Malvern was in flames. Most of its inhabitants and a very large proportion of his armed forces had been killed or injured. The survivors were being hunted down just for the dubious thrill of the chase.

To be fair, the surviving Vikings didn't look particularly healthy. Their numbers had been decimated, and if it hadn't been for the arrival of Thor, they would have lost.

Every Malander had a unique responsibility. They had a power that could only be used once in their term as a Duke. It had never been used in living memory. There were no paper records of it ever being used. It could only be used in a dire emergency when the hills themselves were at risk. If they were used inappropriately, then the duke would die.

The old prophecy spoke the words:

> *To capture the Hills of Prophecy,*
> *Will encounter beasts of great monstrosity,*
> *Nothing will prepare you for its progeny,*
> *These killing, fire-breathing monsters of astrology.*

Now was the time, but he would need help from his wife, assuming that she was still alive or Thomas, wherever he was.

Perhaps there was more magic in the world than he realised, as Thomas tapped him on the shoulder.

Thomas, 'It's time, isn't it?'

Lord Malander, 'How did you find me? How did you know?'

Thomas, 'I've always known, the Hills talk to me.'

Lord Malander, 'Don't be silly.'

Thomas, 'There is more magic in the world than you realised.'

Lord Malander, 'How did you know that I was thinking that?'

Thomas, 'The Hills told me.'

Lord Malander, 'Perhaps you are right. I've got the spell written down. I will just get it out of my pocket.'

Thomas, 'There is no need. I will say it, and you can repeat it, but you must be word perfect. Are you happy with that?'

The duke nodded.

Thomas, 'You know that if you use this power, there will be consequences?'

Lord Malander, 'If I don't use the power, then there will be consequences.'

Thomas, 'In that case, are you ready?'

The duke nodded again.

Thomas, 'I call upon the Hills of Prophecy.'

Lord Malander, 'I call upon the Hills of Prophecy.'

Thomas, 'To save us from Thursday's astrology.'

Lord Malander, 'To save us from Thursday's astrology.'

Thomas, 'And free the beasts of great monstrosity.'

Lord Malander, 'And free the beasts of great monstrosity.'

Thomas, 'To aid the Hill's human progeny.'

Lord Malander, 'To aid the Hill's human progeny.'

And then nothing happened.

Lord Malander, 'Nothing is happening.'

Thomas, 'Believe me, it is.'

There wasn't a lot to believe in.

56
Is it an Eruption?

The wrath of Thor seemed to have no end. He, or possibly it, was just a ruthless, merciless killing machine. He had probably personally killed between ten and fifteen thousand individuals. It was genocide on a scale never seen in Grand Britannica before.

It wasn't a volcano, but it was an eruption from a volcanic hill. No one who lived locally would ever believe it. It was almost beyond comprehension. It was not of this reality, but then neither was Thor.

Three truly enormous fire-breathing dragons broke free from the tops of the hills and started their hunt. They knew who the prey was, and they knew where he was. The Valkyries lined up in front of their Nordic god, protecting him from the fabled dragon's breath.

Valkyries are formidable entities in their own right. They were the almost invulnerable collectors of dead warrior's spirits. They were of multiple dimensions and feared no one. Well, they should have feared the incandescent dragons as, one combined fiery breath, and the Valkyries were no more. They were just embers floating in the ether.

Thor was next. He shot bolt after bolt at the three marauding dragons to no effect. He threw Mjolnir at them to no effect. He swore at them to no effect. The dragons didn't play; they just used their fiery breath, and a god ceased to exist. Odin felt a massive disturbance in Yggdrasil, the Nordic Tree of Life.

Odin knew that his son had died. It was almost impossible to believe. What could have killed him? Odin decided to terminate his travels and investigate. Someone would suffer the might of his revenge.

57

A Strange Conversation

Lord Malander was over-joyed to see the death of a god. He was a bit surprised when the largest of the three dragons landed next to him in Guarlford. He was even more surprised when the giant white dragon started a conversation.

Alexander, 'Good Evening, Lord Malander, it's nice to speak to you. My name is Alexander.'

Lord Malander, 'I didn't know that Dragons could talk.'

Alexander, 'Not a lot is known about us. There is some truth in the myths, but most of it is rubbish.'

Lord Malander, 'I wasn't sure what to expect when we made the spell.'

Alexander, 'But surely the clues were in the prophecy: "Beasts of great monstrosity and killing, fire-breathing monsters of astrology". We are the only creature in Chinese astrology that is mythical.'

Lord Malander, 'Well, you are not that mythical as you are standing next to me.'

Alexander, 'I suppose you are right, but until today you didn't believe in dragons, did you?'

Lord Malander, 'No, that is a fair point.'

Alexander, 'Anyway, it's really nice to have a real conversation. I think it's the first one I've had in over a thousand years.

'I have to ask you if our task has been completed to your satisfaction. If yes, I can go back to my sleep.'

Lord Malander, 'I can honestly say that you have completed your task with great efficiency, and it has been a pleasure meeting you. Have a good slumber.'

Alexander, 'I have to point out that there will be consequences.'

Lord Malander, 'I know. Do you have any idea what they might be?'

Alexander, 'I don't know, and if I did, I couldn't tell you. But the killing of a god would have more serious consequences than most.'

Lord Malander, 'I understand, and I wish you well.'

Alexander, 'And I wish you well, my Lord. We will not meet again, but I will get to know your son quite well. And please give my regards to Merlin.'

Lord Malander, 'Before you go, how do you get the poems to the appropriate places?'

Alexander, 'How did you know?'

Lord Malander, 'The clue is in the prophecy itself.'

Alexander, 'So it is.'

Lord Malander, 'So it was you.'

Alexander, 'It was us. Now you have found out I don't think I will bother doing the poems any more.'

Lord Malander, 'That's a shame.'

And in the flick of an eyelid, the three dragons were gone.

Thomas, 'Were you saying something, my Lord?'

Lord Malander, 'I was talking to Alexander.'

Thomas, 'Alexander who?'

Lord Malander, 'Alexander, the giant white dragon.'

Thomas, 'Can they talk?'

Lord Malander, 'You must have seen him.'

Thomas, 'I'm sorry, my Lord. You have me at a loss.'

Lord Malander, 'Why do we call you Thomas when you are really Merlin?'

Thomas, 'I've always been called Thomas, so I'm happy with it. But during the Slimenest war, there were two of us, so I kept the name Thomas as a differentiator.'

Lord Malander, 'Now that is settled, I've got to go and see if my wife is still alive.'

Thomas, 'She is alive, my Lord, but I don't know where she is.'

Lord Malander, 'That's a huge relief. So it's just a case of finding her.'

Thomas, 'Yes, my Lord.' Thomas didn't want to say that Lady Malander had cast a spell stopping anyone from finding her.

58
The Aftermath

After most battles, the leaders would often say that the aftermath was worse than the battle. In this case, it was true. There were almost sixty thousand dead bodies or parts of bodies that had to be disposed of. There were twenty thousand wounded men and women who needed urgent treatment. You could call it inhumane, but the Viking wounded were given the option of a quick death or a slow lingering death caused by their wound. There was little mercy to be had.

Nearly every building in Malvern had been badly damaged. A dozen or more had been burnt to the ground. The Citadel, being made of stone, was reasonably intact, and the factory was still fully operational. Every cannon had been destroyed by Thor, but new ones were being constructed already.

General Winterdom's hair was a bit greyer. He was trying to do a roll call, but it was proving almost impossible as his forces were so scattered. He still had ten thousand troops on Bredon Hill that had not taken part in the hostilities. Of the rest of that force, almost half had been lost. The Northern Army that came from Worcester had losses of over sixty per cent. He was a hardened soldier, but he shed a few tears. He lost a lot of good men and some life-long friends, but that was his job.

Major Lambskin carried out a similar roll call. His two regiments based at Gloucester were almost intact, but the Malvern regiments had practically been wiped out. He could barely make one regiment out of the eight that fought.

Major Bandolier's mounted archers had fought everywhere and were a significant part of the British Army's success until Thor turned up. He had lost about half of his force. He wasn't sure what had happened to the squadrons sent to Newport.

Major Dragondale's archers had more or less been eliminated as a fighting force. Thor had killed even the ones based in the forts along the Severn. She wondered what the future had in store for her.

Lord Hogsflesh almost drunk himself to death. He had failed to do his job. He had not thought it possible that the Vikings would attack over the hills. It showed a certain lack of intelligence which is not good for an intelligence officer.

Lady Malander had vanished from the face of the Earth. Her husband was worried sick. He had actually been physically ill, thinking about the worst. He needed her, and he needed his son-to-be.

Thomas or Merlin had enjoyed the cannoning but was troubled by the death and destruction that had struck his beloved Malvern. It seemed so unfair that one small town should have been the focus of two different wars.

Major Mainstay had built up a significant force in the south-east, which was available if required.

Captain Clutterbuck was annoyed that his cannons had been destroyed but relieved that his factory was still standing. He was pleased that he had been promoted to Major.

And what about the Vikings? The majority had been rounded up and executed. Again, that might seem harsh and inhumane, but that was their wont. Some had escaped and were fleeing back to Newport. Mounted archers were tracking them.

59

The Fleet

While the Battle of Malvern was underway, Major Bandolier sent some mounted archers from the Forest of Dean to Newport to determine if they could destroy the Viking fleet. When they got there, they found nearly two hundred longships guarded by about seventy men.

The expedition leader, Captain Drainwater, couldn't decide whether to destroy the fleet with flaming arrows or to capture it. Destruction was an easy option, but capture was challenging as the fleet would need to be moved to protect it, and none of them had any naval skills.

In the end, she decided to eliminate the Vikings and then decide. A pitched battle broke out between the Viking spears and the British arrows. The arrows won as they gradually picked off the Viking sentries one at a time. To be fair, they only offered token resistance as the guards left behind were either wounded or too old for fighting.

Captain Drainwater now had two hundred intact longships, but there was a real danger that the owners would return for them. There was no way that they could manage two hundred, so they selected twenty to man, and they decided that they would just let the rest loose. The incoming tide would push the rest inland. Some of the riders would go ahead and seek advice.

Each crewed boat managed to pull two or three longships behind them. The archers had no idea how to crew a vessel, but it wasn't that difficult, and the sails pushed them along at a decent speed. So, Captain Drainwater became the first admiral of a British Navy.

The fleet had only just departed in time as the remnants of the defeated Viking Army started arriving in Newport so that they could flee home. They were startled to see the fleet leaving. Some managed to swim out and secure some of the freed boats that had been stranded on mudflats. Some of these became so over-crowded that they sank.

The Vikings were being followed by fresh regiments of mounted archers who were giving them no quarter. A few of the Viking ships managed to escape, but most of the Vikings either drowned or experienced the sharp end of an arrow.

60
Who was Raped?

Lady Malander had been taken prisoner by a small group of Vikings that had taken over a residence in Eastnor. They were waiting for things to quieten down before they made their escape. In the meantime, they decided to have a bit of fun at Lady Malander's expense.

There were a dozen unwashed, grizzly ruffians. Not the sort that Lady Malander would normally associate with. They had lust in their eyes, and from what she could see, the tools to put it into practice. The fact that she was a lady made her even more desirable.

She fought, as that was expected of her, but her dress was ripped off, and the under-garments were soon on the floor. The Vikings relished her beautiful nakedness, and hands were soon caressing her voluptuous breasts and fingering her most hidden of places. The Vikings started fighting over who would fuck her first. Eventually, an order of precedence was agreed upon, and she was raped.

Then she was raped again and again, but she did not conceive. It may seem strange that she allowed this to continue as she could easily have escaped at any time. In fact, the facts were not as they appeared. She had engineered the whole thing. She made them hide in Eastnor. She made them particularly lusty. She made them rape her, not that they needed much encouragement.

But not one of the twelve men got her pregnant. Perhaps she was the problem in their marriage after all. Not everyone knows that a female magician knows exactly when conception is achieved.

Now it was time for revenge as some of the Vikings were considering a second raping session. She conceived a horrible death for them. One that fitted the crime. She made their willies grow in length so that they were long enough to enter their rectums. She then made them fuck themselves. While this was going on, she increased the girth to over a foot so that they fucked themselves to death.

It wasn't long before the lounge was full of dying Vikings screaming in agony as they gradually bled to death.

Then an old friend knocked on the door. It was Thomas. She ran at him, and her hugs almost crushed him in her enthusiasm. Thomas was conscious of her nudity and was finding it hard to control his reactions.

Thomas, 'So your plan didn't work?'

Lady Malander, 'No, I was fucked by twelve different men, and not one of them got me pregnant.'

Thomas, 'That's hard to believe as you got pregnant before.'

Lady Malander, 'I know.'

Thomas, 'Lord Malander is worried sick about you.'

Lady Malander, 'I'm sure that he is, but I'm not going home until I get pregnant.'

Thomas, 'You can't leave him in that state.'

Lady Malander, 'In that case, you better do the decent thing.' She could feel his erection through his tights. It was actually rubbing against her fanny as they hugged.

Lady Malander, 'I can tell that you want me.'

Thomas, 'But I couldn't cheat on his lordship.'

Lady Malander, 'I'm doing this for him.' She placed her hand inside of Thomas's tights and rubbed his penis. It was already rock hard. She needed it in her before it came of its own accord.

She lifted his cock out of his tights and pushed it into her vagina. That was no challenge as her receptacle had received gifts from twelve men already. It wasn't a case of sloppy seconds but very sloppy twelfths.

Lady Malander gently fondled Thomas's balls and played with his scrotum. She knew that he was resisting, but no man could resist her administrations for long. She grabbed his penis and thrust it hard into her pussy. That was too much for Thomas, and he came, and within seconds she knew that she had conceived.

Lady Malander, 'Thomas, you are going to be a daddy.'

Thomas, 'Never.' And they hugged and hugged.'

Lady Malander, 'Take me home.' And it was never mentioned again. Lord Malander was going to have a son.

61
Victory Meeting

Lord Malander called his fourth War Council, but this time it was a victory meeting. The attendees were as follows:

- Major Mainstay, South-East Region
- Major Bandolier, Mounted Archers
- Major Clutterbuck, Engineering
- Lord Hogsflesh, Scout
- Major Lambskin, South-West Region
- Major Dragondale, Archers
- Thomas Merlin, Mystical Arts
- Lady Malander, Mystical Arts
- General Winterdom, Northern Army.

Lord Malander, 'We won. We beat the invaders. It's hard to believe. But at what a terrible, heart-breaking cost. We need to honour the dead by having two minutes of silence.'

It was a particularly poignant moment as there was no one in the room who had not lost a friend or a loved one.

General Winterdom, 'The losses wouldn't have been that bad if Thor had not intervened.'

Major Lambskin, 'But just think how much worse it would have been without the dragons coming to our aid.'

Thomas, 'The dragons were amazing. Why didn't we use them before?'

Lord Malander, 'The old legend says that a Malander can only call upon them once during his tenure as the duke. That was our one and only time.'

Major Dragondale, 'It was a good call. We have swept the Vikings from Grand Britannica.'

Lord Malander, 'Alexander said that he would get to know my son well.'

Major Clutterbuck, 'And who is Alexander?'

Lord Malander, 'He is the white Dragon.'

Major Clutterbuck, 'Are you saying that they can talk?'

Lord Malander, 'Yes, we had a good chat.'

Thomas, 'I didn't hear him say a word.'

Lord Malander, 'That is strange. He said that there would be consequences and killing Thor would result in serious consequences.'

General Winterdom, 'Did he say what they were?'

Lord Malander, 'No. He is not allowed to say, but I got the feeling that serious means serious.'

Major Clutterbuck, 'Do you think the Vikings will come back?'

Lord Malander, 'Almost certainly.'

Major Dragondale, 'What is driving them?'

Lord Malander, 'Treasure, land, honour, it's hard to tell.'

Lord Hogsflesh, 'Women, they are after our women. And I'm not having it.'

Lord Malander, 'That may be true, but would that drive them across dangerous seas?'

Major Clutterbuck, 'I would say yes, I think Lord Hogsflesh is right.'

Lord Malander, 'Anyway, they will come again, partly to get revenge. What do we know about the Norse gods?'

Lady Malander, 'Very little. I've heard of Loki and Odin, and there are some female gods.'

Lord Malander, 'They might want revenge. Let's assume that they are coming back and that they will have more resources than before. What are we going to do?'

General Winterdom, 'I need to rebuild the Northern Army and garrison the coastal towns.'

Lord Malander, 'Do we build castles?'

General Winterdom, 'That would be an excellent idea if we had the time and money.'

Lord Malander, 'Let's assume that money is not an issue.'

Major Clutterbuck, 'We need to decide where the likeliest invasion spots are going to be.'

Lord Malander, 'Could I ask you, General Winterdom and Major Lambskin, to agree on the fortification sites and then discuss with Major Clutterbuck.'

They all agreed.

General Winterdom, 'We will need another recruitment campaign.'

Lord Malander, 'Let's get that underway. What are your views, Major Lambskin?'

Major Lambskin, 'More troops would be useful, but what I really want are cannons. They were magnificent.'

Major Mainstay, 'I agree, give me cannons.'

Major Clutterbuck, 'We will have much smaller, hand-held versions shortly.'

Major Lambskin, 'Never.'

Lord Malander, 'I would like Major Bandolier to create a force of musketeers and cannoneers. Gradually we will distribute these forces to the divisions. Is that acceptable?'

Major Bandolier, 'It certainly is.'

Major Clutterbuck, 'I will need more resources to achieve that.'

Lord Malander, 'What do you need?'

Major Clutterbuck, 'My Lord, I think they call it a foundry, more metal workers, craftsmen of all sorts.'

Thomas, 'My Lord, we have lots of new ideas to develop,'

Lord Malander, 'Give me a list, and we will get it organised.'

Lord Clutterbuck issued pencils to everyone. They had seen them before, but here was a veritable hoard. There was a clamour to get as many as possible.

Lord Hogsflesh, 'I would like to offer my resignation for my failure to scout properly. I should have had scouts in Herefordshire and Wales.'

General Winterdom, 'Yes, that was a failure in intelligence, but I would never believe that they would go over the hills.'

Lord Malander, 'Resignation not accepted. We all did our best, and it's going to get tougher. We are going to need all of the expertise we currently have and more. But Lord Hogsflesh, you can buy us a round of drinks.'

Lord Hogsflesh, 'I'm not sure if my pockets could handle that sort of expenditure.'

Lord Malander, 'And now, my Lady, what do you plan to do regarding mystical services?'

Lady Malander, 'I'm handing everything over to Thomas due to my pregnancy.'

Lord Malander was stunned. What a time and place to announce it. What happiness. There was an outbreak of goodwill.

62
Odin

Odin called a Thing of all the Nations. These meetings were only called once in a lifetime, usually in a crisis. Odin decided that the death of his son was a crisis, not because he loved him or even cared for him. As far as he was concerned, he was a disrupter, a disturber of the peace, and a real pain in the arse. No, it was more about respect.

You can't just go around killing gods. It was rude. It was an affront to their dignity, and especially his dignity. And for a god, dignity was seriously important. Without dignity, you couldn't really be a god.

Odin had gathered together all of the Viking warlords throughout Europe. He had liberated their sobriety through liberal quantities of beer and mead. These meetings were never very organised affairs, but usually, a decision was made. Once a decision had been made, the planning process kicked in but was never particularly well-organised. And once a plan was made, it was subject to immediate change due to the whim of the gods or a cock-up. They had invaded the wrong country on one occasion after following the process.

There were a few hours of drinking to wish Thor well on his journey to wherever dead gods go. That was all a bit vague because he wasn't in Valhalla. But then dragon magic was very powerful, but Odin had every intention of annihilating them.

The drinking stopped, and the fucking started. A large number of captured slave-girls were brought in to help set the scene. The warlords were told that these were all British girls and that Grand Britannica was over-flowing with nubile beauties, and most of them wanted real Viking men as opposed to the rather limp Brits. That wasn't the impression that the slave-girls gave as they were being ravished.

Once the drinking and the fucking had ended, or rather petered out due to exhaustion or the death of too many slave-girls, it was time for the meeting to start. Those who could still sit, sat. Those that were too tired slept, knowing that they would be subject to the decisions made.

Odin stood up, displaying his godly demeanour, and showing a fair amount of dignity. He banged the floor with his staff and said, 'We invade Grand Britannica.'

There was a huge cheer. Some of them weren't sure what they were cheering for, but a decision had been made. Odin had always been good at managing meetings. He then decided to go and help himself to a fair British maiden. By the time he got there, she certainly wasn't a maiden.

63
The Long Pregnancy

Lady Malander realised that she shouldn't have blurted out her pregnancy at the meeting. She should have chosen the right time and place to share the information with her husband. As far as he was concerned, this was her first pregnancy, but she had almost reached term when time was previously reversed.

She often wondered about her first child. What would he be like now? How would he get on with his father? Would he have survived the recent tribulations? Would he be happy? Anyway, it was all speculation.

Then she wondered about Thomas. At one level, she saw him as her son. At another level, he was an object of desire or was that just another aspect of mothering? At least she had made her husband happy and kept the line going.

And now she was pregnant again. In some ways, it seemed like one long pregnancy. She decided, if the fates allowed, to take this pregnancy nice and easy. She was going to relax. It would give Thomas the opportunity to develop the team without her interference.

Dinner was called, and she sat down with her husband to eat roast chicken. Nowadays, he was just one big smile. He was going to be a father. His line was guaranteed. He had beaten the Vikings with a little bit of help from a few others, and he had a new mate called Alexander.

Lady Malander, 'What are you going to call your son?'

Lord Malander, 'Is it definitely a boy?'

Lady Malander, 'There is no doubt.'

Lord Malander, 'Something regal like Timothy, Ivor, Hugh or Victor.'

Lady Malander, 'Is that the best you can do?'

Lord Malander, 'You know his name, don't you?'

Lady Malander, 'I do, but the future is not totally fixed. There are many threads that are woven. And he will have his own path to tread.'

Lord Malander, 'Are you going to tell me his name?'

Lady Malander, 'No, because later you are going to tell me what it is.'

Lord Malander, 'I do hate all this mystery and suspense.'

Lady Malander, 'It is the price you pay for falling in love with a sorceress. You do love me, don't you?'

Lord Malander, 'I'm surprised that you even had to ask.'

Lady Malander, 'All women and especially me need to hear the answer.'

Lord Malander, 'I've always loved you, and I will always love you.'

Lady Malander, 'Is that my personality you love or my body?'

Lord Malander, 'You have caught me out. It is your fanny that I love.'

Lady Malander, 'You bastard. It's nothing special.'

Lord Malander, 'That's not my view.'

Lady Malander, 'Let's go and check it out.'

Lord Malander, 'But you are pregnant.'

Lady Malander, 'That's not going to stop me having a good fuck.'

64
Magical Training

Thomas felt that Lady Malander had put him in a very difficult situation. She had taken advantage of her position and their special relationship. Whenever he saw her son in the future, he would think about this moment, but then that didn't make sense.

As far as he was concerned, he couldn't father a child. Why had he suddenly become fertile? Was he really the father? Was Lady Malander deliberately creating a bond between them? What if his lordship found out? Part of him wanted to run, but a much bigger part of him wanted to stay. He was besotted with Lady Malander. He knew that he was falling in love with her. He was desperate to fuck her again.

While all of these thoughts were swirling around in his head, his class had turned up. Rather ironically, the lesson was called 'Divining the truth'. Thomas wasn't sure, if it was an area he had any expertise in.

There were now over forty magicians in training. About half a dozen were excellent, another dozen were competent, and the rest were journeymen with no destination. They would be useful in handling the mundane.

One of the problems with magic is that you can't be trained to be a magician. You can be trained to be a better magician. Even that is more about someone showing you the possibilities of a situation. Thomas suffered this problem himself.

He explained to his pupils that a house was on fire. How could you put the fire out? Most would shout water. What if you couldn't magic up any water? What else can you do?

Then the room would go silent. A magician has to think of alternatives, and the class would brainstorm the problem.

Typical answers would be:

- Use a different liquid
- Use sand

- Remove the air
- Turn the house to stone
- Move the house into a lake
- Get a dragon to pee on it

A good magician has to think on his or her feet.

Thomas realised that his mind was wandering again and that he wasn't really focussing on the class. Something was bothering him, and then an image entered his mind. It was Odin, and he was on his way.

He rushed to the Manor House to let Lord Malander know.

Lord Malander, 'Morning Merlin.'

Thomas, 'Good morning, my Lord.'

Lord Malander, 'You are in a bit of a hurry.'

Thomas, 'I think they are on their way.'

Lord Malander, 'Who?'

Thomas, 'The Vikings, my Lord.'

Lord Malander, 'What makes you think that?'

Thomas, 'I stood on Odin's longship.'

Lord Malander, 'In a dream?'

Thomas, 'No, I was there.'

Lord Malander, 'How do you know?'

Thomas, 'You just do.'

Lord Malander, 'Tell me about Odin.'

Thomas, 'He is a big man by any standard. Over seven foot tall, barrel-chested, a long grey beard, piercing eyes, cloaked with a staff in his hand. He had a strong, determined presence.'

Lord Malander, 'Did you like him?'

Thomas, 'Strangely, yes. Thor had an evil streak. He liked and lusted for battle. He enjoyed killing people. Odin seems wise, astute, intelligent. He is the sort of man you would like as an uncle.'

Lord Malander, 'What about the ship?'

Thomas, 'It was larger than your typical longship with a black sail. It was part of a fleet of two or three hundred vessels.'

Lord Malander, 'What was your impression of their mission?'

Thomas, 'I got the impression that the war had started. They were on their way here, or they were still planning to come here.'

Lord Malander, 'I guess that we need to plan our defence. By the way, I need an update on the witch situation.'

65

The Fleet

Lord Malander, 'Morning, Victor. Are you still down about your crap scouting performance?'

Lord Hogsflesh, 'Thank you, my Lord. You have that rare gift of kicking a person even harder when he has already been kicked pretty hard.'

Lord Malander, 'Your problem is that you are far too sensitive.'

Lord Hogsflesh, 'Thank you, my Lord. No one has ever accused me of that crime before.'

Lord Malander, 'Anyway, how is my navy going?'

Lord Hogsflesh, 'I'm not sure if it's your navy any more. Every ship is commanded by a Hollander but with a British crew. It's strange when you think about it. We are an island race with no maritime tradition.'

Lord Malander, 'We have just started a tradition.'

Lord Hogsflesh, 'I think we probably have.'

Lord Malander, 'So, how big is the fleet?'

Lord Hogsflesh, 'We have sixty-two Viking longships and thirteen Hollander ships. Not much, but it is a start.'

Lord Malander, 'When will they be ready to fight?'

Lord Hogsflesh, 'Give them six months.'

Lord Malander, 'I doubt that they will have two months. Possibly less than a month.'

Lord Hogsflesh, 'How do you know that?'

Lord Malander, 'Thomas has seen Odin leaving Russia.'

Lord Hogsflesh, 'How does he know that he is coming here?'

Lord Malander, 'I guess that he doesn't know for sure, but how do you know anything when it comes to magic?'

Lord Hogsflesh, 'So what you are saying is that we better get prepared and better get in position.'

Lord Malander, 'I think so.'

Lord Hogsflesh, 'You do realise that if they come in force, we will be simply pushed out of the water.'

Lord Malander, 'True, but we need to make them think that we have a substantial force. I even wondered if we could put a cannon on the ships?'

Lord Hogsflesh, 'That's a brilliant idea. It might work on the Hollander ships, but the longships are probably too low in the water. But I will see what I can do.'

Lord Malander, 'You might need one of Thomas's illusions.'

Lord Hogsflesh, 'I will have a chat with him. By the way, thank you for sticking with me.'

Lord Malander, 'We are in this together. I was thinking that you might need more spies in Europe.'

Lord Hogsflesh, 'I had thought about it, but communications are so slow.'

Lord Malander, 'But it is slow for both sides, and some communication is better than no communications.'

Lord Hogsflesh, 'Sometimes I wonder about that.'

66
Planning the Next Victory

Lord Malander called his fifth War Council, but this time it was not about victory but about planning the defence of the Grand Britannica. The attendees were as follows:

- Major Mainstay, South-East Region
- Major Bandolier, Mounted Archers
- Major Clutterbuck, Engineering
- Lord Hogsflesh, Intelligence and Navy
- Major Lambskin, South-West Region
- Major Dragondale, Cannons and Musketeers
- Thomas Merlin, Mystical Arts
- General Winterdom, Northern Army.

Lord Malander, 'I'm glad that you could make it. It's time to plan our defence. Thomas believes that the campaign against us is underway. He has seen Odin in his black longship.'

Major Bandolier, 'Are you sure that Odin is on his way here?'

Thomas, 'I saw him on his longship and certainly got the feeling that the campaign against us is underway.'

Lord Hogsflesh, 'Talking to my Hollander friends who have suffered many Viking incursions, things are definitely afoot. They think that there has been a call to arms.'

General Winterdom, 'At least the signs suggest that we need to prepare ourselves.'

Lord Malander, 'What resources do we have at our disposal?'

Each commander listed his forces:

General Winterdom
- Northern Army — fifty thousand

- Garrisons — twenty-five thousand
- Militiamen — say one hundred thousand.'

Major Mainstay
- Southern-Eastern Army — thirty thousand
- Garrisons — fifteen thousand
- Militiamen — say two hundred thousand

Major Lambskin
- South Western Army — twenty-five thousand
- Garrisons — ten thousand
- Militiamen — say one hundred and fifty thousand
- Malvern Army — twenty-five thousand

Major Bandolier
- Mounted Archers — five thousand

Major Dragondale
- Cannoneers — one hundred

Lord Hogsflesh
- Naval Personnel — one thousand
- Scouts — one thousand

Thomas
- Forty-six Magicians

Lord Malander, 'That is quite a force, but the following things are obvious:

- We need to convert the militia into regulars
- We need more cannoneers and musketeers as soon as possible
- We need to grow the size of the Navy.'

Major Dragondale, 'We are recruiting more artillerymen, but we still are waiting for the equipment.'

Major Clutterbuck, 'Manufacture is underway, but we keep coming up with new innovations.'

Lord Malander, 'That is all very commendable but we need weaponry now.'

Major Clutterbuck, 'I understand. I will now focus on production.'

Lord Malander, 'And the muskets?'

Major Clutterbuck, 'They are actually more complex to make than the cannons. I'm waiting for the woodworkers to arrive. Then we can get a production line going.'

Lord Malander, 'Sorry, I'm not being critical, but your weaponry might be the difference between success and failure.'

Major Clutterbuck, 'I do understand, and I will now focus on production.'

Lord Malander, 'Thank you.'

Thomas, 'I would like the Council to think about rockets.'

Lord Malander, 'Rockets?'

Thomas, 'Yes, these are similar to cannons but are self-propelling explosives that you fire up into the air, and they land on the enemy from above. They can be quite terrifying.'

Major Clutterbuck, 'That sounds interesting.'

Lord Malander, 'The more weaponry, the better. Who knows what we are going to need to defeat Odin?'

Lord Hogsflesh, 'We won't have the dragons this time. Without them, we couldn't have stopped Thor.'

Major Lambskin, 'And Odin might be worse.'

Lord Malander, 'Any suggestions, Merlin?'

Thomas, 'I don't think our magic can stand-up to the power of the gods.'

Major Lambskin, 'Would the Druids help?'

Thomas, 'I was wondering about calling a meeting of all the magical races in the land.'

Lord Malander, 'That sounds like a good idea, but we need those witches eradicated first. General Winterdom, do you have the site details?'

General Winterdom, 'We have a list of sites that should be fortified but do we have time?'

Major Clutterbuck, 'I have the plans for wooden forts, but not the resources.'

Lord Malander, 'Won't they just burn down?'

Major Clutterbuck, 'Not straight away. Typically, it takes eighteen months to build a decent stone castle. I would suggest that we target every Lord Protector to start building one, especially in the areas where we have identified that we need them.'

Lord Malander, 'I accept that suggestion and will action it. Moving on, how do we propose tackling the Viking incursions?'

General Winterdom, 'I would suggest the following:

- Firstly, we need a network of lookouts along the coast to warn us of their impending arrival
- Then we use whatever resources we can muster to stop them from landing: the Navy, magic etc. But there is every chance that they will land
- We must counter-attack immediately
- Other forces from around the country must be ready to support the defending Army
- We defeat them in battle.'

Major Lambskin, 'They could attack in multiple places at the same time.'

General Winterdom, 'The plan still stands.'

Major Lambskin, 'Do we have our three regional armies and a central Army that will come to the aid of the others.'

Lord Malander, 'I guess we already have that with the Malvern forces. 'These are my orders:

- Lord Hogsflesh to set up a network of coastal observers with fire warnings and horseback couriers
- General Winterdom to continue to build up the Northern Army and improve defences
- Major Lambskin to continue to build up the South Western Army and improve defences
- Major Mainstay to continue to build up the South Eastern Army and improve defences
- Lord Hogsflesh to build up the Navy and to charter further vessels as required
- Lord Hogsflesh to build up a network of continental spies
- Major Clutterbuck to focus on the production of cannons and muskets

- Major Clutterbuck and Thomas to work on rockets as long as it doesn't impact the manufacture of other weaponry
- Major Clutterbuck to build up the supply of arrows and munitions for the cannons
- Major Dragondale to recruit more cannoneers and musketeers
- Thomas to eradicate the witches
- Thomas to assist Lord Hogsflesh in stopping the Vikings landing
- Lord Hogsflesh to attack the Viking fleet or fleets
- We will follow General Winterdom's plan
- Thomas to talk to other magical entities
- I will talk to the Lord Protectors about the building of forts.

'Let's get cracking. We have an island to defend.'

67
Rockets

Major Clutterbuck, 'So how do you make a rocket?'

Thomas, 'You need a thin tube that can be internally divided into two. You can put gunpowder into both halves. Then make it aerodynamic like an arrow with wings at one end and a point at the other. The winged part has a fuse.

'Put the rocket into a container which is really another tube. You will need easy access to the fuse. When it is lit, the rocket flies out of the container and lands on the opposition.'

Major Clutterbuck, 'I guess that the firing tube's elevation defines the trajectory of the rocket.'

Thomas, 'Exactly.'

Major Clutterbuck, 'I understand the requirement. What was the other thing you were going to show me?'

Thomas, 'It's called shrapnel. In its simplest form, it is just a collection of metal pieces or musket balls usually put into a bag. On firing from a cannon, the bag splits, and the shrapnel pieces spread out, killing and maiming anyone in their way.'

Major Clutterbuck, 'It all feels rather ungentlemanly. At least with a sword, it is man against man.'

Thomas, 'I know where you are coming from, but we didn't ask them to invade us.'

Major Clutterbuck, 'But shouldn't peace be the objective?'

Thomas, 'I agree. I've got the task of eradicating the witches. I'm not really happy about it, but they have attacked us many times. They have brought it upon themselves.'

Major Clutterbuck, 'And the enemy are ruthless. They would have no qualms about killing us.'

Thomas, 'That is the difference. We are fighting for our survival.'

68
Plymouth

Lord Hogsflesh and Lord Malander were both at Plymouth reviewing the first Navy of Grand Britannica.

Lord Malander, 'It looks impressive.'

Lord Hogsflesh, 'I think it is as a first attempt. But we are going to be outclassed in terms of the number of ships and seamanship. I suspect that their very best, are going to confront us.'

Lord Malander, 'Is there any way we can fit a cannon on a longship?'

Lord Hogsflesh, 'I would say no. They are built for speed, and you will notice how shallow their draft is. They can travel up rivers, only three foot deep. Although they are made of oak, they are light enough for men to carry. In fact, they are often turned upside down to act as shelters.'

Lord Malander, 'There must be a way of installing a cannon.'

Lord Hogsflesh, 'Both ends are curved upwards, so they couldn't be placed there. I guess that one could be placed where the mast meets the hull, which is called the kerling. It's pretty strong there, but it means that they can only fire sideways.'

Lord Malander, 'Can we ship one to Major Clutterbuck so that he can consider the installation of a cannon?'

Lord Hogsflesh, 'Of course.' He thought it was a stupid idea, but he had learnt that Lord Malander's stupid ideas were often world-beaters.

Lord Hogsflesh, 'I will introduce you to your admiral.'

They walked to the harbour office to find the Hollanders knocking back a few drinks. Lord Hogsflesh introduced them to Lord Malander, focusing on the fleet leader: Captain Peter van Dijk.

Lord Malander, 'What would happen if the Vikings turned up now?'

Captain Peter van Dijk, 'The Vikings avoid naval battles. They are just a means of transporting troops and goods.'

Lord Malander, 'How would you stop the Vikings from landing?'

Captain Peter van Dijk, 'I would plan to be in the vicinity. That should be enough to put them off.'

Lord Malander, 'That is hardly fighting talk.'

Captain Peter van Dijk, 'What do you want me to do?'

Lord Malander, 'I want you to attack their ships and stop them from landing.'

Captain Peter van Dijk, 'That has never been done before.'

Lord Malander, 'That doesn't mean that we can't do it.'

Captain Peter van Dijk, 'I will think about it.'

Lord Malander, 'And why are all the ships here?'

Captain Peter van Dijk, 'Where would you prefer them to be?'

Lord Malander, 'Why can't they patrol the coast.'

Captain Peter van Dijk, 'I can organise some patrolling if that is what you want.'

Lord Malander and Hogsflesh walked off.

Lord Malander, 'Find me a British captain.'

Lord Hogsflesh, 'I wish I could.'

Lord Malander, 'Those Hollanders will be off when the shit hits the pan.'

Lord Hogsflesh, 'I agree, but I can't find an alternative.'

Lord Malander, 'What about a rogue Viking who would join our cause?'

Lord Hogsflesh, 'Leave it with me.'

Lord Malander, 'I will, but time is running out.'

69

Hunting down those damn Witches

Robin took on the job of neutralising the witches. She divided her magicians into ten teams of two. Each group was allocated ten men at arms.

Lady Malander's detection spell had been used during the Slimenest war. Every witch's head was turned orange. There was a downside in that it also coloured those who had the witching powers but weren't actually practising witches.

The other danger is that once exposed, the witches could turn nasty and cause havoc. They might see that as a viable alternative to the traditional punishment of being burnt alive on the stake. There were no plans for mass burnings or capital punishment of any sort. They planned to turn them into orange sheep. Then they could live out their days in a sheepish fashion.

Rather than turn all of the witches orange in one go, it was decided to tackle the problem region by region. Obviously, the news would get out, and some havoc would be caused. Every orange witch, would be interviewed, and if they were confirmed as a witch, they would be 'sheepised'. If they simply had unused latent skills, they would be released but monitored. A monitoring spell would be used and would take the appropriate action if any witchery was detected.

The campaign started with considerable success, but then the witches went into hiding. It became more and more difficult to track them down. In some cases, they were turned into orange sheep without meeting them. There were many amusing stories of sheep being stuck up chimneys and found in impossible places.

Slowly a very lucrative market developed in orange sheep. They were hunted down for their meat. Some were used for more primal purposes, knowing that a witch was entombed in the sheep. It was not a good time to be a witch.

Robin carried out a steady but dedicated campaign. Everyone in the local communities thanked her. Gradually she became a national celebrity and was named 'Witchfinder General'. She even found that she enjoyed it, although she felt pity for the men and women who had latent powers as they were effectively cursed forever.

70
A Magical Conclave

Thomas put out a call for a magical conclave on Midsummer Hill. He had no idea what sort of reaction he was going to receive. He wasn't sure if the Vikings were seen as better or worse than the British. In reality, they were both human and probably both equally cursed.

Anyway, it was worth a try. The invitations were sent to the following:

- The Unicorni
- The Goblini
- The Elementi
- The Dragoni
- The Fauni
- The Asrai
- The Pixi
- The Elfi
- The Mersi
- The Bansheei
- The Leprechauni
- The Gremli
- The Impi
- The Famili
- The Fairi

Thomas wasn't sure if they all still existed. He had assumed that The Dragoni were extinct, but he was proved wrong. And although most of them were members of the Fay Council, he wasn't sure how much magic they had between them. Were they strong enough to counter Odin?

He also added the Druids to the list. He ignored the giants, ogres, trolls, mermen, and an assembly of others as they weren't members of the Fay Council and tended to veer towards the dark side.

He choose Midsummer Hill as it had been a traditional meeting place. That was one of the reasons that the elders came to Malvern. That and the strength of the ley lines.

The date selected was the next Friday, the thirteenth, which is a very lucky day for the Fay, but not always for the humans or ploughmen as they call us.

As Thomas and Lady Malander had called the meeting, there were several actions that had to be carried out, including:

- Spells of safety and security
- Blessing of the oaks and the sycamores
- Dressing of the yew trees
- Dressing of the local fountains
- Ample supply of Malvern water
- A berry feast
- Food requirements for each type of Fay
- Artificial light as the meetings were held at sunset
- Lodgings for all
- Seating
- Gaia celebrations
- Opening and closing ceremonies, and more.

Lady Malander, 'The Enchantress of Evermore would have loved all of this.'

Thomas, 'She does. She is here now. I can feel her excitement.'

Lady Malander, 'I didn't realise how much work was needed.'

Thomas, 'I could certainly do with Robin's help.'

Lady Malander, 'Where is she?'

Thomas, 'Busily converting witches into sheep.'

Lady Malander, 'That has to be done.'

Thomas, 'I believe that she plans to choose a different animal to stop the locals from eating them. Witch meat is now regarded as a culinary delicacy.'

Lady Malander, 'What animal is she thinking of?'

Thomas, 'A cat.'

Lady Malander, 'Good idea, but that will probably curse a cat forever. They will be seen as being familiar with a witch.'

71
Odin does the Rounds

Although Odin had got a universal agreement to attack Grand Britannica, the decision had to be reinforced. It was partly because the Viking warlords couldn't remember what they had agreed to or a new warlord had been appointed. Or they were just too lazy.

Odin had about twenty different territories to visit. So Thomas had been right; the campaign was underway, but the invasion was still some time off. Once a warlord had agreed to the invasion, Odin had to take that fleet with him to the next territory; otherwise, they would wander off. This meant that Odin's fleet was getting steadily larger. This meant that they had to attack and pillage the locals to obtain sustenance.

It wasn't long before pillaging led to raping and so on. From a Viking perspective, this was quite acceptable until one group of Vikings attacked another group of Vikings. This tended to cause a breakdown in relationships and bloody warfare. Vikings quite enjoyed attacking Vikings as they liked Viking women and they could steal their longships. However, it didn't help Odin's cause.

As his tour continued, the problems of feeding the multitude and maintaining peace just got worse. The Vikings respected Odin, but they were their own masters. They only did things if there was profit involved. They had never been an Army. They were raiders and damn good at it.

The normal Viking tactic was to raid a coastal or riverine town over and over again. Often, they would depopulate a whole area. Then they would land a settlement group who would take over the local properties and farms. From there, they would gradually increase their sphere of influence until the country belonged to them. Here Odin was planning an invasion fleet, but who would settle the land? How would they claim it as their land? Odin was simply interested in revenge.

Odin was also up against nature. The waters around Helsinki were starting to freeze. Game was in short supply. Ships needed to be repaired. Men wanted to go home. It was not all easy sailing for a god.

72
Clutterbuck's Calculations

Major Clutterbuck's team were gradually getting their act together. The foundry and metal workers were knocking out cannons, rocket tubes, musket frames and munitions at a consistent rate. The carpenters were creating cross-bows, carriages, musket bodies and arrows at a rapid pace. The concept of a production line was now fully understood.

Fay Mellondrop was doing a great job of sourcing components and managing the stores. She was definitely the power behind the throne. Major Clutterbuck needed her. The production line would fail without her constant attention to detail. He knew it, and she knew it.

Thomas was impressed with the new cannons. They were held in place on wheeled carriages with a screw device that would allow the cannoneer to change the elevation as required. The finishing off was much better. He was surprised by how many were being produced. He had never seen so much metal in one location.

Thomas was amazed by how impressive the factory was looking. The storeroom was now a secure, shelved area under Fay's guardianship. There was a separate off-site gunpowder store. Horse-drawn carts and carriages were now moving stocks about. The need for proper roads was becoming apparent. There was even an array of lifting apparatus.

Thomas, 'Morning, Lindsey. I must admit that I'm very impressed with the way the factory looks.'

Major Clutterbuck, 'I have to confess that a lot of the inspiration and hard work is down to Fay.'

Thomas, 'Nevertheless, you must be proud.'

Major Clutterbuck. 'I am rather proud. I can't help myself. And a lot of it is down to you. I would never have thought of those innovations.'

Thomas, 'And I could never have manufactured them.'

Major Clutterbuck, 'What do you want to see? Cannons, rockets, muskets, shrapnel, cross-bows?'

Thomas, 'No, I have another simple idea for you. It's called a bayonet.'

Major Clutterbuck, 'What's that?'

Thomas, 'Say you had a large group of musketeers who were under close attack, and were unable to reload. What would they do?'

Major Clutterbuck, 'I guess that they would grab their sword.'

Thomas, 'Exactly. Well, a bayonet is a dagger that goes over the top of the musket so it can be used a bit like a spear.'

Major Clutterbuck, 'Draw me a picture.'

Thomas did, and Major Clutterbuck said, 'That is so simple.' He called one of his metalworkers over and told them to make one.

73
Too Many Cats

Robin had to stop the conversion of witches into sheep as people were queuing up to take them away for butchering. The demand far outstretched the supply, and as far as Robin was concerned, it was cannibalism. Neighbours were happy to eat neighbours. It was a sad indictment on the human condition.

But then her decision to switch the spell to cats was backfiring. Every cat turned out to be black and was generally unwanted. At least they weren't being eaten, but their long-term chances of survival were slim. But then she decided that life was rarely fair.

Robin had heard that Thomas wanted her back to help with the Magical Conclave, and to be honest, she was desperate to attend. It was a once in many lifetimes event. She was fairly confident that her team could handle the witch hunt on their own. You had to be fairly tough, particularly with the younger witches, as they looked so innocent. Then you had to be prepared for the sudden outbreaks of violence. Two of the younger magicians had lost their lives, and some of the men at arms had been severely mutilated.

Then there were the frequent battles of spells. Tackling one witch was generally achievable, but when a coven was involved, you needed back-up, but generally, witches were solitary individuals.

The trouble now was that the witches were expecting them. They had prepared counter-measures such as spiritual beasts, traps, mind-games, illusions, inter-dimensional portals, demons, poisons and so on. They were not stupid, but it was good training for the magicians who had to be alert at all times.

Sometimes the witches attacked the magicians, particularly at night. The two magicians who lost their lives fell straight over a cliff edge chasing a witch. The witch was caught, and the locals ate her after being converted into a sheep, and Robin felt no sympathy for her whatsoever.

74

The Frustration of Odin

Odin, although a mighty god, was wondering whether he should give in. It was a bit like herding cats, except cats didn't usually answer back. His fleet was now huge but going in the wrong direction as the Vikings in Russia still had to be signed up. Once that was done, the invasion could begin.

Lord Hogflesh's spies now knew what was going on. Almost everyone in Europe had heard about the massive Viking fleet that had been brought together in the Baltic Sea. Most of the ruling classes in Europe wondered what the target destination was going to be. It was a time of great danger. A time of intrigue and alliances. But not for the British. They knew that trouble was coming their way.

The only good news was that they had been given time to prepare their defences. Stone and wood castles had been erected all along the coast by the Lord Protectors. It was amazing what could be done when lives and property were threatened.

Four reformed armies had been established with the Northern Army at York, the South-Eastern Army split between London and Portsmouth, and the South-Western Army split between Plymouth and Bristol. The Central Army was spread between Malvern and Coventry. Each Army now contained infantry, mounted archers, musketeers, cannoneers and magicians. The armies were designed to help each other as required.

The militia had been trained like they had never been trained before. The main objective was to give them enough confidence to stand their ground. Historically, most militias had never been in a battle. They had never seen blood and guts. Mock battles had been organised, which sometimes turned quite violent. There were always numerous battle casualties.

Lord Hogsflesh had been on a bit of a roll. He had established look-outs along the entire coast. Not just England but also Wales and Scotland. It had been a massive undertaking, but there had been a lot of support from the local population. And to be fair, it was in their interest. He even had spies in Eire just in case.

Lord Hogsflesh had also set-up a network of spies along the Baltic and Dutch coastlines, but the Viking fleet's location was hardly a closely guarded secret.

His roll continued. Lord Hogsflesh had found a Viking warlord who had married a British wife and was more than happy to be the British fleet's Admiral. He had been declared an 'outlander' by the Vikings and was consequently a non-human. He wanted revenge.

Lords Hogsflesh and Malander met with all of the Lord Protectors to explain their plans and invite their involvement. Most agreed to build up defensive forces. It had been a remarkably successful meeting. Lord Malander felt that everyone was pulling in the right direction.

Robin had cracked the witch problem, although it would be sometime before it would be eliminated. The magical conclave had been scheduled.

Major Clutterbuck's production targets had all been exceeded, and further stocks of weaponry were being distributed.

Lord Malander reviewed all of the updates and wondered what could possibly go wrong. His confidence level had reached a new high. Then Odin appeared in the Malander Manor House and calmly slashed his adversary's throat.

75

The Murder of the Mighty

Lord Malander wasn't the only victim. Majors Lambskin and Dragondale had also been murdered in their sleep, and the new admiral had been a victim of the blood eagle.

This was a disgusting Viking ritual where the victim is stripped naked, and then his penis and testicles are sliced off. His tongue is then sliced down the middle, both ears are cut off, his nose is smashed with a hammer, but his eyes are left intact so that he can enjoy the spectacle.

The arms and legs are tied together to prevent any sort of movement. The victim is then placed on a large stone with the back fully exposed. The body is then punctured by the coccyx and then slit upwards towards the neck, exposing the spine.

One by one, each rib is shattered using a large hammer and exposed outwards, leaving the victim's internal organs fully displayed. Once all of the ribs have been broken, each lung is laid out like the wings of an eagle. A salt and water mixture, is then thrown onto the victim's back to increase the agony.

What was worse was that his wife and three young children suffered the same fate.

What was even stranger was that the factory just ceased to exist along with Fay Mellondrop. There was nothing there. No buildings, no stores, no personnel. But the gunpowder store survived.

The Academy of Mystical Arts was also missing. The building had just disappeared into the ether. Fortunately, most of the magicians were out, either witch-hunting, or they had been allocated to the regional armies. But there were two serious losses: Lionel Wildheart and Tinton of Taverton.

And then six hundred Viking longships were seen sailing up the Thames.

76
Tears and More Tears

Lady Malander wasn't surprised, but that didn't stop the heartache. She knew that it was coming. She knew that her unborn child would never know his father. He would never know what a brilliant human being he was. She didn't know the date, but she knew that Odin would be his killer.

She also knew that they would lose half of the country to the Vikings despite all their hard work. But she told no one and had no intention of telling anyone because the future can be changed. She had to believe that it could be changed.

Her only concern now was her son, the future King of England. She had to find ways of protecting him. She knew that Thomas, or rather Merlin, was the key to that challenge. The fact that Thomas thought that he was the father was part of her plan. A plan hatched many years ago.

When Thomas learnt of Lord Malander's death, he felt guilt. He should have protected him, but what was he compared to a god? What chance did Lord Malander have? What was going to happen now? Who would take over the command of the British forces?

Thomas was even more devastated when he learned about the deaths of Majors Lambskin and Dragondale and then the loss of the factory and Fay. How did Odin know about the factory?

Lady Malander and Thomas hugged and cried together. And then cried some more. Thomas wondered if his sister was safe. Then they cried for the loss of Tinton and Lionel. And then they cried some more.

Thomas, 'I feel your loss but not your surprise.'

Lady Malander, 'You feel right.'

Thomas, 'You knew that this was going to happen?'

Lady Malander, 'Promise me one thing. Just one thing.'

Thomas, 'What's that?'

Lady Malander, 'That when the time comes, you will save Arthur.'

Thomas, 'Arthur?'

Lady Malander, 'My husband named him yesterday. That's when I knew that Lord Malander's days were numbered. I didn't expect it to happen that quickly. So promise me.'

Thomas, 'I promise that I will look after your son.'

Lady Malander, 'For the rest of his life.'

Thomas, 'I promise that I will look after your son for the rest of his life.'

Lady Malander, 'You won't regret it, I promise you. You will have so many adventures together.'

Thomas, 'You sound as if you are not going to be around.'

Lady Malander, 'See, you are getting more perceptive.'

Thomas, 'What are you saying?'

Lady Malander, 'It won't be long before I will be joining my husband.'

Thomas, 'That can't be true.'

Lady Malander, 'I've known my fate for some time. And that time is getting nearer. I have no regrets. I welcome what is coming, but I will miss my son growing up, but then I have already seen it.'

Thomas felt that his life was falling apart. His hero had died. His friends had died. His substitute mother or lover was going to die. The factory and the school had disappeared from the face of the Earth. And the Vikings were on the doorstep.

77
General Winterdom

General Winterdom was horrified when he learnt about the death of Lord Malander and Majors Lambskin and Dragondale. It was a good tactic to kill the leader of your adversary on the eve of battle. It often caused confusion, disillusionment, and disarray. The first move had been made in the forthcoming battle.

But General Winterdom was made of sterner stuff. He ordered the following:

- That he would take over as Commander-in-Chief
- That Colonel Walsh would take over as Commander South-West
- That Major Bandolier would take over as Commander Central
- That the Bristol regiments would take on the Vikings coming up the Severn
- That the Plymouth regiments would march to the aid of Bristol
- That the London regiments would take on the Vikings sailing up the Thames
- That the regiments in Coventry should prepare to go to the aid of London if requested
- That the manufacturing facilities should be restored as quickly as possible.
- That the fleet should attack the Viking fleets on the Thames or the Severn depending on wind and tidal conditions.

London was a relatively easy target as nothing was guarding the Thames. It wasn't long before London, with its closely packed houses, was ablaze. By the time the British Army had arrived, the Vikings were gone. The Army spent most of their time rescuing Londoners from the flames rather than doing their job.

It wasn't long before Chelmsford and Colchester were also on fire. This was soon followed by Ipswich, Lowestoft, and Norwich. There was no way that a land-based Army could keep up with the marauding Vikings. They were playing to their strengths as raiders, but to conquer the land, they would have to disembark.

Whilst this was going on, Lord Hogsflesh got warnings that a further three fleets had been sighted off the English coast. He was also told that the main fleet in the Baltic was near Copenhagen.

The Viking cards were being played. General Winterdom realised that these initial engagements were just warming-up sessions with the intention of causing confusion. There were many small fires, but where would the main conflagration be?

General Winterdom was conscious that he could wear his resources out by marching up and down the county. So he decided to wait. He also ordered that senior military personnel, should sleep with an armed guard in case Odin returned.

And Odin did return. General Winterdom woke up to find two of his guards wrestling with what looked like a dirty old man. The alarm was raised, and a musketeer shot Odin in the chest. Odin collapsed on the floor from a mixture of shock and heart damage. He had never seen anything like it. Then Odin fell asleep.

Colonel Walsh hadn't been so lucky. Odin killed him before he even got to his post.

78
Naval Tribulations

The British Navy had lost its leader, and although they had mastered basic seamanship and cannonading, they had no idea about tides or the intricacies of the British coastline. Despite this, they had been ordered to attack either of the Viking fleets in the Thames or the Severn Estuary.

They did their best and left Portsmouth and made good progress along the south coast towards Plymouth, where they sheltered for the night. The next day, a storm off Land's End destroyed a third of the fleet. Leaderless, they carried on trying to navigate the Cornish and Devon coastlines, which were fraught with danger.

They saw no sign of any Viking ships, but that wasn't surprising as they had just entered the Severn estuary. Their lack of knowledge regarding the Severn became obvious when they floundered on the sandbanks. Even then, they weren't sure what to do. They tried pulling the longships to the shore, but the sinking mud prohibited that. So all they could do was sit and wait.

In the meantime, the Vikings were attacking Bristol. Fortunately, the South-West Army was on-hand to resist their incursions, and they were fought off. This wasn't a problem for the Vikings as they were only a diversionary force. Instead, they decided to plunder the Devon and Cornwall coastal towns.

On their way back down the Severn, they were surprised to see a foundered Viking fleet. As they got nearer, they were surprised to see that it was manned by British seamen. That was unheard of. As they got even nearer, they were even more surprised to be bombarded by shot and shrapnel. They were totally surprised when their longships sunk.

So the British had their first naval victory. Eventually, they refloated, and the ships captained by the brave went off to the Thames. They wondered what the sandbanks were like there.

79
What do you do with a God?

Odin was unconscious and under lock and key. General Winterdom wasn't sure whether to simply kill him, as he had murdered Lord Malander and his colleagues, or use him as a bargaining chip. He was also potentially very dangerous.

If nothing else, the General was pragmatic. He didn't like the idea of killing a prisoner, but the Vikings did it as a matter of course. Slowly the idea of killing Odin grew on him until he reached a decision. He was going to do it. It might save the lives of thousands of his troops and possibly stop the invasion. He decided that it was the right thing to do.

General Winterdom grabbed his dagger, and as he readied himself to do the deed, Odin smiled. He continued smiling as the blade pierced his heart. He laughed as a massive burst of energy erupted from his body, demolishing most of Yorkshire. The entire Northern Army, including General Winterdom, simply ceased to exist in the overwhelming outpouring of energy.

Rather than saving his Army and helping British resistance, he had probably achieved the opposite. In the future, a debate took place on whether Odin planned this or not. Was it part of a great scheme or just opportune?

80
What happened in Yorkshire?

Lord Hogsflesh was trying to understand what had happened in Yorkshire or rather the huge crater that was Yorkshire. His spies all reported an explosion so great that it must have been the work of a god. And, of course, they were right.

The entire county was a crater, and nothing within fifty miles of York had survived. There was no Northern Army and now no leader. Lord Hogsflesh suggested that Commanders Mainstay and Bandolier met with him and Merlin in Oxford to agree on the best way forward.

As far as Lord Hogsflesh was concerned, they now had two principal armies and a smaller central force. They had the benefit of gunpowder, but how could they cope with another Yorkshire? There were three further Viking fleets off the coast and a massive thousand plus fleet on its way. That probably equated to two hundred thousand warriors. But where were they going to disembark? It could be Yorkshire as there would not be any opposition, but the crater was a bit of an obstacle.

He still had look-outs around the coast, except for the north-east, but there were still so many towns and villages burning in the east. Vikings were still stomping through the countryside, causing mayhem. Normally he could work out a strategy, but he wasn't sure what to do. Should they attack every Viking incursion, or should they retreat to a 'home' territory and defend it to the last.

Lord Hogsflesh was worried about a Viking horde coming down from the north and attacking their forces from the rear, cutting them off in the south-east. He was a master-spy, not a soldier, but then he had seen it all before. A good leader such as Lord Malander could make things succeed, and they could drag success from disaster. Even General Winterdom could make things happen through hard work and grit, and a never say die attitude. Those that were left were the followers, the doers, the managers of men but not the leaders. And he included himself in that.

81
Friday the Thirteenth

Thomas wasn't looking forward to the Magical Conclave. With the recent deaths and the whole Odin experience, there wasn't much point in having a meeting. The original plan was to use the combined magical strength of the Fay people and humanity to counter the powers of the gods. Now Thor was dead, and possibly Odin was no more.

Nevertheless, Thomas, and especially Robin, decided that it had to go ahead. Lady Malander didn't want any part of it, partly because she was mourning and partly because she was pregnant, and partly because she just couldn't care less.

Most of the preparation had been done. Layer upon layer of protective incantations and spells had been placed on, in and around Midsummer Hill. Surrounding the hill, there were also mounted archers and musketeers, although they were not allowed on the hill.

All of the nearby oaks and sycamores had been blessed, and every yew tree within fifty miles of Midsummer Hill had been dressed. Over a hundred natural fountains on the Malvern Hills had been dressed to represent the various members of the Fay Council and other attendees. Food and lodgings had been prepared with great attention to detail as the Fay were very demanding and very jealous of anyone getting special attention.

One of the key objectives was to avoid bloodshed. The Fay as a group were not the friendly, easy-going fairy types that humanity often imagined. They ranged from slightly aggressive to downright bestial. They had filthy habits, despicable morals, and unbridled greed. Some were cannibalistic, some sucked blood, and most stole human babies and human souls. And generally, they hated each other. They generally hated each other more than they hated humans, and they hated humans a lot.

The opening ceremony was a key part of the conclave, with each member of the Fay Council making a formal entrance. The Unicorni arrived first though the portal. Thomas saw them as magnificent horses with horns on their heads. Apparently, they were sentient, but he had never heard one communicate, but then he had never seen one before. Robin thought that they were beautiful, mysterious creatures that inspired awe and admiration. As far as she was concerned, a lifelong ambition had been achieved.

The second entrants were the Goblini. Thomas was disappointed that they turned up as the Goblini were nasty, grotesque, malicious little bastards that always caused problems. Thomas remembered that he and his sister used to go on goblin hunts to eradicate infestations. If you let them breed, they would steal all of your property. They had voracious and unsatisfiable appetites for gold and silver.

Their delegation contained a variety of different goblin types, including brownies, kobolds, gnomes, duendes and hobgoblins. Thomas had assigned some junior magicians to monitor them. He knew that they had to be invited as they were part of the Fay Council, but he also knew that their contribution would be negligible or even seriously negative.

The next delegation was the Elementi. There were four separate groups:

- The Nymphi, representing water elements
- The Sylphi, representing air elements
- The Pygmyi, representing earth elements
- The Salamandi representing fire elements

Their characteristics, attitude to life, skills etc., were dependent on the type of elemental. Some had been known to attract humans to their death. Others had sacrificed themselves to save humans in distress. They were one of the few members of the Fay Council that could mate with humans, thereby acquiring a soul.

Generally, Thomas liked them, and they could be a good ally against the Vikings, although they were very easily distracted.

The more Thomas thought about it, the more he was convinced that the conclave was a total waste of time. It was going to take hours to complete the procession. Then he got a note requesting his attendance at a War Council in Oxford, which was a few hours away on a fast horse.

82
Viking Confusion

The Admiral of the main Viking fleet wasn't sure where he was going. That had to be considered as a bad thing as he had a fleet of over twelve hundred longships. He had no way of contacting Odin and therefore had to make his own decision. He knew that London and many of the towns along the eastern coast were burning and were presumably still being Vikingised, so he decided to go to Yorkshire. He had fond memories of ravishing some of the locals.

The Humber looked very inviting, but when they sailed inland, they found a desert. Grimsby, Hull, and Goole were completely flattened. There was hardly any vegetation and certainly no human population. It was as if a giant wind had just flattened everything. Search parties were sent north, and they found a massive crater with a crystallised centre. It just didn't make sense.

In the end, they camped at Scunthorpe. The rations they brought with them had all been consumed. Anyway, their modus operandi was always to live off the land: the enemy's land! But there was nothing to live off. They would have to march south fairly quickly just to eat.

The three smaller Viking fleets that were circling the south coast combined and entered the Thames. The city was still on fire from the earlier Viking incursion, but nevertheless, they were determined to secure the city. The British forces were poorly positioned and decided to retire to Finchley, where they had a good view of the city. If Commander Mainstay had been in place, he would probably have stayed his ground, but he was on his way to Oxford for a meeting of the War Council remnants.

Just to make things more confusing, the British fleet entered the Thames estuary and cannonaded the Viking fleet that was anchored along the Thames Estuary. Who said that cannons would never work at sea? Rather ironically, it forced the Vikings to stay and fortify London as now they couldn't escape.

83
The Witches fight-back

Witches used to be burnt on the stake. Then they were magically transformed into sheep, killed, and roasted over an open fire and then eaten as human steaks. It turned out that quite a few of them weren't killed before being turned into a Sunday roast. Some were still alive when slithers of meat were shaved off or skewers were used to test their tenderness.

And to make it worse, some of these so-called witches had never practised witchcraft or even knew that they were witches. Some of the more junior witches were easily bullied by the locals into denouncing young women as witches so that they could take advantage of them. And a naked witch being slowly roasted has little protection from lusty locals.

The northern witches who had survived the Odin-blast ganged up and hunted down the witch-hunters. It wasn't long before the hunter became the hunted and ended up as a kebab. The witches had nothing to lose and everything to gain by orchestrating a reign of terror. Lancashire became the land of the witches. There were even warlocks blockading the main roads.

The witchery infestation spread south, with Warrington becoming a hotbed of activity. There were rumours that Satan had taken over that town, and it would forever be his headquarters on Earth. Demons were supposedly attacking Widnes and Wilmslow.

Thomas and Robin were too busy to devote any attention to this latest problem. There was still a serious lack of senior magicians. Thomas needed to find more naturally skilled wizards. The training programme had highlighted the difficulties in training the average. After detailed training, they were still average. Sometimes the training had dulled their natural ability by killing off their spontaneity.

84
The Oxford War Council

It was the smallest War Council ever, consisting of the following:

- Lord Hogsflesh, Intelligence
- Commander Mainstay, Commander South-East
- Commander Bandolier, Commander Central Forces
- Commander Mannering, who had taken over from Commander Walsh, who had taken over from Commander Lambskin.

There was no sign of Thomas, and Major Clutterbuck was too busy trying to rebuild the factory. Without that, there would be no munitions.

Lord Hogsflesh, 'Thank you for making your way to Oxford. I know that you are all very busy, but we need to rethink our strategy. Firstly, we need to appoint a new leader, and it shouldn't be me.'

Commander Bandolier, 'I would like to nominate Commander Mainstay as Commander-in-Chief.'

Commander Mannering, 'I second that.' And the job was done. Commander Mainstay wasn't sure that he wanted the job, but there was no real alternative. They were in the shit, and it was his job to shovel them out of it.

Commander Mainstay, 'Somehow, we need to assess our current situation. Lord Hogsflesh, you might have the best overall picture.'

Lord Hogsflesh, 'I guess that the first point is that there is so much confusion, almost everywhere, but I will have a go at summarising the situation:

- Yorkshire has been obliterated by a massive explosion that destroyed York and most of the local towns. We have no idea what caused it, but it seemed to involve Odin
- The entire Northern Army and General Winterdom were lost in the

explosion

- The following were killed by Viking treachery: Lord Malander, Commanders Dragondale, Lambskin and Walsh, Fay Mellondrop, and some of the senior magicians
- The factory and the Mystical Arts school were destroyed
- A Viking force in the Severn Estuary was destroyed by Commander Lambskin's forces and our Navy
- London and towns along the East Coast are on fire
- Commander Mainstay's forces retook London, but I'm told that those forces have retired to Finchley due to the arrival of three further Viking fleets.'

Commander Mainstay, 'What? I told them to hold London no matter what.'

Lord Hogsflesh, 'I don't have any further detail. Anyway, I will continue:

- Our fleet then destroyed the Viking fleet in London
- Meanwhile, the main Viking Army landed in the Humber Estuary and is now in Scunthorpe and planning to head south
- Lancashire and part of Cheshire have a serious witch infestation.'

Commander Mainstay, 'Let me get this right. There are large Viking forces in Scunthorpe and London and possibly further Viking parties in some of the eastern coastal towns.'

Lord Hogsflesh, 'That's correct.'

Commander Mainstay, 'What numbers are we talking about?'

Lord Hogsflesh, 'The fleet that landed in the Humber Estuary had one thousand, one hundred and seventy longships with just over one hundred and ten men per ship. That gives us one hundred and twenty-nine thousand warriors.'

Commander Mainstay, 'A significant force. And in London?'

Lord Hogsflesh, 'It's a much more confusing picture, and there has been a considerable amount of fighting. But I would estimate between twenty-five thousand and forty thousand warriors. Probably the lower of the two figures. What resources do we have?'

Commander Mainstay, 'I've about thirty thousand regulars and one hundred thousand militiamen in the London area and about one hundred thousand troops in Portsmouth.'

Commander Bandolier, 'My forces are more or less intact:

- Malvern Army — twenty-five thousand
- Mounted Archers — five thousand
- Militiamen — say one hundred thousand.'

Commander Mannering, 'I'm told that I have the following forces:

- South Western Army — twenty-five thousand
- Garrisons — ten thousand
- Militiamen — say one hundred and fifty thousand

I would assume that we lost some men in the Bristol battle.'

Commander Mainstay, 'So numerically we are stronger than the Viking forces.'

Lord Hogsflesh, 'That's correct, and we have gunpowder.'

Commander Mainstay, 'What has happened to Thomas?'

Lord Hogsflesh, 'He was meeting with the Fay.'

Commander Mainstay, 'What's the point? Those thieving, murdering, child-stealing scumbags should be eradicated. They are far worse than the witches. I hate them all.'

Lords Hogsflesh, 'I didn't know that you felt so strongly about them.'

Commander Mainstay, 'They stole my son and gave me a changeling. Anyway, let's get back to our Viking problem.

'We need to confine the London Vikings and confront the northerners.'

Commander Bandolier, 'I agree. Where should we form the line?'

85
It wasn't Natural

Lady Malander had been talking to her unborn son. For her, it wasn't that unusual as it happened with her previous pregnancy. She had wondered if it was going to be the same boy, but it wasn't. Arthur was a very different kettle of fish.

Arthur was inquisitive, intelligent, strong-willed, and kind. From what she could gather, he had a calm but serious demeanour but with a sense of fun. He was already advising her on household chores. It was difficult to keep secret from him as their minds were in tune. It wasn't exactly mind reading. It was more like acting as a single mind.

She kept reinforcing that his father was Lord Malander, but no one except her knew the truth. Perhaps, Alexander, the white dragon, had an inkling. She was also desperately hiding the fact that she would never see him growing up. He kept asking her why she was so sad. The loss of her husband was a good cover.

Lady Malander also knew that Arthur's life was not always going to be a bed of roses or indeed a single rose. He would experience love and great friendship, heroic deeds, and adulation, and sadly, deceit and betrayal. But that was the way of the world.

What was most worrying, was the development of the foetus. Lady Malander had assumed that she would have at least eight months to go, but Arthur was probably halfway there already. If this rate of gestation continued, she would be giving birth in a month!

She had only a month to prepare everything. She needed Thomas.

86
Friday the Thirteenth, Part 2

Thomas was being torn in lots of different directions. He needed to complete the magical conclave, although it was probably pointless. He had missed a War Council meeting that might have decided the fate of Grand Britannica. There was a serious amount of witchery about, and Lady Malander was demanding his urgent attention. And Clutterbuck needed help; otherwise, there would be no munitions.

His head was spinning, but he was not surprised to see that the Dragoni hadn't turned up, since they hadn't turned up for a thousand years. Then the fawns arrived. Thomas wondered what it would be like to be half man and half goat. They were all male with their genitals on display and proud of it. He had never seen a female fawn and wondered how they procreated.

The Asrai then arrived. Thomas had never seen them before. They were beautiful but ethereal. They were naked, about four feet tall with webbed feet. They were water creatures who could transform their legs into tails when it suited them. They could not countenance direct sunlight, which dissolved them.

The next two groups were the pixies and the elves. In many ways, they looked very similar with the same height, stature and pointed ears. The pixies were mischievous, child-like, and fun-loving. They loved dancing and wrestling. The elves were nasty malevolent creatures that caused humankind nothing but trouble. Their greed for gold, silver and human babies was legendary, but they were a lot brighter than most of the Fay.

The Mersi never made the conclave meetings as they were totally aquatic. They were normally represented by the Asrai.

The Bansheei actually turned up. Sometimes they came but were only heard. They were a mysterious lot as they didn't fit into a specific profile. Some were very tall, whilst others were shorter than an elf. Some were portly, whereas others were almost skeletal. Most were 'blackish', but some had red hair. They could certainly shout. There were no male banshees, and

Thomas once again wondered about procreation, but then he often thought about procreation. He did rather fancy some of the female elves, he knew that they were off-limits, but it didn't stop him from desiring them.

Whilst he stood there, Lady Malander turned up and demanded an audience.

Lady Malander, 'Thomas, I need you now.'

Thomas, 'Does it have to be this very moment?'

Lady Malander, 'We are talking about the future of Grand Britannica.'

Thomas, 'I will need to excuse myself from the conclave.'

Lady Malander, 'No, don't do that. See me afterwards.'

Thomas knew that her needs were pressing, but they weren't critically urgent. He could tell that she was being driven by distress. He hated to see her like that. While that was going on, he missed the entrance of the Gremli and Impi, but unfortunately, he did see the Famili.

They were the dregs of the Fay world and included every type of sucker you could think of. From vampiric bloodsucking familiars to energy or soul-sucking monsters. They literally sucked whole towns or even regions dry. As far as Thomas was concerned, they were not welcome in Malvern. You could almost feel yourself being sucked as they walked by.

He wondered if the Fairi would turn up as wizened old crones or delightful gossamer-clad darlings.

87

The Oxford War Council draws the Line.

Lord Hogsflesh, 'I suggest that we create a defensive line from Finchley, London to Liverpool. It will be divided into three zones: North, Central and South. A commander with sufficient forces will guard each sector.

Commander Mainstay, 'You are giving a fair amount of land away.'

Lord Hogsflesh, 'They effectively have it although we have no idea what is happening north of Yorkshire.'

Commander Bandolier, 'And we can always take it back at a later date.'

Commander Mainstay, 'Easier said than done.'

Lord Hogsflesh, 'At least it gives us a fighting chance.'

Commander Mainstay, 'My orders:

• Commander Bandolier will take eighty thousand militiamen and twenty thousand regulars and defend the northern part of the line or zone one

• The five thousand mounted archers will act as a mobile reserve along the line

• Commander Bandolier will leave twenty thousand militiamen and five thousand regulars to defend Malvern

• Commander Mannering will take one hundred thousand militiamen and twenty-five thousand regulars to defend the central part of the line or zone two

• The garrison troops will remain behind

• My one hundred thousand troops in Portsmouth will defend the southern part of the line or zone three

• I will use some of the London troops to defend the line depending on what I find when I return to London.

• Cannons to be installed on as many strategic points as possible

• Commander Bandolier to find out what the situation is with Thomas

• The Fleet is to attack the Viking fleet on the Humber. If nothing else, it will stop them from going back to get reinforcements.'

Lord Hogsflesh, 'So that gives us roughly three hundred and fifty thousand troops on the line.'

Commander Bandolier, 'But there is no in-depth defence and only five thousand mounted archers as a reserve.'

Commander Mainstay, 'The distances are too large to provide a decent reserve.'

Lord Hogsflesh, 'What do we do if the Vikings break the line? Which they will probably do as they could throw all their strength at one point.'

Commander Mainstay, 'We could shorten our line by giving up more territory. Alternately we could go on the attack, but we would need to stay aware of their London forces.'

Commander Mannering, 'I say let's go with Commander Mainstay's plan but be proactive if we have to be.'

And the orders were put into action.

88
Friday the Thirteenth, Part 3

They were all waiting for the arrival of the Fairy Queen. Apparently, it was the pièce de resistance, a spectacular that shouldn't be missed. Firstly, two smartly dressed courtesans exited the portal, followed by a dozen classic fairies with gossamer wings and pixie dust. It was both pretty and expected.

Then the Fairy Queen made her entrance accompanied by the most exquisite music. The music somehow contained every piece of music that you had ever loved. And the smell was literally magical. Somehow it comprised every smell that you had ever loved. And there she was, probably the most beautiful creature he had ever seen. But that's what a glamour spell does. You see the best of everything, but Thomas had to admit he really enjoyed the experience.

If he didn't know better, he would think he was in love with her. But he did know better. But he didn't expect what happened next. Midsummer Hill was suddenly filled with blue-skinned Druids on a killing spree. They showed no particular preference. They killed any Fay creature that they could get their hands on.

They killed them with spears, knives, hatchets, and their bare hands. The Fairy Queen was decapitated, and she returned to her true grotesque form. It was a massacre as the Fay had no weapons or defensive measures of their own. They had relied on the Malvern magicians to defend them. They had guaranteed their safety.

There was no way of knowing, but the Druids had probably killed every representative of the Fay. Most of their leaders had been exterminated.

Vortigern, the Druid leader, said, 'What did you think of that?'

Thomas, who was almost speechless, said, 'What have you done?'

Vortigern, 'Just helping you with the extermination of the unclean. I've admired the way that you have hunted down the witches. Turning them into sheep and eating them was a masterstroke. Sheer genius.'

Thomas, 'I don't believe it.'

Vortigern, 'And when you invited us to the Magical Conclave, we knew exactly what you intended. What a plan. It went brilliantly. You should have seen the look on the elf faces when we stomped their heads in. It was classic. And chopping the unicorn's horns off and using them to kill them was so poetic.

'Believe me. The world is a much better place without blood-sucking, soul-stealing scum-bags. We are all safer tonight now that we have declared war on the fay people.'

89
More tears

Thomas walked into Lady Malander's dressing room to find her almost naked. She looked at him. He looked at her. Her eyes questioned him, and he burst into tears.

Lady Malander grabbed Thomas's head and dragged it towards her breasts, and cuddled him. His sobbing tears rolled down between her cleavage on to the Arthur bump. He struggled to stop. It was as if the sobbing was in automatic mode.

Lady Malander, 'There was nothing that we could have done to stop it.'

Thomas, 'You knew.'

Lady Malander, 'You must have sensed it. Magic is leaving this world. This was just another step in a long, drawn-out process.'

Thomas, 'That can't be true.'

Lady Malander, 'Betty, Tinton, Lionel, Thor, Odin have all gone. I will be gone shortly.'

Thomas, 'Odin's gone.'

Lady Malander, 'That explosion was his demise. I bet he was pleased that he took a lot with him.'

Thomas, 'But the Fay folk will never forgive us.'

Lady Malander, 'They are all gradually dying. There are few young Fay.'

Thomas, 'I can't believe it.'

Lady Malander, 'Well, you are killing off the witches. They are magical entities.'

Thomas, 'But that had to be done.'

Lady Malander, 'Desperate times need desperate measures, don't they?'

Thomas, 'But they tried to kill us.'

Lady Malander, 'We have been killing them for centuries.'

Thomas, 'I thought that you supported their eradication.'

Lady Malander, 'I went along with the rest for my own reasons. Now you are going to demand that we punish the Druids, aren't you?'

Thomas, 'But they can't go unpunished.'

Lady Malander, 'They are dying out. Their days are numbered. Magic is leaving this world.'

Thomas, 'Do you really believe that?'

Lady Malander, 'Apart from you and your sister, we haven't found a decent new magician in two hundred years. Have you found any?'

Thomas decided to carry on sobbing, and then they made love. It took some careful manoeuvring to achieve orgasm.

Lady Malander knew that she would never make love again.

90

Siblings United

Robin, 'What should we do?'

Thomas, 'What can we do?'

Robin, 'Shouldn't we apologise?'

Thomas, 'Who to? Most of the leaders are dead. And they will never believe that it wasn't planned. We are guilty because we are human.'

Robin, 'But I feel terrible.'

Thomas, 'So do I. I cried most of yesterday.'

Robin, 'In Lady Malander's arms. I suppose you fucked her.'

Thomas didn't answer, but she knew.

Robin, 'How could you? Her husband only died a few weeks ago, and she is heavily pregnant.'

Thomas, 'You don't understand.'

Robin, 'I understand that you can't control your cock. How could you do that immediately after the disgusting and deceitful murder of innocent Fay folk.'

Thomas, 'Lady Malander knew that it was going to happen.'

Robin, 'That's not possible.'

Thomas, 'She knew that her husband was going to be murdered by Odin. She also said that Odin was dead.'

Robin, 'Did she tell you that before or after she fucked you.'

Thomas, 'She also said that she was going to die in childbirth and that magic was leaving this world.'

Robin, 'That can't be true.'

Thomas, 'It seems that everyone we know is moving on.'

Robin, 'So what are we going to do?'

Thomas, 'We carry on. We help fight the Vikings. We put down the witch infestation, and we carry on.'

Robin, 'What do you want me to do tomorrow?'

Thomas, 'Focus on the witches. I will go and see old Clutterbum.'

Robin, 'Don't die on me.'

Thomas, 'Let's keep the magic alive.'

91
Bandolier on the Move

Thomas, 'What's going on?'

Commander Bandolier, 'Where have you been?'

Thomas, 'I'm not sure if I can talk about it.'

Commander Bandolier, 'Is it top secret?'

Thomas, 'No, it was just such an awful experience.'

Commander Bandolier, 'Tell me.'

Thomas, 'Yesterday was Friday the thirteenth and the meeting of the Magical Conclave. All of the Fay folk were represented. Everything was going well, and then the Druids attacked and murdered all of the Fay.'

Commander Bandolier, 'I knew about that.'

Thomas, 'What do you mean?'

Commander Bandolier, 'Well, everyone in Malvern knew about it. The druids didn't make a secret of it. We even helped them carry some of their equipment up the hill. No one likes those Fay bastards. They give you the creeps, don't they?'

Thomas, 'I can't believe what I'm hearing. Fuck you.' And Thomas stormed off to find Robin.

Robin was where the academy of Mystical Arts used to be.

Thomas, 'What are you doing?'

Robin, 'I just thought I would see if anything was left, but there is nothing.'

Thomas, 'Most of the humans knew that the Fay were going to be massacred and did nothing about it.'

Robin, 'I know.'

Thomas, 'How come?'

Robin, 'Everyone is talking about it as if it was great news. Even the junior magicians are happy about it.'

Thomas. 'It must be us that are out of sync with the rest of humanity.'

Robin, 'It looks that way.'

Thomas, 'Can you send a junior over to Commander Bandolier to let him know that Odin is dead.'

Robin, 'Is that important.'

Thomas, 'Just do it.'

Robin, 'Yes, Sir.'

Commander Bandolier was getting his men ready to move. Shifting a hundred thousand men northwards a hundred miles or more was a major logistical task. Two regiments of the mounted archers and some of Lord Hogflesh's men were already scouting ahead.

Supplies were being loaded onto wagons, and the Malvern defences were being activated.

Commander Bandolier was still wondering why Thomas was so upset, but then that's magicians for you: temperamental at the best of times.

92

Mainstay in a Mood

When Commander Mainstay got to Finchley, he was already in a mood. He regarded the potential loss of London as a disaster. It was the largest port in the country, the financial capital, and the national centre for the arts. There had even been talk about moving the elders from Malvern to London at one time.

When he spoke to his captains, he could see their logic. They thought that the Viking fleet sailing up the Thames Estuary was the main enemy force with over one hundred and twenty thousand men. Then they saw another fleet arriving with possibly another thirty to forty thousand warriors. Together those forces might be overwhelming, especially when you added those warriors already in London.

They weren't to know that the second fleet was British, and, on reflection, they agreed that they should probably have stayed. Anyway, the British had a commanding position overlooking London, and the Viking fleet had been destroyed.

Some of the London regiments were reorientated towards Kingston and Reading, and the Army based in Portsmouth was ordered north to man the line.

Commander Mannering's Army had four targets: Stafford, Birmingham, Warwick, and Northampton. The line was not fully guarded. There were points of great strength with scouts in between to detect any enemy activity. Lord Hogsflesh had managed to track the Vikings who were in four separate, disorganised columns making their way to the Peak District above Derby.

It looked like they were heading towards Birmingham, but they could easily turn towards Stoke or even Chester or North Wales. Commander Mainstay ordered the campfires to be lit to give the impression that there were significant forces defending the line. He also ordered double the number of guards in case of night attacks.

93
Clutterbuck is depressed

Thomas, 'How are you today?'

Major Clutterbuck, 'Depressed, demoralised and downright despondent. They stole my lovely factory.'

Thomas, 'Come on, man, pull yourself together.'

Major Clutterbuck, 'Where did it go? Factories, although I haven't had that much experience of them, don't just disappear.'

Thomas, 'That's a very good question.' It certainly got Thomas thinking. How would he make a factory disappear? He could think of ways of making it invisible. Then he thought about other dimensions, but he knew nothing about them. Major Clutterbuck suggested that it could be a trick of time. That was a good idea, but most magicians, and presumably gods, avoided time magic as it was so unpredictable.

Then Thomas got on his hands and knees and searched the hard earthen floor and hey presto, he found it. He called Major Clutterbuck over and showed him a miniature version of his factory in his hand. Odin had simply shrunk it.

Thomas took some time to work out the expansion spell. Clutterbuck wanted the factory moved slightly to catch the early morning sun. Once positioned, the factory started expanding. Major Clutterbuck hugged Thomas and thanked him profusely. Inside there had been some minor damage, but they also found a very hungry Fay Mellondrop. Fay and Lindsey hugged each other like long-lost lovers, and that is what they became.

Thomas dashed off to do the same trick with the school. Robin was genuinely amazed until she released what Odin had done. Why didn't she think of it?

94
Elder Plans

Deputy Chief Elder, 'Fellow elders, the cards are now stacked in our favour. Most of the players are in position.'

Elder Two, 'Are we ready to move onto the next phase?'

Deputy Chief Elder, 'Almost. A few more strings need to be pulled, and we will be back in power.'

Elder Two, 'You mean back in our rightful position.'

Elder Four, 'But the old hag is still alive.'

Deputy Chief Elder, 'Not for much longer. She will die during childbirth in the next few days.'

Elder Two, 'And her progeny?'

Deputy Chief Elder, 'You mean the future King of England.' And they all laughed.

Elder Two, 'Exactly.'

Deputy Chief Elder, 'The Malander witch, has been fucking Merlin in an attempt to gain his loyalty. He is her only hope, and we have plans to neutralise him.'

Elder Two, 'Excellent.'

Elder Five, 'Are you sure that we can trust the Vikings?'

Deputy Chief Elder, 'So far, they have followed the plan. They took out Lord Malander and destroyed the Northern Army. There is no reason to suspect foul play. They have a lot to gain.'

Elder Five, 'And is your son ready to do his bit?'

Elder Seven, 'To be honest, he was very reluctant at first, but now that he sees the bigger picture, he is onboard.'

Elder Five, 'You don't sound that confident.'

Elder Seven, 'He did take some convincing. He has been fighting the Vikings for some time and naturally saw them as the enemy. Now he understands his duty to the family and to the elders.'

Elder Five, 'He thought that we were paying too high a price.'

Elder Seven, 'I can understand that, but it is for the general good.'

Elder Five, 'That is what I said, and he replied, "Who's general good?" But he will do what he has to do.'

Deputy Chief Elder, 'You better keep an eye on him.'

Elder Five, 'Believe me. It is under control. But what about the Druids?'

Deputy Chief Elder, 'You can believe me. They are under control.'

Elder Two, 'It looks like everything is under control.'

Deputy Chief Elder, 'It better be. We are playing for the future of Grand Britannica.'

Elder Six, 'And Lord Hogsflesh will follow his instructions?'

Deputy Chief Elder, 'He will, or his parents will die a lingering and painful death.'

Elder Two, 'And who is to say that they might anyway.'

95
Lord Hogsflesh does his Bit

Lord Hogsflesh had always done his best. Sometimes it wasn't good enough, but it was his best. He spied and bartered, bribed, and planned, and carried out skulduggery on a massive scale to meet the aims of his masters. He wasn't always proud of what he had to do, but that was the role of a fixer.

But who were his masters? Lord Malander was dead. So were the elders the official power in the land? Had they always been the official power? He wasn't sure any more, but it looked like they were now in control.

But now, it was down to pure ethics. Should he save his parents or do the dirty on his long-term colleagues? What would they do in his position? And what about his parents? They had a very poor opinion of him. They saw him as a whoring, worthless alcoholic. Of course, there was some truth in that, but they had no idea that he was Spymaster Extraordinaire with nearly five thousand spies working for him.

He did what any good Spymaster would do and used his resources to track his parents down. He could not betray his comrades. He would not dishonour the family name.

Anyway, he had a meeting with Commander Mainstay regarding the London situation.

Commander Mainstay, 'Morning old chap.'

Lord Hogsflesh, 'Morning, John.'

Commander Mainstay, 'Did you want a beer?'

Lord Hogsflesh, 'Not really, I thought that I would just update you on how I see the London situation, and then do a runner.'

Commander Mainstay, 'That would be interesting.'

Lord Hogsflesh, 'There are only about sixteen thousand Vikings in the city. Quite a few of them were ordered north. It wouldn't take much effort for your forces to seize the city. Once that is done, you could put more regiments onto the line.'

Commander Mainstay, 'That is good news.'

Lord Hogsflesh, 'I'm now hopeful that we can give the Vikings a good thrashing.'

Commander Mainstay, 'And what is the situation up north?'

Lord Hogsflesh, 'I'm not sure if I should tell you, but the elders wanted me to tell everyone that the Vikings are heading south, but they actually plan to attack Commander Bandolier's Army.'

Commander Mainstay, 'And why would the elders do that?'

Lord Hogsflesh, 'I've no idea, but my spies are on the case. They also threatened to kill my parents if I didn't comply.'

Commander Mainstay, 'That really doesn't make sense.'

Lord Hogsflesh, 'If I didn't know better, I would think that the elders are in cahoots with the Vikings.'

Commander Mainstay walked over to his desk, picked up a dagger, and rather nonchalantly sliced some dry skin off his hand.

Commander Mainstay, 'All I can say is sorry old friend.' As he plunged the dagger deep into Lord Hogflesh's body, Commander Mainstay would never forget the look of shocked horror on his old friend's face.

Commander Mainstay called for the guards as there had been an assassination attempt on his life, and Lord Hogsflesh had been killed. The assassin was never found. He then called for a messenger to inform Majors Bandolier and Manning that the Vikings were heading to London and that, sadly, Lord Hogsflesh had been killed in the process of obtaining this information.

96
Commander Bandolier has a Rest

It took a couple of days for Commander Mainstay's messenger to reach Chester. But the message was well-received, except for the death of Hoggy. It didn't make sense as he was indestructible. His troops were exhausted from the long march from Malvern. They could now rest and recuperate before what was going to be a long march to their next assignment.

There was a big cheer when the regiments were told to stand down. The gunpowder was put back into dry storage, and the party began. There was singing and dancing, card-playing, drinking and some whoring with the local ladies.

The last thing they expected was a hundred thousand Vikings attacking them from the east and an unknown number of Druids and witches attacking them from the west. It was worse than a massacre: it was a total slaughter of the unprepared. Their camps were a charnel house filled with the gory remains of a once fine military force.

About thirty thousand prisoners were captured. Five thousand were given to the Druids to be sacrificed and eaten, and the rest were being ritually murdered. Some were simply clubbed to death. The officers were skinned alive and then rubbed with salt to intensify their agony. It was a totally uncalled for culling of the innocent, but the Vikings enjoyed themselves, and the Druids had full stomachs.

Commander Bandolier had been stripped and chained so that he could be easily sodomised, which in Viking eyes made him less than a man. He was kept alive on the orders of the elders. He later learnt that he was going to be a present for the witches.

97
Making Sense of the World

Thomas was struggling to sleep as his mind was trying to make sense of the world. So much had happened in such a short period of time. The only stable thing in his life was his sister, and she was still in shock over the Fay massacre.

And then there was a knock on the door, and his sister entered his room. She wore a simple light smock which displayed her figure to good effect. Her hair had been freed from its normal entanglements, and it gently rolled down each side of her face softening her countenance.

She sat on the side of the bed and lent forward to kiss his forehead, giving Thomas a fine view of her assets. Her breasts were well-formed, with fully erect nipples crowning their glory. She placed her hand on the bed by his thigh and said that she couldn't sleep and that she would like a cuddle.

Thomas lifted the sheet so that she could get closer, although he was conscious of his nudity. That didn't seem to worry her, and she clambered in and turned her back to him so that they could get closer. Either accidentally or deliberately, her smock had been lifted so that his penis was brushing against her buttocks.

Robin must have felt the rigidity of his penis, and Thomas was finding it hard to resist her charms, especially when she kept wriggling her arse. It was as if she was trying to suck him in.

She whispered, 'You can take my virginity if you like.'

Thomas was too shocked to say anything.

Then she whispered, 'If you are worried about getting me pregnant, you can fuck me up the arse.'

Thomas jumped out of bed and said, 'What are you playing at. Get out of here.' And a crying Robin left the room.

Thomas found it even harder to get to sleep. His rigid penis kept him awake.

98
Commander Mannering wondered what to do

The destruction of Commander Bandolier's Army was a complete shock to Commander Mannering. How could they have got things so wrong? And why did the Druids attack them?

He planned to withdraw his forces south as he was in danger of being out-flanked. He didn't want to do that without Commander Mainstay's approval, as his withdrawal would expose his flank, but there was no response from him which was strange.

In the end, he had no choice but to withdraw as the situation was getting precarious. He had no idea how far south he should retire to, but he was obviously thinking of Malvern, as there was a defensive structure to support him. He started questioning Commander Mainstay's ability to command. He wondered if he should take over.

He also took command of the regiments of mounted archers as they were leaderless. They had not received any orders in days. Even the spies were asking him who they should report to following the death of Lord Hogsflesh.

99

My Sister is a Slut

Thomas woke up to find his sister naked, sitting on him. The sheet had been pulled back, and she was grinding her fanny against his cock. She looked beautiful with the light streaming in behind her and her voluptuous breasts swinging backwards and forwards in line with the gyration of her thighs.

Thomas looked into her eyes and could only see lust.

She said, 'You know that you want to fuck me.'

Thomas, 'I don't. You are my sister.'

Robin, 'My cunt is as good as Lady Malander's.'

Thomas, 'Get off. I don't want to fuck you.'

Robin, 'That is not what your cock is saying. Put it in me and have your wicked way. You have always had a secret desire to do that.'

Thomas, 'That's not true.'

Robin, 'Just fuck me. Do as your sister tells you. No one will know.'

Thomas, 'No.'

Robin, 'Give me your seed.'

Thomas, 'No.'

Robin, 'Do it, No one will ever know.'

And then Robin walked in, wondering what all of the noise was about. She said, 'I will know.'

It's not often that you have two identical sisters in the room. But then the naked one disappeared.

Robin, looking at Thomas's cock, said, 'Put that away.' And Thomas did. Although once again, he decided that the world was just getting stranger and stranger. And he was probably right.

100
The Elders Celebrate

Deputy Chief Elder, 'Fellow elders, as I said before, the cards are very much stacked in our favour, and the play is well underway. As always, there have been a few setbacks, but we will persevere.'

Elder Two, 'I hear that Lord Hogsflesh refused to play ball, and he paid the price.'

Elder Seven, 'My son, Commander Mainstay, did what was required of him. He proved his loyalty by killing one of his friends.'

Deputy Chief Elder, 'Yes, he did well. We haven't decided yet on how we plan to dispose of Hogsflesh's parents. Any suggestions?'

Elder Two, 'How about boiling them alive in oil.'

Elder Four, 'Why oil?'

Elder Two, 'It's considerably more painful.'

Deputy Chief Elder, 'That does seem a bit tame.'

Elder Two, 'What does the mother look like?'

Elder Four, 'Not bad.'

Elder Three, 'We could throw her to the troops. That's always quite entertaining.'

Elder Ten, 'What is this obsession with pain? Aren't we committing enough crimes without making it worse?'

Elder Two, 'You have no sense of fun.'

Elder Ten, 'I don't see how you can construe torture as being fun.'

Deputy Chief Elder, 'Just tell the jailer to dispose of them in any way he wants. We need to move on.

'I also need to inform you that our Viking friends and the Druids massacred Commander Bandolier's Army.'

There was clapping all around except from Elders Ten and Eleven.

Elder Ten, 'Why are we clapping the murder of one hundred thousand British soldiers?'

Deputy Chief Elder, 'It was part of the plan.'

Elder Ten, 'I understand that, but why are we clapping their deaths. I understand that thirty thousand brave soldiers were ritually murdered after surrendering, and five thousand were sacrificed and eaten. How can we celebrate that?'

Elder Eleven, 'I have to agree with Elder Ten.'

The Deputy Chief Elder called in the guard and asked them to kill Elders Ten and Eleven. There was no hesitation as both their throats were cut, and they were left there to bleed to death. There was some more clapping.

Deputy Chief Elder, 'We are still waiting for Lady Malander to die. When she does, we will need to move quickly to secure the child and eliminate Thomas.

'The temptation of Thomas also failed because his actual sister turned up at the wrong time.'

Elder Two, 'That was unlucky. So we haven't got his seed.'

Deputy Chief Elder, 'Not yet. It would be useful but not critical to the plan.'

Elder Two, 'What do we plan to do with the other two British armies in the field?'

Deputy Chief Elder, 'Commander Mainstay's Army will stay in London and collaborate with the Vikings.'

Elder Two, 'Does he know that?'

Deputy Chief Elder, 'Not yet.'

Elder Four, 'What about Commander Mannering's Army, which I understand is on the way back here?'

Deputy Chief Elder, 'Yes, I've been wondering about them. They need to be eliminated.'

Elder Three, 'Why don't we send them to Snowdonia. That will keep them out of the way for some time.'

Deputy Chief Elder, 'I think Strathclyde makes more sense. That will keep them out of the way for a long time.

'Once that is done, there is nothing to stop the Vikings from taking over.'

101
General Mainstay Regrets

Commander John Mainstay wasn't sure what to do. He had just killed one of his best friends, who had more principles than he could muster. He tried to save his friend's parents, but they had already been boiled alive in oil. He couldn't see any reason for doing that. It was simply unnecessary.

His message to Commander Bandolier had resulted in the gruesome deaths of over one hundred thousand brave British soldiers by Vikings, Druids, and witches. And for what reason?

He had just ordered Commander Mannering and his Army to go to Strathclyde without providing a logical reason. That was bound to cause more unnecessary deaths. And now, he had been instructed to report to the Viking leader in London and take instructions from him. What was he going to tell his commanders and troops?

But what options did he have? He could refuse and be killed. He could report to the Vikings and would almost certainly be asked to do something unacceptable. His refusal would mean certain death. In fact, most options seemed to lead to death.

He decided not to carry on, and his body was found hanging from the rafters.

102
Robin

Robin and Thomas were sitting down with Major Clutterbuck in the factory.

Robin, 'So what is going on?'

Thomas, 'What do you mean?'

Robin, 'For a start, nearly everyone we know is dead.'

Major Clutterbuck, 'Who exactly?'

Robin, 'I will list them: Lord Malander, Major Hogsflesh, General Winterdom, Commanders Walsh, Lambskin, Dragondale and Mainstay, Lionel, Tinton and Betty.'

Major Clutterbuck, 'That's nearly the whole team.'

Thomas, 'And Major Bandolier is a prisoner of the Vikings.'

Major Clutterbuck, 'They don't keep prisoners for long.'

Robin, 'So who is in charge of the Army?'

Thomas, 'I guess that it must be the elders.'

Robin, 'Two of them were murdered the other day.'

Thomas, 'How did you know that?'

Robin, 'I keep my ear to the ground.'

Major Clutterbuck, 'Where is the Army now?'

Thomas, 'Commander Mannering is on his way to Strathclyde, and there is still a large Army near London.'

Major Clutterbuck, 'So what are the Vikings doing?'

Robin, 'I heard that they are on their way here.'

Major Clutterbuck, 'Then we better leave.'

Thomas, 'I'm just waiting for Lady Malander to give birth.'

Major Clutterbuck, 'I think we need to make our plans to escape, us three, Fay and Lady Malander.'

Thomas, 'Lady Malander is not going to survive the birth of her son.'

Major Clutterbuck, 'How do you know that?'

Thomas, 'We know.'

Major Clutterbuck, 'Does Lady Malander know?'

Thomas, 'She does.'

Major Clutterbuck, 'Then that's another one for the list.'

Robin, 'When her Ladyship gives birth, how are you going to smuggle the baby out?'

Thomas, 'I haven't really thought about it.'

Robin, 'Then you better start.'

Major Clutterbuck, 'Let's get our critical possessions packed into carts and be in a position to go at a moment's notice. I can bring a few loyal engineers with us who can multi-task as guards.'

Thomas, 'That sounds like a good plan to me.'

Robin, 'And who was that naked wench in your bed that looked like me?'

Major Clutterbuck, 'Sly devil. No one told me about that.'

Thomas, 'I woke up with a naked copy of my sister on top of me demanding my seed. I must admit I was very close to letting her have it.'

Robin, 'Dirty bugger. You men are all the same.'

Thomas, 'I've no idea who she was.'

Robin, 'I know who she was.'

Thomas, 'How do you know?'

Robin, 'It's just come to me. It was Rachel.'

Thomas. 'Are you sure?'

Robin. 'I just used a spell to analyse her image in my mind's eye. It's her all right.'

Thomas, 'So what does she want?'

Robin, 'We know the answer to that. Your seed.'

Thomas, 'But why does she want it?'

103
The Witches' Revenge

The witches were very pleased with their present: a fully-fledged commander of the British Army. Commander Bandolier wasn't that excited about being a present. He had been tied to a pole in the middle of a circle. At least it made a pleasant change from being sodomised by groups of filthy, barbaric Vikings, although he wasn't expecting the evening to be a good result.

The coven leader spat all over his face and then fondled his penis until it was stiff.

Coven leader, 'We have got a live one here.'

Witch Tanith, 'I'm surprised that it's still intact. The Vikings usually chop them off for fun.'

Coven leader, 'What shall we do with it?'

Witch Amanda, 'How big is it?' The coven leader went back and massaged it a bit more.

Coven leader, 'I would say that it's an average size, about six inches.'

Witch Tanith, 'Does anyone fancy a fuck or shall we whip it off?'

Coven leader, 'Before we do that shall we choose his fate?'

Witch Miranda, 'I quite fancy doing what they do to us. Turning him into a sheep and then eating him.'

Coven leader, 'Did we want to torture him first?'

Witch Alison, 'Can I torture him now?'

Coven leader, 'What are you thinking of?'

Witch Alison, 'Ears, nose, fingers, toes, tongue, all the normal stuff. Rip them off and then blind him.'

Coven leader, 'That's all been done before. Many times.'

Witch Alison, 'But it is quite amusing.'

Witch Tanith, 'It would be quite interesting watching him starve to death.'

Coven leader, 'We need to make our minds up before dawn.'

104
The National Governance Meeting

The National Governance Meeting was organised for Banbury and had the following delegates:

- Deputy Chief Elder
- Remaining elders
- War Chief Eric Bloodaxe
- War Chief Harald Ironside
- War Chief Ragnor Godwinson
- War Chief Gunred the Strong
- War Chief Sweyn Thorson
- Coven Mistress Annabel
- Druid Leader Bryrona
- Druid Leader Celestina
- Druid Leader Camma

Deputy Chief Elder, 'Ladies and gentlemen, welcome to the National Governance Meeting. I believe that we are in a position to agree on the following:

- That Grand Britannica will become a formal member of the Viking Empire and will follow Viking laws and customs
- That a Viking King will be appointed
- That the remaining elders will be appointed as Dukes with the nominated estates as per the agreement
- That the capital of the country will be London
- That the British Army and Navy will be dissolved
- That the Vikings will be responsible for the defence of the country
- That the Druids will have the province of Wales
- That witchcraft will be legalised

- That all magicians will be sentenced to death
- That all members of the Malander family will be treated as traitors and executed
- That all officers in the British Army and Navy will be treated as traitors and executed
- That all Fay creatures will be hunted down and executed
- That all property is now under the control of the king and his ducal supporters
- That all courts will be closed down
- That all Lord Protectors will be treated as traitors and executed
- That each port will be controlled by a Viking port master.

'Are there any objections?'

There were no objections, and the National Governance regulations were accepted.

Scribes produced multiple copies for signature.

105
It is the Day

Lady Malander called for Thomas as she knew that it was time.

Thomas, 'Is it time?'

Lady Malander, 'It is.'

Thomas, 'How do you want to handle this?'

Lady Malander, 'Firstly, there are spies everywhere. They want me and the baby dead. As soon as I give birth, they will kill both of us.'

Thomas, 'If that is the case, why don't they kill you now?'

Lady Malander, 'They are frightened of my powers. Anyway, I've created a double who has just started the birthing process. As you know, it can take hours. Now I need to find somewhere safe to give birth. I need to warn you that it is not going to be your usual process.'

Thomas, 'What about the factory?'

Lady Malander, 'I think they would suspect that.'

Thomas, 'Shall we just leave town and then find somewhere safe?'

Lady Malander, 'That makes sense.'

Thomas, 'If we can secrete you across the road, then Major Clutterbuck will pick us up in his wagon. Robin will prepare some spells to hide our departure. Her spells are the best.'

It wasn't long before Major Clutterbuck arrived, and they surreptitiously left town. Robin's spell worked like a dream. Mind you, three wagons with ten people onboard was an unusual sight, but it couldn't be helped. They travelled for a couple of hours when Lady Malander announced that she wanted to give birth under the oak tree that she was pointing to.

She stripped and laid down on a bed of acorns with her baby bump pointing towards the sky. She chanted a few incantations and then called Thomas over.

Lady Malander, 'Take this dagger and slice me downwards from my chest to my vagina.'

Thomas, 'I can't do that, my Lady.'

Lady Malander, 'Do it, or the baby dies.'

Thomas, 'But that will kill you.'

Lady Malander, 'I'm going to die regardless. Now cut me.' Robin came over and said that she would do it. She was made of sterner stuff than Thomas.

Lady Malander, 'It must be Thomas, and he must do it now.'

Thomas took the dagger and placed it between her pendulous breasts, and started the cut. He was crying as slowly the line of blood reached her black triangle. Lady Malander didn't utter a word.

Lady Malander, 'Now cut me across the highest point of the bump.'

Thomas, still crying, took the marvellously sharp dagger and made the second cut. The pain must have been unbearable, but still, Lady Malander didn't utter a word. You could see the pain in her face, but she didn't utter a sound. Thomas had seen many a brute of a man, scream in agony over a minor flesh wound. He would never forget her courage.

Lady Malander, 'Now unfold me.' Thomas wasn't sure what she meant.

Robin, 'Take the cut skin and pull it apart.' Thomas did as instructed, and was amazed. In front of him was a baby floating in the universe. He could see the moon, the planets and then the constellations.

Lady Malander, 'I'm off now, look after Arthur, won't you?'

And then, from within him, he heard the Enchantress of Evermore say, 'Thank you for looking after me. It has been a brilliant adventure. You have got such an interesting future. Don't give up. I love you.'

Lady Malander, 'Bye Merlin, we are both off now.' And then Lady Malander's body turned into a flutter of bright blue butterflies, leaving a very healthy-looking baby boy looking for a cuddle. Robin picked him up straight away and fell in love with him.

Major Clutterbuck, 'We must get on our way.'

106
The Time of the Cull

The rumours went out that Lady Malander was giving birth. The elders sent out their bodyguard to kill her and the baby only to find magic afoot. When the Deputy Chief Elder found out, he went into a rage.

Deputy Chief Elder, 'Kill every magician in Malvern. Then kill every Army officer. Then hunt down the criminals and hang them.'

The Master of the Elderguard didn't like the idea of attacking the magicians and certainly hated the idea of killing fellow officers, but he knew how ruthless the elders were, and so followed orders.

Three junior magicians were killed whilst they were asleep, but the alarm had been raised, and war erupted. It was a dozen magicians against nearly a thousand guardsmen, but then, as some of the Army officers had also been targeted, the rest of the officers came to the aid of the magicians.

There was no love lost between the bodyguard and Army, and it was time for old scores to be settled. The officers organised their musketeers, and the Elderguard were soon being mowed down. The Master of the Elderguard was forced to surrender, which suited him. In his pocket, they found a copy of the National Governance proclamation.

The information was soon circulated to the Army, which caused an uproar as the Vikings were universally hated. Army scribes quickly copied the proclamation, and couriers were organised to send the documents to Commander Mannering and the London Army and as many other officers as possible.

The remaining members of the Elderguard quickly ushered the elders out of their stately home and rushed them off on fast horses towards Evesham. The elders weren't happy as in their secluded naivety they had assumed that most of the common people had the same views as themselves. Surely the Vikings would be preferential to a military dictator?

The remaining magicians tried to find Thomas, Robin, and the genuine Lady Malander, but their tracks had been too well-hidden.

107
Bandolier's Post

Commander Bandolier was rather surprised that he was still alive. He was freezing, stuck to a post on a hilltop, but he was still alive. He had been sexually abused quite a few times by a variety of witches, but as they couldn't agree on his fate, he had been left.

But they would be back. He couldn't think of a way of escaping until a shepherd's dog came running by. And where there was a shepherd's dog, there was usually a shepherd. And there was a shepherd of the female variety.

Shepherdess, 'What have we got here?'

Commander Bandolier, 'I'm Commander Bandolier of the British Army.'

Shepherdess, 'No, you are not. You are a naked plaything. I expect the witches left you here to die after enjoying your predicament.'

Commander Bandolier, 'You know about the witches?'

Shepherdess, 'I've found many a dead body tied to these posts. You are the first live one. Normally they are horribly mutilated with their eyes pecked out.'

Commander Bandolier, 'Well, at least you can release me.'

Shepherdess, 'I couldn't do that. I wouldn't be safe. The witches will hunt me down and torture me. My Fred wouldn't know what to do with himself.'

Commander Bandolier, 'I could pay you.'

Shepherdess, 'What with. From where I'm standing, your pockets don't look too deep.'

Commander Bandolier, 'Could you get a message to anyone in the Army?'

Shepherdess, 'There are some officers in the village, but I would still want a fee.'

Commander Bandolier, 'That won't be a problem. Please make contact as soon as possible.'

Shepherdess, 'I've still got to complete my round.'

Commander Bandolier, 'Please hurry.'

It wasn't long before two junior officers were tramping up the hill. One of them immediately recognised the Commander, and he was released. A coat was handed over.

Captain Pellett, 'What happened to you, Sir?'

Commander Bandolier, 'There has been treachery. The Vikings and Druids destroyed my Army after I received misleading information.'

Captain Pellett, 'We know about that, Sir. Those fucking Viking bastards murdered thousands of our comrades.'

Commander Bandolier, 'Then I was handed over to the witches as a present. They need to be punished.'

Captain Pellett, 'We can organise that, Sir, but we are reforming due to this.' And he handed over a copy of the proclamation.

Commander Bandolier, 'I can't believe it, but at least I now understand what has been going on. Do you know the current position?'

Captain Pellett, 'It's all a bit vague, Sir. Commander Manning's Army was sent to Strathclyde. I'm not sure how far he had travelled before he got a copy of the proclamation. Commander Mainstay committed suicide.'

Commander Bandolier, 'I can't believe that.'

Captain Pellett, 'It's true, and his Army has been told to report to the Vikings.'

Commander Bandolier, 'Where is the main Viking Army?'

Captain Pellett, 'Somewhere in the Midlands. I heard that they were going to Malvern, but I'm really out of date.'

Commander Bandolier, 'In that case, we need to go to Malvern.'

Captain Pellett, 'What about the witches?'

Commander Bandolier, 'Leave them for now, but I haven't forgotten about them. Let's get on our way.'

108
She has Gone?

Robin, 'It's hard to believe that she has gone.'

Thomas, 'That's true. I don't think that I've started the grieving process yet.'

Robin, 'It's hard to grieve when there is so much going on.'

Thomas, 'Anyway, grieving is about ourselves. She has gone. We know that we will never see her again. Our memories will never be updated with her presence, and that makes us sad.'

Robin, 'I know that, but I will miss her calm presence.'

Thomas, 'She was calm, wasn't she?'

Robin, 'And at the same time so full of life.'

Thomas, 'She meant a lot to me as a mother, a mentor and a friend.'

Robin, 'And as a lover.'

Thomas, 'That was accidental.'

Robin, 'Fucking a woman is hardly ever accidental.'

Thomas, 'What I meant is that I never intended to make love to her. It just happened.'

Robin, 'So she seduced you?'

Thomas, 'It was more mutual. It was the right thing to do at the time. And I don't regret it for a moment.'

Robin, 'You men are so weak.'

Thomas, 'That might be the case, but I loved her.'

Robin, 'I know you did.' And they both cried.

Thomas, 'Do you believe that she is dead?'

Robin, 'No. She is still alive in some form. What was that whole celestial thing about?'

Thomas, 'It's beyond me. Did you know that she had lived for more than a thousand years?'

Robin, 'I expected as much.'

Thomas, 'She knew more than we will ever know. And now there is no one to teach us.'

Major Clutterbuck, 'You guys can chat as much as you like later, but you need to tell me where we are going.'

Thomas unfolded the piece of paper that Lady Malander gave him, and it just contained an arrow, and that is the way they went.

109
The London Army

Acting Commander Squire had received a summons from the Viking Warlord in London demanding his presence and that of all his officers. It stated that they should come unarmed. Fortunately, he had received a copy of the proclamation. He knew that he would be walking towards his death.

He surreptitiously put his Army on full alert. They were ordered to march into London, ready to engage the Vikings. This covert operation went down well as they wanted to avenge their colleagues who had been ritually murdered by the barbarians. And the task was going to be fairly easy as they outnumbered the Vikings ten to one.

Commander Squire arrived at the Viking camp with his officers and a regiment of two hundred musketeers. There weren't even any sentries. Most of the warriors were utterly drunk to the point where they couldn't stand. It was hard work living off the land.

War Chief Harald Ironside, 'I ordered you to come unarmed.'

Commander Squire, 'None of the officers here are armed.'

War Chief Harald Ironside, 'What are they?' He was pointing at the musketeers.

Commander Squire, 'You mean our bodyguard?'

War Chief Harald Ironside, 'Order them to disarm.'

Commander Squire, 'I will when I receive my written orders.'

War Chief Harald Ironside, 'What fucking written orders?'

Commander Squire, 'The ones that give you command of my forces.'

War Chief Harald Ironside, 'You will do what I tell you, or I will rip your head off.'

Commander Squire, 'That's not the attitude of a professional soldier.'

War Chief Harald Ironside, 'I will give you fucking professional. If you don't do as I say, I will skin you alive.'

Commander Squire ordered his musketeers to present arms and said, 'I have to warn you that my men will fire if you approach me.'

War Chief Harald Ironside knew that Commander Squire was far too weak a man to do that. So he stood up, took out his knife and lunged at Commander Squire, who ordered his men to fire. Two hundred muskets converted the Warlord's command structure into human mincemeat.

The sound of the muskets was the signal for the main Army to attack the London Vikings. It wasn't pretty. The British Army had a grudge, and they went for it. There was enough blood and gore to keep the rat's stomachs fed for quite a few weeks. There were no prisoners, which wasn't a surprise.

Commander Squire left half of his Army to defend London, and the rest marched on Malvern.

110
Ride a Cock Horse

The elders and their few remaining guards fled to Banbury. They consumed a plate from the local patisserie and convened a meeting.

Deputy Chief Elder, 'Clearly, the pack of cards has not fallen in our favour, but we have other cards to play.'

Elder Seven, 'What is the point of all this? My son is dead.'

Elder Five, 'Stop going on about it. He was just weak.'

Elder Seven, 'So having principles is being weak. We had principles once.'

The Deputy Chief Elder called the guard and asked him to escort Elder Seven to his room, which was actually an extermination command.

The remaining Elders continued the conversation.

Elder Two, 'So what is the situation with Lady Malander?'

Deputy Chief Elder, 'They have evaded our security staff.'

Elder Three, 'So they have escaped.'

Deputy Chief Elder, 'That is one of the possibilities.'

Elder Three, 'What other possibilities are there?'

Deputy Chief Elder, 'Malvern is still infested with magicians.'

Elder Six, 'What happened to the Elderguard?'

Deputy Chief Elder, 'The enemy got hold of a copy of the proclamation, and the Malvern troops turned on the guard.'

Elder Twelve, 'I can't say I blame them as it is more or less a death warrant.'

Elder Three, 'That probably means that all of the British forces know about our plan.'

Deputy Chief Elder, 'Possibly.'

Elder Three, 'What do you think their reaction will be?'

Elder Nine, 'Revenge. Pure unadulterated revenge. They will come for the Vikings and us.'

Elder Three, 'Can the Vikings protect us?'

Deputy Chief Elder, 'Possibly. It's hard to tell. We need to work out the numbers:

- Mannering has got one hundred and twenty-five thousand troops
- There are about one hundred and fifty thousand in the London Army
- There are twenty-five thousand in Malvern
- There are five thousand mounted archers.'

Elder Nine, 'So what's the total?'

Deputy Chief Elder, 'About three hundred thousand.'

Elder Nine, 'And the Viking Army?'

Deputy Chief Elder, 'The main Army has one hundred and twenty thousand, and there are probably another forty thousand in London.'

Elder Nine, 'So we are outnumbered two to one.'

Deputy Chief Elder, 'It looks that way.'

Elder Three, 'What are we going to do?'

111
The Fleet Prevails

The British were encouraged by their successes. Their seamanship was improving, and they were probably, indeed almost certainly, the best maritime cannoneers in the world. But there was a lot of trial and error.

After destroying the Viking Fleet in the Thames Estuary, they were tasked with destroying the main Viking fleet on the Humber. The problem was that none of the crew knew where the Humber was. There were no maps and few knowledgeable locals.

As a consequence, they were forced to investigate every inlet and estuary along the eastern coastland. A difficult and dangerous journey for those with little nautical skills. The sea was terrifying, and the sand dunes were a constant danger. There were miles of marshland which made navigation really challenging.

Along the way, they had many collisions, capsized ships, fires, hull breaches, ripped sails, mutiny, groundings, lost oars etc. The list was endless, but every disaster was a learning exercise. Eventually, they reached the Humber. They were astonished to see such desolate and depressing scenery. They made a mental note not to return.

As was the Viking tradition, their fleets were either unguarded or manned by old men and young boys. Rather than set fire to them, which was the plan, they managed to tow most of the ships out to sea, where at least half were lost to the elements.

The rest were used to double the size of the British fleet. The Vikings now had no transport to return home.

112
Baby Delivery

It was a delightful journey as they left Worcestershire and entered Shropshire. The piece of paper continued to guide them. They were worried about how they were going to feed Arthur as they had no baby milk, but Arthur kept silent all the time.

They avoided Ludlow, as it was likely to have some Government forces, and they weren't sure who was friend or foe at the moment. Lady Malander's piece of paper guided them towards The Striperstones, where they stopped for the night. Not once did little Arthur cry out for food, although he was quite happy to suck a finger.

In the morning, after a dry breakfast, the paper made them change direction towards Long Mynd Hill. Here the scenery was spectacular but very hard work for the horses. As they climbed the hill, they were directed along a rickety path that came to an imposing but slightly worn country house.

As the three carts meandered their way into the courtyard, a small party from the house came out to meet them.

The carts stopped, and the fattest of the five residents put his hand out to shake Thomas's hand.

Squire Ridgeway, 'Merlin, it is a huge honour to meet you. I'm Squire Ridgeway, and this is my wife Doris, my daughter Emily and our two servants.'

Thomas, 'The pleasure is mine. This is my sister.' And they shook hands.

Squire Ridgeway, 'Not Robin. She is almost as famous as you.'

Thomas, 'And this is…'

Squire Ridgeway, 'Mr Clutterbuck, the most famous inventor in Grand Britannia. I'm so honoured to meet all three of you. I understand that you are delivering my son, Arthur.' Some more handshaking went on.

Thomas, 'Well, yes.'

Squire Ridgeway, 'I have a wet nurse in the house. The poor boy must be starving.' And he was.

Thomas, 'Clearly, you were expecting us.'

Squire Ridgeway, 'We have been tracking you since you left Malvern. Now there is no time to lose. Lady Malander said to give you this document. I hope that you understand it.'

The document said:

'Dear Merlin, Robin, and Lindsey,

Thank you for delivering my son to Squire Ridgeway. They will look after him and bring him up as their own son.

Do not grieve for me as I have my own destiny to fulfil. There is a chance that we will meet again.

Once you have read this, you will forget everything about this journey, and you will forget about Arthur. Turn your wagons around and return to Malvern. After ten miles, stop and read this note again, and you will understand what you still have to do.

I love you all.

Sheila Malander.'

113
Viking Dilemmas

The Viking Army was enjoying itself plundering Walsall. The head of the Viking forces, War Chief Ragnor Godwinson, wasn't sure what he was supposed to be doing. After the proclamation, all British military forces were supposed to stand down, giving the Vikings a free hand. Indeed, it was their land to do with as they pleased.

But War Chief Ragnor Godwinson was picking up some very disturbing rumours. Firstly, he had heard that the Viking occupation in London had ended. The British Army under Commander Squire had defeated them and was on its way west.

The second rumour was that the elders had fled to Banbury and that they were expecting him to rush there and defend them.

Then he heard that their fleet on the Humber had been destroyed. This didn't sound like a stand down of the British military. With the fleet gone, there was no way of requesting reinforcements.

In addition, Commander Mannering had abandoned the trip to Strathclyde and was returning to Malvern.

War Chief Ragnor Godwinson wasn't keen on dividing his forces, so he had to choose one option:

1. Reclaim London and avenge his dead brothers
2. Capture Malvern
3. Head to Banbury and discuss options with the elders.

After much deliberation, mixed with some alcohol, he selected options two and three, which went against his initial thinking. He would crush Malvern once and for all and save the elders.

114
The Message

Thomas, Robin, and Lindsey followed the instructions to the letter. At exactly, the ten-mile mark text started appearing on the note. They stopped, eager to see what Lady Malander had to say.

It said:

'Thank you, friends, for following my request. You will always have my sincere gratitude.

And now for some guidance:

- *Firstly, beware of the deputy Chief Elder. Things are not what they seem*
- *There will be a battle at Banbury, but save the elders*
- *There will be a desperate battle at Malvern, but keep faith*
- *In the end, the losers are the Vikings but let them have part of the country. It will be called The Danelaw. It is Grand Britannica's destiny*
- *Old friends will return.*

Fulfil your destiny, and the gods will be forever grateful.

Take care, my friends.

Love Sheila.'

Robin, 'What is she thanking us for?'

Thomas, 'I've no idea.'

Major Clutterbuck, 'I'm trying to remember where we have been.'

Thomas, 'At least we have an insight into the future.'

115
The Battle of Banbury

The Battle of Banbury was never planned: it just happened. The British Army in London formed two columns. One left Finchley and headed towards Watford and then Aylesbury and Bicester on their way to Malvern. The other column took the Oxford to Cheltenham route.

The Vikings were heading south after giving Walsall a good pulverisation. Their journey took them via Solihull and Warwick. In theory, the two armies should have missed each other. It looked like either scouts made contact or probably lost battalions. Battles caused by the lost was a well-known military phenomenon. Anyway, contact was made, and an escalation developed.

From a Viking perspective, just more and more warriors were thrown into the fray. From a British perspective, scouts were simply clashing swords. Then the British vanguard of two mounted regiments of archers joined the action causing devastating casualties amongst the Vikings. The open countryside suited their hit and run tactics. But they were being threatened by the sheer number of enemy warriors.

They were countered by three regiments of pikemen and men at arms with supporting archers. At the same time, Commander Squire found a vantage point to check out the lay of the land. The Vikings simply attacked anything in front of them. It often worked as it didn't give the enemy any time to organise themselves, but here it was going to be a battle of sheer animal ferocity against organised tactics.

The fact that the Vikings simply surged forwards gave Commander Squire an advantage in that all he had to do was to hold them and then let them loose into a playground of his choosing, and then the play would commence.

Commander Squire, 'My orders:

- Three more regiments of infantry will support the existing regiments in action

- All mounted archers to attack the Viking flanks but avoid any serious action
- Cannons to be positioned on Steepness Hill
- All Musketeers to be positioned on Steepness Hill
- Infantry regiments to be based out of sight on the flanks of Steepness Hill
- Send messengers to order the column moving towards Oxford to divert to the west of Banbury at full speed.'

His aides rushed off to deliver the orders.

The British infantry were being battered, but they held their ground. In many ways, they were simply 'delaying fodder' used to secure a victory. It was fortunate that they accidentally held the higher ground and that the Vikings were already exhausted from excessive drinking, fornicating, pillaging, and some rapid marching, or in their case, traipsing.

Commander Squire waited for the right moment to issue further orders:

- All forces on Steepness Hill to prepare for battle
- Mounted archers to press the flanks to funnel the enemy
- All engaged infantry to retreat on the sign of a flaming arrow.

Once again, aides rushed off, and the flaming arrow was fired. An organised retreat for infantry was a particularly difficult and dangerous operation. It meant exposing themselves to the enemy, especially as the pikemen had to abandon their pikes. The men knew that probably half of them would die. They had learnt that retiring in small groups was the better method as they could protect each other, and this was often done in battalions. A single fleeing infantryman was an easy target for a sword in the back.

The Mounted archers tried to protect the infantry as best they could, but they had their own job to do. Then the Viking spotted the British troops on Steepness Hill. It wasn't called Steepness without a reason, and it was hard going for the Vikings. It got even harder when every other cannon fired, taking out huge swathes of hairy, horned berserkers. Then the second round went off, decimating the Viking ranks. As they got nearer, the Musketeers joined the bombardment. Cannonballs shot down the hill, taking a dozen Vikings at a time. Shrapnel simply removed dozens of heads.

The blood, gore and wet grass simply made the hill impassable. Commander Squire wondered if he had invented the concept of continuous bombardment, but it was working a treat.

The regiments at the base of the hill entered the slaughter, and the Viking leader, War Chief Ragnor Godwinson, ordered a readjustment of the battlement. In British speak it was a retreat. In some ways, the Viking Army's survival was not due to Ragnor Godwinson but to Commander Squire using his hillside infantry too early. More Vikings could have easily been cannonaded to death.

The Vikings readjusted to Banbury, and the British followed, eager to press home their advantage.

116
Save the Elders

Thomas and Robin looked at each other as they received a message from the now-dead Lady Malander. In simple terms, it said, 'Go to Stratford-Upon-Avon and save the elders.'

Firstly, they didn't care a damn about the elders. Given a choice, they would like to see them dead. They certainly deserved death after putting personal greed before the lives of British men and women. They were, directly and indirectly, responsible for most of the horror and anguish seen in Grand Britannica over the last few years.

Secondly, they had just travelled from an unknown destination and were looking forward to a proper meal, a wash, and a good long rest. The last thing they wanted was yet another long journey, especially on horseback.

But then Lady Malander, dead or alive, was the boss. They had no choice but to be guided by her wisdom.

When they reached Malvern, they obtained fresh horses and galloped off to Stratford-Upon-Avon, wondering what they would find there. Major Clutterbuck decided to join them as it felt right.

On the journey, they chatted away as brothers and sisters do. Then Thomas said, 'Who do you think our parents are?'

Robin, 'We know who our parents are. The butcher and his wife.'

Thomas, 'I know that they brought us up, but don't you think it strange that two of the world's most powerful magicians were born to them.'

Robin, 'That's a bit condescending.'

Thomas, 'I know, but you know what I mean.'

Robin, 'I know exactly what you mean. I used to dream that I was a foundling and that my real parents turned up out of the blue and claimed me.'

Thomas, 'I'm assuming that they were royalty.'

Robin, 'Of course, and wealthy beyond compare.'

Thomas, 'Have you gone back and seen the parents who brought us up?'

Robin, 'Not for a long time.'

Thomas, 'But they were really good to us. So why don't we go and see them? And don't say that you have been too busy.'

Robin, 'Because they are unbelievably boring.'

Thomas, 'There is some truth in that.'

Robin, 'I don't need them as long as I've got you.'

Thomas, 'It won't be long before you find a lover, and then you will be off.'

Robin, 'I don't think so. We are a team, and that's the way I want it to be.'

Thomas, 'Me too. Let's pledge to stay together.' And they did.

117
The Second Battle of Banbury

So the British won the first battle of Banbury. How would they fare in a town where street to street fighting might better suit the Viking skill set? The Vikings rushed back to Banbury in a disordered mess, but that was their normal routine.

The British reformed back into regiments. Commander Squire liked organisation and structure, and he found that the men liked it as well. It gave them confidence and belief in their own abilities. It gave them a hierarchy of order. By the time they were in a position to move on, the second column from Oxford had arrived. They were given time to rest whilst the first column set off to Banbury. Commander Squire and his command team went ahead to review the Banbury environment.

The elders were still hiding in Banbury with a couple of hundred Elderguards. They knew that the first battle of Banbury wasn't the success that the Vikings claimed it was. Apparently, the Vikings had never lost a battle. But their definition of loss was total annihilation. If one warrior survived, then they hadn't lost. This wasn't the elders' definition of loss, and they started getting nervous about their position. Should they flee?

Commander Squire circled the entire town. It was basically a small market town on several important commercial routes. It serviced a large part of Oxfordshire, with the locals calling it Banburyshire. Its most notable features, were the crossroads with its ancient inns and a market square. Currently, it was crowded with hammer-fighting, hard-drinking, shaggy louts.

The problem with the louts was that it was both easy and difficult to work out a strategy to defeat them. They just came at you. In this case, there was probably still a hundred thousand of them. When that number come at you, it is difficult to stop them. Therefore, you need a strategy to concentrate them into a single, easily defended killing ground or divide them into more manageable units and defeat them one by one.

Commander Squire had to decide what to do as his Army were not far away. The Vikings would expect him to come from the south, so that was the first thing to avoid. But then, three things happened. Firstly, he was under attack. Secondly, the column nearing Banbury was being attacked, and thirdly the sky filled with Valkyries, a few thousand of them.

Before this started, the elders had done their normal trick whenever danger was likely: they fled. Two hundred-odd riders headed towards Stratford-Upon-Avon straight into forces controlled by the returning Commander Bandolier.

Commander Squire managed to escape to join his main column where the Valkyries were causing havoc. He ordered a general retreat. He was particularly angry as he had lost some good men in this attempted ambush.

So you could say that the Vikings won the second battle of Banbury.

118
Commander Bandolier versus the Elders

Commander Bandolier had managed to collect about three thousand troops from the various encounters and garrisons and was travelling across country to Malvern, trying to avoid the main routes in case of enemy activity. And then they collided with two hundred riders coming in the opposite direction.

He recognised them immediately as Elderguards. They started to turn, but they were soon outnumbered and surrendered. Commander Bandolier called over the Master of the Elderguard.

Master of the Elderguard, 'You have no right to stop us. We represent the elders, the rightful rulers of this land.'

Commander Bandolier, 'Since the proclamation, the elders have no right to live, let alone rule the land. They are traitors to everything we hold dear.'

Master of the Elderguard, 'How dare you criticise the elders. I will have you arrested for treason.'

Commander Bandolier, 'You and whose Army? I guess that would be the Viking Army.'

Master of the Elderguard, 'What are you suggesting?'

Commander Bandolier, 'I'm not suggesting anything. It is a fact that the elders are in cahoots with the Vikings.'

Master of the Elderguard, 'What proof have you got?'

Commander Bandolier, 'The proclamation says it all.'

The Master knew that Commander Bandolier was right. Deep down and, despite his position, he was full of contempt for the elders and hated the Vikings as much as any Briton.

Master of the Elderguard, 'What are you going to do with us?'

Commander Bandolier, 'I want you to tell me where the elders are.'

Master of the Elderguard, 'I can't tell you that. My men and I have sworn to protect them. We would rather die than betray them.'

Commander Bandolier, 'In that case, you are of no use to me.' He shouted to Captain Pellett to prepare ropes for hanging.

Master of the Elderguard, 'You can't hang us.'

Commander Bandolier, 'Why not? You are on the side of the traitors, and I'm sure that you have carried out traitorous acts.'

Master of the Elderguard, 'But my men have only been following orders.'

Commander Bandolier, 'But they followed them. I'm going to order my men to hang ten of your guards now. They don't have to follow my orders, but if they do, then they are complicit.'

Commander Bandolier ordered Captain Pellet to select ten of the Elderguard and place ropes around their necks. This was done.

Master of the Elderguard, 'You can't do this.'

Commander Bandolier, 'But we are. Tell me where the elders are, or the hangings will start.'

Commander Bandolier ordered Captain Pellett to tie the men's arms together and put them on horseback. This was done.

Master of the Elderguard, 'In the name of the elders, I command you to stop this.'

Commander Bandolier approached the ten victims and said, 'Are you willing to tell me the elders' location?' No one responded.

Commander Bandolier 'Your lives are in your hands. This is your last chance.' No one responded.

Commander Bandolier ordered Captain Pellett to continue with the execution. The ropes were thrown over the branches of nearby trees, and nine men choked to death. One of the branches collapsed due to the weight of the body. The nearest soldiers stabbed the poor victim in the neck.

Commander Bandolier, 'Select the next ten volunteers.'

Master of the Elderguard, 'You can't continue. This is uncivilised.'

Commander Bandolier, 'Captain Pellett, I believe that the Master of the Elderguard has volunteered.'

Captain Pellett, 'That's correct, Sir. I spotted that too.'

Master of the Elderguard, 'You can't kill me. I have the personal protection of the elders.'

Commander Bandolier once again approached the ten victims and said, 'Are you willing to tell me the elders' location?' No one responded. And they were hung.

Commander Bandolier admired their courage and dedication and said,

'Captain Pellett, continue with the executions.'

The next ten contained an elder disguised as an Elderguard. As soon as the rope was put on his neck, he broke ranks and proclaimed that he was an elder.

Commander Bandolier, 'I see no reason to stop the executions.'

Captain Pellett, 'Yes, Sir. I will continue.'

119
The Magicians to the rescue

The three travelled to Stratford-Upon-Avon as fast as they could, and when they got there, they couldn't find anything out of the ordinary. There was no sign of any elder activity.

Then Lady Malander gave further instructions, 'Go to Hatton Rock. Save the lives of the elders.' That meant another five or six miles by horseback. When they got there, they easily found the military forces and saw the nineteen bodies hanging from the trees with another ten in preparation.

Thomas just shouted, 'Stop.'

Commander Bandolier immediately recognised his old friends. They were genuinely pleased to see each other. There were handshakes and hugs all around.

Thomas, 'So what's going on?'

Commander Bandolier, 'Well, we caught these traitors fleeing from Banbury where there has been a battle.'

Thomas, 'Who won?'

Commander Bandolier, 'From what I understand, we won the first battle of Banbury but had to retire from the second battle due to hundreds of Valkyries.'

Thomas, 'I thought that the Valkyries had gone.'

Commander Bandolier, 'So did I. Anyway, we offered these guards every chance to tell us where the elders are.'

Thomas, 'Why are you persecuting the elders?'

Commander Bandolier, 'That suggests that you haven't seen the Proclamation. I will read it to you:

- That Grand Britannica will become a formal member of the Viking Empire and will follow Viking laws and customs
- That a Viking King will be appointed

232

- That the ten elders will be appointed as Dukes with the nominated estates as per the agreement
- That the capital of the country will be London
- That the British Army and Navy will be dissolved
- That the Vikings will be responsible for the defence of the country
- That the Druids will have the province of Wales
- That witchcraft will be legalised
- That all magicians will be sentenced to death
- That all members of the Malander family will be treated as traitors and executed
- That all officers in the British Army and Navy will be treated as traitors and executed
- That all Fay creatures will be hunted down and executed
- That all property is now under the control of the king and his ducal supporters
- That all courts will be closed down
- That all Lord Protectors will be treated as traitors and executed
- That each port will be controlled by a Viking port-master.'

Thomas, 'I can't believe this.'

Commander Bandolier, 'I accept that it is hard to believe, but they have committed one traitorous act after another. Whole armies were wiped out due to their ruthless and deceitful actions. They deserve to die.'

Thomas, 'I can see that.'

Commander Bandolier, 'Anyway that guard there with a rope around his neck claims that he is an elder.'

Thomas, 'Let's interrogate him.' He was taken off the horse and dragged over.

Commander Bandolier, 'So who are you?'

Elder Six, 'I'm Elder Six.'

Commander Bandolier, 'Why are you dressed as a guardsman?'

Elder Six, 'To disguise ourselves in case of capture.'

Commander Bandolier, 'Well, clearly that hasn't worked. Who are you trying to avoid?'

Elder Six, 'The enemy.'

Commander Bandolier, 'And who are they?'

Elder Six, 'I can't comment.'

Commander Bandolier, 'Captain Pellett, please return Elder Six to the hanging tree.'

Elder Six, 'You wouldn't dare.'

Commander Bandolier, 'Captain Pellett, please continue with the executions.' Elder Six and nine guardsmen met their end. Thomas thought about intervening but couldn't build up the enthusiasm. He looked at Robin to see what her thoughts were, but she didn't appear to have any objections.

But then they got another message from Lady Malander pleading for the elders to be saved. Apparently, the future of humanity depended on it.

Thomas, 'Commander Bandolier, could I have a word.'

Commander Bandolier, 'Of course.' They walked to a spot where they couldn't be heard.

Thomas, 'This is really difficult to explain, but Lady Malander is dead.'

Commander Bandolier, 'How?'

Thomas, 'She died in childbirth giving Lord Malander a son.'

Commander Bandolier, 'I'm so sorry.'

Thomas, 'But she is not completely dead. Somehow her consciousness lives on. She sent us here to save the elders. She claims that this is necessary for the future of humanity. I've no idea what she means.'

Commander Bandolier, 'So you want me to stop the executions?'

Thomas, 'I just want the elders captured and imprisoned. I don't care what you do with the guard, although I wouldn't execute them, but that is up to you.'

Commander Bandolier, 'So how do we identify the elders?'

Thomas, 'I think I can do that with a spell. Put the Elderguard in a line, and I will do the rest.'

Captain Pellett did the lining up, and Thomas did his spell. There were now seven naked humans in the line: the elders had been exposed in more ways than one. But what they discovered was shocking.

120
Another Magical Conclave

The Fairy Queen, 'The time has come to decide which side we are going to fight on.'

Goblin Master, 'We need to kill as many ploughmen as possible.'

Pixi Master, 'Do you mean every sort?'

Goblin Master, 'Just kill them all.'

Pixi Master, 'But the ones that attacked us were the blue ones. The pink ones were trying to stop it.'

Elfi Master, 'What about the hairy ones with the two horns?'

Mersi Master, 'You mean the Vi-queens. They and the elders have issued a proclamation to kill us.'

Gremli Master, 'Why would they do that?'

Famili Master, 'Much hate us.'

Pixi Master, 'All hate us. So we kill the blue ones and the hairy ones.'

Leprechauni, 'Elders want to kill us too.'

Goblin, 'Why not hide? Let ploughmen kill ploughmen.'

Impi Master, 'Ploughmen are very, very good at killing ploughmen.'

Gremli Master, 'They much hating each other.'

The Fairy Queen, 'The prophecy has marked this as the time of decision. It is not whether we fight or not fight. It is about who we fight with.'

Elementi Master, 'Is magic leaving this world?'

The Fairy Queen, 'It is, the time of magic is behind us. It may be gone in our lifetime.'

Asrai Master, 'That can't be the case.'

The Fairy Queen, 'How many new-borns have you had this year?'

Asrai Master, 'You know the answer to that.'

The Fairy Queen, 'I do, and the answer is none. I'm the last fairy queen. There is no fairy queen in waiting.'

Gremli Master, 'So do we need to fight?'

The Fairy Queen, 'The Vi-queens and elders want to eradicate us. We need to protect our interests and guard magic for as long as we can.'

Elfi Master, 'So you are saying that we have to fight.'

The Fairy Queen, 'Yes.'

Elfi Master, 'In that case, there is no choice. We have to fight with the Learned.'

The Fairy Queen, 'I agree. The magicians are our only choice.'

Elfi Master, 'So is that a decision?'

The Fairy Queen, 'It is unless someone objects.'

There were a few attempts at an objection, but the Fairy Queen wasn't having it. The Fay, were going to war with the magicians against the Vi-Queens.

121
Naked Elders

Thomas, Robin, Lindsey, and Commander Bandolier were shocked. There were seven people: six men and one woman. Then the woman went on the attack, and Captain Pellett dropped down dead. Killed by a spell.

Thomas and Robin countered, but they were up against a very talented magician who knew her way around both attacking and defensive spells, but it was two to one. And Thomas and Robin knew their stuff. It suddenly dawned on Thomas who she was. It was his long-lost treacherous ex-girlfriend: Rachel.

Rachel knew that they were probably the only two people in the world that she couldn't defeat and consequently decided to do a runner. She needed a distraction before she could implement a disappearance spell. And what a distraction she came up with: a super-bright nova-flash which blinded everyone. And before she disappeared, she stabbed Robin in the guts knowing that her agonising death would hurt him more than his own death. And then she was gone.

By the time that Thomas got his sight back, Robin was on her last agonising death throes. Thomas immediately cradled her and shouted for help, but Robin was beyond help and died in Thomas's arms. His anger was incandescent. He wanted to kill Rachel and every elder and possibly every Viking.

Then he heard Lady Malander, 'Robin is with me now. I will look after her. Don't kill the elders as you will need them later.' That helped but did nothing to quell his anger.

Commander Bandolier, 'You should have let me hang them all.'

Thomas, 'I wish with everything in my heart that I didn't stop you now, but that murderous female is a very powerful magician called Rachel. She has been emulating the Deputy Chief Elder and has caused all of this misery in her desire for power.'

Commander Bandolier, 'I still should have hung her.'

Thomas, 'It would never have happened. Somehow, she would have escaped.'

Commander Bandolier, 'What do we do now?'

Thomas, 'I plan to bury Robin on the hills that she loved so much. I would like you to take the six remaining elders as prisoners and take them to Malvern.'

Commander Bandolier, 'What about the Elderguard?'

Thomas, 'I would offer them the chance to join you. Those that genuinely want to accept. Those that wish to join the Vikings, I would kill.'

Commander Bandolier, 'So be it.'

The deeds were done, and they got on their way. Thomas had never felt so low before. Suicide had even crossed his mind, but he had too much to do. Too many people were depending on him. What he did know was that Rachel would pay.

The surviving elders weren't too sure what had just happened. Somehow their Deputy Chief Elder had just turned into a beautiful naked girl. Then two of the enemy's team died, and the naked girl disappeared. It was all too much to comprehend. And now, for reasons they didn't understand, they were going to be imprisoned.

122
Mannering's Manoeuvres

Commander Mannering was determined to take his anger out on someone. He had marched his men up from Gloucester and Portsmouth to man the line at Stafford, Birmingham, Warwick, and Northampton. When Bandolier's Army was defeated, and Mainstay offered no communication, he started the long withdrawal to Malvern.

Before he got there, the elders ordered him to Strathclyde without giving him any reason for going there because there was no military objective. He had got as far as Blackburn when he got a copy of the proclamation. At that point, he decided that the elders were now an illegal organisation and decided to return to Malvern.

Despite his better judgement, he decided to rest his Army for a week. They were not in a fit state for a forced march or even a gentle stroll. They needed time to make some new shoes and simply rest. They had done him proud, but they were angry at the pointlessness of it all. The proclamation document had been circulated to the troops, and they soon realised who the enemy was.

Commander Mannering enjoyed the week. The Army did what all resting armies do: drinking, eating, singing, gaming, whoring and more drinking. He always wondered where they found the women, but whenever there were large groups of men, it wasn't long before the ladies of the night arrived. He used to have a poor opinion of them, but, as he got older, he realised that his profession was very dangerous and you had to take your pleasure where you could.

He wouldn't mind a little sample himself, but he always wanted to set a high example to the men. In reality, they couldn't care a shit.

The week was up, and the Army was on the move. Scouts and mounted archers formed the vanguard, and the rest followed. As he got nearer to Malvern, he would reorganise the structure, but there was a long way to go.

123
Goodnight, my Dear Sister

Thomas, Lindsey, and Commander Bandolier reached Malvern. The town was on full alert, and they were stopped by sentries. The Garrison Commander heartily welcomed Merlin, the famous wizard, and three thousand more troops would make a very valuable contribution to their forces. He was also pleased to see Commander Bandolier as he could hand over command to him being the senior officer.

Major Clutterbuck went immediately to his beloved factory, where he found Fay doing a brilliant job. From a production point of view, he wasn't really needed. Fay was a remarkably capable and talented woman, and he loved her. He couldn't wait to express his love, and she had to run to protect her modesty. But it wasn't long before she was caught, and her modesty was in shreds, and she loved it.

Thomas was still seriously depressed, as you would expect. The ladies in Malvern washed Robin's body, did her hair, and put her in a silken shroud. Thomas kissed her on the lips before her head was covered.

A group of soldiers had dug a hole on Midsummer Hill, a truly magical place, and carried her body there with Thomas following. He tried his hardest to stop the tears but failed. He tried his hardest to stop the sobbing, but he failed. He didn't want to be seen as a sop in front of the hardened soldiers, but they had seen death a thousand times and respected him for his grief. It was what they would have wanted at their demise.

The soldiers, showing huge respect, lowered her body into the grave. Thomas's crying affected them, and most had tears in their eyes. They had huge admiration and a little fear of both Robin and Thomas as they were genuine heroes and magicians.

The soldiers raised the swords and clashed them with their opposites and sang a simple song. That was a huge honour not usually offered to the non-military. Thomas threw several items into the grave, including an acorn, a coin, a bobbin, and a comb. Don't ask why, but it was the done-thing. Thomas then threw some soil on top of the body, and the soldiers completed the task of burying her.

The soldiers left Thomas to his grief. He sat down on the grass next to her and chatted. He thanked her for being his sister, not that he had much choice. He apologised for not protecting her. He promised to get revenge, not that Robin was a vengeful sort of person. He promised to remember her forever. He told her that he loved her and that he now felt emptiness. There was a hole in him that might never be filled.

It doesn't usually take long for grief to turn into self-pity. He moaned about his loneliness and the fact that he had no one to talk to. Everyone he loved had gone. What was the point of carrying on?

Then Lady Malander said, 'Pull yourself together. You have still got a lot to do. Robin thinks you are quite sweet but get a move on.'

124
Vikings on the move

There was no alcohol left in Banbury or any of the nearby towns. So it was clearly time to move on. The target was Malvern. They still had over ninety thousand warriors, although they now knew that the London contingent had been wiped out.

During one of their long drinking sessions, it was decided that although they had never lost a battle War Chief Ragnor Godwinson had failed to secure a substantial enough victory. The warlord was so drunk that he even agreed to his own blood eagle ritual.

The ritual didn't go too well due to alcoholic intoxication, which is always rather dangerous when Vikings are involved. They accidentally smashed in his jaw. Well, these things often happen. Then they accidentally crushed his wedding tackle with a horse's hoof. It could accidentally happen to anyone.

Then his eyes were accidentally ripped out and pushed into his mouth, followed by two crushed testicles. Again, this sort of mishap wasn't that unusual. Then they tried pulling his lungs through his arse, a technique not recommended by most medical practitioners. Just when things were hotting-up, War Chief Ragnor Godwinson died. That was typical of him.

Normally they honour a warlord by burning, but they pushed him into a cesspit. His son kept a mental record of all the Vikings involved, and their time would come.

The half-sleepy, half-drunk, half exhausted Army was on the move. There was every chance that they were going in the right direction. There was some concern as there was no leader. None of the other warlords were keen on the top job after seeing what happened to Godwinson, but usually, a leader emerged out of necessity.

125
The Current Picture

It was hardly a War Council, but someone had to assess the current military situation. The attendees were as follows:

- Commander Bandolier
- Major Clutterbuck
- Captain Gray, Garrison Commander
- Thomas.

Commander Bandolier, 'So what do we know?'

Captain Gray, 'We have received regular updates, although there is still some confusion:

1. The Vikings are heading this way from Banbury
2. Commander Squire defeated the Vikings at Banbury but had to retire from the second battle due to Valkyries. He is now heading towards Malvern
3. Commander Mannering is marching south from Blackburn and is probably nearing Wolverhampton by now
4. There is still a sizeable British force in London.'

Major Clutterbuck, 'Can we map it?'

Captain Gray, 'Of course.' And he proceeded to draft out the positions of the various armies on the map.'

Commander Bandolier, 'How big are these forces?'

Captain Gray, 'We haven't got the detailed figures, but my estimates are as follows:

Army	Size
Viking	90,000
Squire	105,000
Mannering	115,000
London	100,000
Malvern	28,000

Commander Bandolier, 'It looks like the Viking Army and the two British armies are likely to arrive in Malvern at much the same time. In that case, we will outnumber them by more than two to one.'

Major Clutterbuck, 'We will have the advantage of a good defensive position, mounted archers, musketeers and cannon.'

Commander Bandolier, 'But they might have Valkyries.'

Captain Gray, 'What if the Vikings get here first? Then the Malvern garrison will be heavily outnumbered.'

Commander Bandolier, 'We need to adopt most of our previous defensive tactics.'

Captain Gray, 'Most of those are already in place: the Severn security system, forts, the Upton Castle etc., but we don't have many cannons.'

Major Clutterbuck, 'I have quite a few completed cannons that we can deploy.'

Captain Gray, 'But we don't have many cannoneers.'

Major Clutterbuck, 'Give me some men, and I will train them. I also need men to fire the rockets.'

Commander Bandolier, 'I'm sure that Captain Gray will find the men you need.'

Captain Gray, 'Yes, Sir.'

Commander Bandolier, 'Send out scouts to determine the Vikings position and that of the two British armies. We also need to update Commanders Mannering and Squire on the current position.'

Captain Gray, 'Yes, Sir.'

126
The Fay go to War

The Fairy Queen sounded the Warinshell, the horn of war. To both humans and the Fay, it sounded silent, but the Fay could sense it. It was a command to go to war that could not be ignored.

Each type of Fay had different customs and practices regarding war. With some Fay, both the males and females fought. More often than not, it was just the females that engaged in war as they were generally much larger and considerably more aggressive. The males would stay at home and look after the offspring, who were now increasingly rare.

Some of the Fay had physical weapons such as the Unicorn's horn, the Goblins' hammer and Elves' bow and arrows. Some relied entirely on magic: the Elementi used fire, water, earth, and air as their weapons, the Gremli used spells of bad luck, many used delusional powers and so on. Some could control the weather or rather create unique micro-meteorological disturbances such as storms, tornadoes, hailstones, and lightning.

Other Fay tribes had giants and trolls under their control. The Famili would suck blood and energy from their enemies and spread doom and despondency. The Mersi would sour pools of water from afar. Air could be solidified, and rain could be turned to acid. Wild animals would attack. Every step the Vi-Queens took would be fraught with danger. And the Fay had the ability to change emotions: fear, hatred, despair, recklessness and so on.

The Vi-Queens were going to be in for a bit of a shock, but the Fairy Queen was worried. She knew that the enemy had powerful resources supporting them: the Norse gods and the Valkyries. They were quite challenging, and she was worried that this might be the Fay's swansong. But if they didn't fight, their days were numbered anyway.

The Fay forces started amassing on Midsummer Hill, and many of them laid a blessing on Robin's grave. The Fairy Queen always acted as

Commander-in-Chief because she was the cleverest and because it had always been that way. She had to find a way of letting the magicians know that they were coming to fight on their side.

127
The even more Current Picture

Captain Gray, 'I have an update re the positions of the various armies:

1. The Viking advanced parties are approaching Broadway, but they are pretty stretched out. There are no signs of the Valkyries
2. Commander Mannering has two columns. One column is in Kidderminster, and the other is in Bromsgrove. He wants to know how you would like his regiments deployed
3. Commander Squire is following the Vikings. He could attack the if you wanted. Again, he is asking for orders
4. Half of the London force is on the way to Malvern. That is about fifty thousand men.'

Commander Bandolier, 'Well done captain.'

Thomas, 'I have to tell you that the Fay are on our side. They are massing on Midsummer Hill.'

Commander Bandolier, 'How do you know?'

Thomas, 'A robin told me.'

Commander Bandolier, 'That's interesting, but can they fight?'

Thomas, 'You will be surprised. They have both physical fighting skills and magical skills. You can rely on them to support your right flank.'

Captain Gray, 'Can I remind you that the Druids are a potential threat.'

Commander. Bandolier, 'I get confused over whose side those murdering bastards are on.'

Thomas, 'I guess that technically they are on the side of the elders.'

Commander Bandolier, 'And whose side are they on?'

Thomas, 'Are they properly secured?'

Captain Gray, 'Yes. They are in individual cells with two guards per elder.'

Commander Bandolier, 'Back to the Druids, they might come from the

Welsh side of the Malvern Hills. Whilst the Vikings attacked from the east, they attacked my Army from the west. Do you know that they cooked and ate five thousand of my men? This is going to be a battle to settle some old scores.'

Captain Gray, 'I have that side covered. Whether the forces are large enough is debatable.'

Commander Bandolier, 'Are the witches likely to be a problem?'

Thomas, 'I would say yes. This is going to be the battle that defines the future.'

Commander Bandolier, 'That's good as I've also got a few scores to settle with them as well.'

Captain Gray, 'Do we have the magicians to counter the witches?'

Thomas, 'Probably not. There will be some magicians returning with the armies but almost certainly too few. On the other hand, a lot of the witches have been ethnically cleansed.'

Commander Bandolier, 'You mean by being converted into sheep?'

Thomas, 'It was the most humane thing we could do.'

Commander Bandolier, 'By being made into lamb stew?'

Thomas, 'I thought that you hated the witches.'

Commander Bandolier, 'I do, but I can see their position. Anyway, let's get down to some planning.'

128
The Blue Wave

Druid Leader Bryrona was approaching Shelsley Beauchamp with about sixteen thousand blue-skinned, drugged berserkers eager for battle. She was a bit confused over her objective.

She had fought with the magicians against the Slimies. She had worked with the Vikings to slaughter one of the British armies. She killed hundreds of the Fay on Midsummer Hill. She had held council with the elders. Whose side were the Druids on? The answer was that they were on the Druids' side.

But who should they support? Who was going to win this epic battle? She knew that the Fay were massing on the hills, and she knew that it was her job to kill them. The Fay were not to be tolerated. She wasn't sure why, but that was the way the Druids were brought up. So if the Fay were with the magicians, then the magicians must be the enemy.

Despite the logic, she didn't really want to be on the Viking side. They were uncouth sexist rapists who had no respect for womenkind. At least the magicians had principles.

Despite all of her deliberations, she was a worried woman. Something told her that magic was dying and that this could be the Druid swansong. She could also see her own death, which was anathema to her as she had not procreated yet.

129
Planning for Victory

Captain Gray, 'I've just been handed a message from one of our scouts that a well-disguised Druid force of about twenty thousand warriors was seen at Monkwood Green.'

Commander Bandolier, 'Where the hell is that?'

Captain Gray, 'About ten miles northwest of Worcester.'

Commander Bandolier, 'Order Commander Mannering's Kidderminster force to intercept them and engage.'

Captain Gray, 'Yes, Sir.'

Commander Bandolier, 'His Bromsgrove forces are to march to Worcester and then deploy themselves to defend the northern part of the Malvern Hills.'

Captain Gray, 'Yes, Sir.'

Commander Bandolier, 'Are you sure that the Fay can defend the southern part of the Hills?'

Thomas, 'Well, let's say that Midsummer Hill is crawling with the Fay. They are our best bet.'

Commander Bandolier, 'Get me a fix on where the London column has got to.'

Captain Gray, 'Yes, Sir.'

Commander Bandolier, 'Order Commander Squire to harass the enemy to delay them and engage if the opportunity presents itself.'

Captain Gray, 'Yes, Sir.'

Commander Bandolier, 'Captain Gray, update me on the Malvern position.'

Captain Gray, 'Yes, Sir:

- We have a total of thirty thousand men
- We have five thousand men in Upton-Upon-Severn. A third are in the castle, another third are in the riverside forts, and the remaining third is in the town

- We have seventy cannons in Hanley Swan, which is the predicted route that the Vikings are going to take. Along with three thousand mounted archers and five thousand infantry and pikemen
- On the hills, we have eight thousand men
- On the west side of the hill, we have five thousand men
- The remaining four thousand men are in the town itself
- There are also fifty rocket teams
- There are also about one thousand men guarding the prison and the factory.'

Commander Bandolier, 'What about you, Thomas?'

Thomas, 'We only have sixteen magicians.'

Commander Bandolier, 'That is not enough.'

Thomas, 'I know.'

Commander Bandolier, 'What are our main vulnerabilities?'

Thomas, 'My view is as follows:

- The Viking Army gets to Malvern before Commander Mannering comes to our aid
- Over-powering witch attack
- The Valkyries and perhaps some Norse gods
- The Fay let us down
- Druid magic
- Bad luck.'

Commander Bandolier, 'Captain Gray, what do you think?'

Captain Gray, 'Before you arrived, I assumed that we would make a gallant effort, but we would be swept away. As far as my men are concerned, we have an extra three thousand troops and some cannon. They still expect to be swept away.'

Commander Bandolier, 'How do we stiffen them up?'

Captain Gray, 'I think a quick tour around the area by you and Thomas would make a great difference.'

Commander Bandolier, 'In that case, let's get on our way.' Just as he left the tent, one of the possible vulnerabilities reared its head: bad luck. The chances were a million to one, but Commander Bandolier was hit in the head by a shot from a dropped musket. The man dropped it because a giant raven crapped on him. Was that just chance or witchery?

130
Witches for Victory

It had been a tough time for witchery. Their kind had been made into pies, stews, kebabs, and meatballs. They had been persecuted for hundreds of years, but their numbers were now the lowest they had ever been in a thousand years. Perhaps more. And if the British won, then the persecution would almost certainly continue.

The National meeting of covens was possibly their last chance to defend themselves. The Grand Master called for the meeting to start. In many ways, it was strange that the leader of an almost totally female calling was a man. But that had always been the case.

Grand Master, 'Order, order. There is only one item on the agenda. Shall we fight, or shall we flee? I ask the two advocates to come forward.'

Witch Gillian, Advocate for fighting, 'Fellow witches, we must fight for the following reasons:

1. Revenge. Our sisters have been ritually murdered by sheep transformation. Literally, thousands have been killed in this heinous, humiliating manner. Their deaths must be avenged.

2. Embarrassment. Our reputation has been tarnished. Our sheep bodies were fought over by the locals who relished our misery. We need to retain and regain our reputation.

3. Prevention. If the British win, then the witch persecution will continue. Our kind will be no more.

4. Loyalty. We fought with the Vikings once. We need to maintain that allegiance to protect our future position.

5. Anger. I have hatred in my soul. I want to kill magicians and kill as many as I can.

6. Future. We need to fight for our long-term future. No one out there cares about us. We must fight.

'My sisters, I rest my case.'

There was an outbreak of cheering and clapping, but nothing like it used to be when the numbers were much larger.

Grand Master, 'Order, order. I ask for the advocate for fleeing to come forward.'

Witch Brenda, 'Fellow witches, we must flee. I have no doubt that it is the time to leave these islands. I'm not frightened of a good fight. I have the scars to prove it, but now is the time to save ourselves and flee for the following reasons:

1. Witch Numbers. There used to be hundreds of thousands of us. Now we have shrunk to a few thousand. Perhaps ten thousand at the most. Further battle would decimate our ranks.

2. Logic. What advantage is there in fighting? My fellow advocate argues allegiance to the Vikings. They don't care a toss about us. There is no guarantee that they won't turn on us. Let's be honest that they are hardly female-friendly.

3. Failure. The British Army is twice the size of the Vikings. They have machines that kill many at the same time. They have better tactics. What happens if the British pig-dogs win?

4. Revenge. I want revenge, too, but not at the cost of our extinction. Let's live to fight another day.

5. Emotion. We should make decisions based on reason rather than hatred, fear, revenge etc.

'My sisters, think of the young ones, think about our future. We must flee.'

Again, there were cheers and clapping but not as much.

Grand Master, 'Order, order. Fellow witches, you have heard the advocates. Now it is the time to vote in the normal manner.'

There were two boxes marked 'Yea' and 'Nea'. Yea was for fighting. The witches lined up and put a crow's eye in the relevant box. It was soon obvious that the witches wanted battle.

A force of three thousand witches was ready to leave Pershore.

131
The Night Before

The Vikings were almost on the bank of the River Severn opposite Upton-Upon-Severn, and, rather surprisingly, they camped for the night. Captain Gray counted the campfires and estimated that there were between eighty and a hundred thousand warriors as per their previous calculations. This was good news as Commander Mannering could get his men into position.

War Chief Eric Bloodaxe wasn't sure if he was the Viking leader or not. He had ordered his men to stop so that the stragglers could catch up. He hadn't expected them to set up campfires, but in reality, it wasn't an army. It was a collection of small raiding parties temporarily fused into a single, disparate fighting force.

The men knew that there would be a major battle tomorrow, and most were looking forward to it. Many knew that they would probably not survive the next day and therefore wanted to put their house in order. One of those loose ends was the slave girls. A girl like Jenny who had been captured in Grimsby, torn away from her probably dead family and regularly gang-raped. She was so close to the Severn that she could smell freedom. In the night, she planned to leave the camp and swim the river to start a new life.

But that wasn't going to be Jenny's fate. At midnight, the slave girls were dragged from their tents, stripped, and fucked. Whilst that was going on, their lovers sliced off their breasts. Traditionally they were converted into purses, but those skills were long gone. Nowadays, they were a good source of meat in an emergency. Whilst the girls were writhing in agony, the Viking men cut out their hearts. It was a truly terrible sight, but many of the men came as the death-throes got them over-excited. There was no way that Britain deserved the Viking culture.

The screams of the female victims could be heard on the other side of the river. Those in Upton wondered what fate had in store for them.

War Chief Eric Bloodaxe hated the way that the Vikings treated women. In the Viking culture, they were just child-bearing necessities. Vikings weren't really interested in relationships. They knew love, but it had little value as it was so fleeting.

War Chief Eric Bloodaxe planned to attack at dawn, but unbeknown to him, the Impi had saturated their camp with sleeping spells. The whole camp woke up two hours later than planned. Then the Elementi caused the Severn bore to overflow the river banks flooding their temporary base. Then a quick freeze froze the waters.

Overnight at least two thousand warriors had been attacked by blood-suckers. War Chief Eric Bloodaxe couldn't understand why he felt so sluggish. He really wanted to go back to sleep, but that was the power of magic.

Eventually, War Chief Eric Bloodaxe rallied his forces, and they started their normal gesturing and weapon raising before they charged. Of course, they would have to charge over a narrow, fortified bridge with a castle or swim across.

132
Squire attacks

Commander Squire could see the Viking encampment ahead of him. He could see thousands of men waving and gesturing. It was just amazing that there were no sentries or guards protecting their rear. It was just very sloppy soldiering.

No one spotted his Army arriving, and no one spotted the cannons being put into position. Not a single Viking spotted anything until the sound of cannons warned them of incoming doom and destruction. Every other cannon had covered the area in deadly shrapnel, which maimed and crippled hundreds. The Vikings turned to charge when the second cannonading took place. That certainly stopped the charge. Then they were hit by an avalanche of arrows. The musketeers were ready, but they needed the enemy to be within range.

War Chief Eric Bloodaxe rallied his men, and ninety thousand Vikings charged the artillery. The cannons fired repeatedly, and the musketeers joined in, but Commander Squire could see that they were going to be overrun. Pikemen placed their long pikes in position, and the archers fired volley after volley of arrows into the oncoming mass.

Commander Squire ordered a tactical retreat, and the Vikings saw it as a victory. They had captured the cannons but had no idea of what to do with them. They didn't even have the means of moving them. Squire used his mobile archers to finish off any stragglers.

War Chief Eric Bloodaxe rallied his men again, and they started the jeering, cheering, gesticulating, and gesturing. Naked bottoms were displayed to those on the other side of the river.

Commander Squire looked at the situation and wondered if he could repeat it again as the cannons were still intact. He ordered everyone back into position. Once again, the Vikings hadn't spotted the arrival of the cannoneers until the cannons started firing. It was another slaughter. This time some of the Viking warriors decided to swim the river. But climbing up a riverbank with arrows and shot coming at you was never easy.

Commander Squire was a great believer in the concept that if it works, then just carry on until it doesn't. The cannoneers fired, and the Vikings died. The musketeers fired, and the Vikings died, and the pattern was repeated with the archers. The expected standard Viking charge happened, and the British retreated. War Chief Eric Bloodaxe was pleased as they had now won two encounters even though it cost them fifteen thousand men.

This time War Chief Eric Bloodaxe left some men to protect his rear. But it wasn't large enough to stop Commander Squire from attacking them. This time he used men at arms on horseback. They were basically horse-riding swordsmen, but it was an innovation. They were swift and hard-hitting, and the Viking rear-guard were soon defeated.

Commander Squire wondered if he dared repeat the play again. If nothing else, it was amusing, and his men were up for it. The cannoneers and musketeers crawled into position. It was hard to believe, but the cannons were roaring again, and the Vikings were dying again. The Vikings had lost some of their enthusiasm in charging partly because there were so many dead bodies in the way.

Then the cannons in Upton started firing at them, but they couldn't charge them because the river was in the way. War Chief Eric Bloodaxe never really wanted to be a leader as his head was blown off.

133
The Fay Attack

To avoid the cannons, the Viking Army split into three. They spread along both banks of the river and across the bridge.

Those that turned left were confronted with the massed armies of the Fay. They looked magnificent but hardly intimidating. The Vikings laughed and rushed at them. That was a mistake as there was a solid but transparent wall between them. Quite a few of the Vikings were crushed to death as they piled into the wall.

The Elves fired thousands of tiny but deadly arrows. In human terms, they were poisoned darts. The poison had several different effects. One liquidised the human body: the warriors simply melted away. Another poison stopped the lungs from working and another caused heart attacks. One made a person super amorous, and the desire to fight was replaced with the desire to make love. It was amusing seeing two fully clad barbarian berserkers going at it hell for leather.

The Goblins had built a series of trap doors along the side of the Severn filled with a range of unpleasantries ranging from stakes to snakes. There was a pit full of raging flames, and some of the pits appeared to be bottomless. These were opened at the appropriate time with the desired effect. The Vikings tried to retreat, but they crashed into another transparent wall that stopped them.

Just when the Fay were building up a head of steam, a hundred witches attacked them on traditional broomsticks. They countered several of the Fay spells, which allowed the Vikings to lay into the Impi. One swipe of a hefty hammer neutralised whole squadrons of the wild-people. The Fay were forced to retreat from the combination of muscle and magic.

Then the witches started falling out of the sky. The Fairies had turned the broomsticks to straw. When the witches landed, they were restrained by the Leprechauni and sucked dry by the Famili. This was hardly fair military practice, but then the Vikings hardly played fair.

The Vikings were still making modest progress when the Unicorni attacked in force. At least four hundred Unicorns with their celebrated horns rushed in and stabbed the Vikings, but the Viking revenge was merciless. The Unicorns were pummelled to death by large men with heavy hammers. It was an awful tragedy seeing such beautiful beasts being smashed to pieces. The other Fay people hated to look on as the Unicorni were held in high esteem by everyone.

The Fairy Queen ordered a no-holds-barred full-frontal attack. The Elementi sucked the air out of the Viking's lungs and set the enemy's hair on fire. The Impi slipped inside the Viking costumes and ripped their skin apart. Then thousands of Goblins attacked with their own hammers and clubs. The Asrai caused confusion and disillusionment. The Vikings were soon on the run, with the Fay in hot pursuit.

The Vikings could hardly claim this as a victory, but they did.

134
Abdilla Attacks

Mannering could hear the sound of cannons in the distance, and he knew that the Battle of Malvern had begun. As instructed, he sent forty-five thousand men from Kidderminster to intercept and destroy the Druids, their one-time allies. Major Abdilla was tasked with the job. He had the full range of military functions: infantry, mounted archers, musketeers, and cannons. He was also allocated all of the available magicians.

Captain Vale was on the north-western part of the Malvern Hills. A messenger instructed him to expect an attack by twenty thousand druids and that Major Abdilla with forty-five thousand troops was on the way to assist him. Captain Vale also had a secret weapon: Thomas. The master magician had analysed the battleground and decided that was where he would be most useful. Certainly, his presence calmed Captain Vale and his rather inexperienced regiments.

Thomas could sense the presence of the oncoming Druids. They were going to arrive before help was going to come. Thomas decided to go on the attack with a series of illusions. The first one was a display showing significant forces on the hill. This worked as Druid Leader Bryrona stopped the progress of her troops to consider the situation. It didn't take long before she realised that it was a trick. On the other hand, it meant that they knew that the Druids were coming. She could also hear the sound of the cannon, which terrified her.

The Fay could also smell the arriving presence of their hated enemies. The Fairy Queen decided to split her forces and sent the Goblini, Elementi, Pixi, Impi, Bansheei and Fauni to attack them. They were desperate to avenge their dead brothers and sisters. They relished the coming confrontation.

Druid Leader Bryrona ordered her troops forward. Her Spellmasters led the attack, but Thomas hit them with another illusion showing rows of cannons. Once again, Bryrona smelled a rat and urged her forces forward.

She realised that she was up against some strong magic, and then she smelled the presence of the Fay. Things had suddenly got worse. Her initial trepidation was proving correct.

Then Major Abdilla did something rather clever. He grabbed several musicians in his force and got them to play stirring music, and ordered his men to sing. This was another first: a military band. Both sides stopped and listened and wondered what it meant, but it did tell Bryrona that there was another player and almost certainly one that wasn't on her side.

Druid Leader Bryrona considered a withdrawal, but that was not the Druid way, but now she knew that there were forces on the hill with a powerful magician waiting for them to attack. A large Fay force was on their right flank, clearly intent on revenge and an unknown music group was on her left flank. The left looked to be the easiest route, but she was wrong.

Her sixteen thousand warriors clashed headlong into battle with forty-five thousand troops armed with cannon and muskets. It wasn't a fair fight. Gunpowder often seems to defeat archaic earth-based magic. It certainly made a mess of naked, blue painted priests and priestesses who charged, screaming their heads off. It wasn't long before their heads were blown off.

The Druids fled, and Major Abdilla's men declined to follow as the battle was still raging elsewhere, and they might be needed. The Fay had a very different view. It was their intention to slaughter every druid they could find in the most painful way possible. Some of the Druid deaths were not pretty and certainly not humane.

Major Abdilla took his men over the hills and formed a position directly over Great Malvern. Captain Vale kept his troops in place just in case. Thomas stood on top of the Worcestershire Beacon and thought about his sister and then his next move.

135
Mannering Attacks

Commander Mannering liaised with the garrison force at Worcester. They were fairly certain that the Vikings hadn't crossed the Severn yet, although there was still a battle going on at Upton-Upon-Severn. Mannering was trying to decide whether he should take his Army down the left or right-hand side of the river.

From Worcester, the right-hand side would put him in a position to defend Malvern. The left-hand side would allow him to attack the rear of the Viking Army, assuming that the battle for Upton was still going on. He didn't want to split his force any further as he wasn't sure how strong the Viking forces were. In the end, he opted for the left bank.

It wasn't long before Commander Mannering's advance guard came into contact with the Vikings at Kempsey about six miles from Upton. Like many battles, it started off as a series of skirmishes and then more forces were just dragged in.

It was the same old pattern. Solid military tactics against barbarian shock attacks. Mannering allowed two or three of his regiments to engage whilst he prepared a line. He had the River Severn on the right flank and woodland on his left. He positioned his mounted archers to guard the forest. As per normal procedure, he formed a line with pikemen, men at arms and archers. Then he placed his cannon and musketeers at strategic points. He knew he was going to win. He wasn't cocky, but he had faith in his technology, his troops, and his own skill as a commander. It wasn't arrogance: it was confidence. And he was right.

The Vikings charged as per normal, and they were mown down as per normal. Mannering had perfected the combination of muskets and cannon so that there was a constant barrage despite the need to reload. It almost became impossible for the Vikings to form a charge partly because of the debris of war and partly because they were blown to bits as they got near.

Commander Mannering ordered the mounted archers to pick the retreating Vikings off as they drove forward. It looked like it was another victory!

136
The London Force

Major Oliver wanted some of the action. His force of fifty thousand men had reached Oxford through a mixture of night marching and forced day time marches. The men were shattered, but Major Oliver didn't really care. He wanted glory, but even he could see that the men needed to rest. That annoyed him, but there was no alternative.

He sent his six thousand mounted archers ahead to scout and to assist if possible. At the current rate of progress, it was still going to take up to two days to get to Malvern. It really was bloody annoying. He contemplated joining the archers, but he felt obligated to stay with his main command.

He also had some vital information about Rachel that he needed to tell Thomas.

137

The Battle of Upton

The Viking Army had split into three parts. Those who had turned left along the bank of the Severn were confronted by the Fay and given a good hiding. Those who had turned right met their demise on Commander Mannering's killing ground. The majority took the direct approach to Upton, which meant crossing the well-defended and fortified Upton Bridge.

Commander Squire's Army was attacking them from the rear, and it wouldn't be long before he was joined by Commander Mannering's Army. There was no retreat for the Vikings. Forward was the only option, but in front of them was a castle, wooden fortifications, and more cannons.

The cannons were already firing shrapnel into the mass of Vikings on the bridge. They were an easy target, but Captain Gray had a problem. He only had five thousand men in Upton-Upon-Severn. Two thousand of them were in the castle, another two thousand were in the town, and one thousand were in wooden fortifications along the Severn. Whatever he did, he was going to be overwhelmed. He also couldn't see a way of avoiding the massacre of his small unit. And the more the castle held out, the more savage the Vikings were going to be.

Captain Gray could see from the top of the castle the following scenario:

- There were about fifty thousand Vikings besieging the Upton bridge
- There were at least another ten thousand Vikings swimming across the river
- Commander Squire probably had eighty thousand troops attacking the rear of the Viking horde
- He could also see Commander Mannering's Army marching along the right bank of the Severn. He estimated that he had at least fifty thousand troops
- Looking towards the hills, he could see a considerable number of

troops on top of them

- He also knew that he had seventy cannons with rockets and nearly ten thousand men at Hanley Swan

It was rather ironic that most of the British troops were on the wrong side of the river. Apart from Upton, the nearest alternative crossings were Worcester and Tewkesbury, which were too far away.

He needed the men on the hills and the Malvern contingent to march to his aid, but even that would probably be too late.

Commander Squire had set his cannons up to just constantly fire into the rear of the Viking force attacking the bridge. It was a bloodbath, but it eventually became pointless as the pile of the dead and dying just absorbed the shot. The cannons hadn't been designed yet to allow angled shots. It was simply straight line ahead.

He sent his musketeers and archers in, but they could hardly stand. All they could do was shoot from a distance.

The castle was doing a valiant job, but there weren't enough apertures to throw ordnance at the Vikings who had now clambered across the bridge. The small defending force of two thousand fled before they were slaughtered, but it was too late in most cases. In the end, the castle was ignored, and at least forty thousand Vikings were over the bridge and on their way to Malvern. They headed towards the hills.

The Vikings, who were swimming, were attacked by the Fay and mown down by troops in the wooden fortifications, but at least five thousand got away and headed towards Welland.

Commander Squire's men were clearing the bridge when Commander Mannering's Army turned up. They didn't know each other that well, but they still hugged. Both had earned their stripes on the field. Captain Gray joined them and was promoted to Major Gray on the spot.

Major Gray was asked to give them an assessment of the situation, which was as follows:

- 'There are probably forty thousand Vikings heading towards Malvern. They will almost certainly take the Hanley Swan route. I have scouts monitoring them
- At Hanley Swan, I have seventy cannons, rockets, three thousand mounted archers and five thousand men at arms.

• There are also eight thousand men on the hills and four thousand in Great Malvern.'

Commander Squire, 'What are rockets?'

Major Gray, 'I've no idea, but we have them at Hanley Swan.'

Commander Mannering, 'Clearly, your men are going to need help. We better get on our way.'

Major Gray and his brave defenders watched Commander Mannering's troops line up and cross the bridge. It looked like a midsummer parade. Commander's Squire's Army followed them. Together there were at least one hundred and fifty thousand troops.

138
Thomas on the Hill

Thomas and Major Abdilla were on top of the Beacon, trying to work out what was happening below. They could see at least twenty miles away, but much was hidden by the forest. They worked out that the Vikings were being pursued by a surprisingly large British force.

Thomas knew that his mate, Major Clutterbuck, was in Hanley Swan with cannons and rockets. After some deliberation, Major Abdilla decided to go to his aid. Soon his forty-five thousand men were on the move. It looked like the Viking horde was doomed.

Thomas had never seen so much activity on his beautiful hills. His heart went out to the locals who once again were suffering for no fault of their own. But then he had his own miseries: Robin, Lord and Lady Malander, Betty and many, many friends.

And as he wallowed in his grief, there was a tap on his shoulder. It was the Fairy Queen with her escort.

Fairy Queen, 'Thomas, we have done well.'

Thomas, 'You have done very well, my lady. Your contribution will be recognised.'

Fairy Queen, 'Ploughmen always say that and then nothing changes.'

Thomas, 'That is true, my Lady. Great deeds are soon forgotten.'

Fairy Queen, 'We just want to be left in peace while magic withers away. Not that most of us will survive this day.'

Thomas, 'What do you mean?'

Fairy Queen, 'You have great untapped powers. Can't you sense it?'

Thomas, 'Sorry, I really don't understand what you mean. We are easily beating the Vikings. We will have a great victory today.'

Fairy Queen, 'The Vikings are not our enemy. They are simply tools.'

Thomas, 'Who is the enemy?'

Fairy Queen, 'It is the old world versus the new.'

Thomas, 'I'm still not sure what you mean.'

Fairy Queen, 'Gunpowder. It has changed the balance of things. It has given the ploughmen the power of the gods. And the gods will be here shortly. All hell is about to break loose.'

Thomas, 'Are you serious?'

Fairy Queen, 'Very serious. As I said earlier, most of us will not survive this day.'

Thomas, 'But everything looks so peaceful.' But then it wasn't.

139
The Battle of Hanley Swan

War Chief Sweyn Thorson wasn't sure if he was in charge or not. It appeared that War Chief Eric Bloodaxe had gone missing, but he was probably dead. Sweyn was really good at organising raiding parties, but he would be the first to state that he wasn't a battlefield commander.

He had no idea what to do. In front of him was a small force, but they had seventy cannons, and he knew exactly what devastation a few cannons could achieve. He could also see the banners of a large force coming to their aid. A force equal in size to his.

Behind him was the main British Army, which was at least four times larger than his, and they had even more cannons. He could see a situation where they would be cannonaded to death. A death that he didn't fancy. It wasn't the Viking way, but somehow, he needed to avoid battle. He even contemplated surrender.

War Chief Sweyn Thorson could contemplate as much as he liked, but the British wanted to finish the job. As the regiments arrived at Hanley Swan, Commanders Squire and Mannering formed their lines of cannons, pikemen, archers, musketeers, and men at arms. It was a truly formidable, battle-hardened force.

At the same time, Major Abdilla deployed his force behind Major Clutterbuck's cannons. Clutterbuck was desperately keen to try out his rockets. The mounted archers took up positions on the left and right flanks of the Viking Army to ensure that they were fully surrounded and that there was no easy escape route.

The Battle of Hanley Swan started with a combined cannonading. Over one hundred and eighty cannons blasted away at the trapped Vikings. The British commanders decided to carry on with this tactic until they had exhausted all of the munitions. The smell of death was in the air. In reality, it was the combined smell of blood, guts, and shit.

It wasn't a battle. It was a slaughter. But then the Vikings did not deserve mercy. Ask the women who had been tortured and raped to see what they thought. Ask the men who had been tortured and castrated to see what they thought. Ask the babies who had been burnt alive and eaten to see what they thought. Mercy had to be earned.

140

Chaos

Suddenly there were thousands of thunderbolts followed by deafening claps of thunder. And hailstones the size of beer glasses fell from the heavens. The Vikings cheered as they knew that help was on the way. The British just stared. Was their victory going to be torn away?

A gap in the sky opened, and out popped a few hundred Valkyries. The British had little defence against these formidable flying female killers. They were heavily armoured, fast, and deadly with both sword and hammer. The Musketeers fired volleys at them, but they weren't that accurate, and the Valkyries were too fast.

The cannoneers continued firing with impressive effect at the Viking mass. As a consequence, the Valkyries started targeting the cannons. It was becoming too difficult to reload them with a screaming Norse killing machine on your back. Then the witches targeted the mounted archers terrifying the horses with the objective of giving the Vikings an escape route.

The Fay countered the witches, who started exploding. It was quite shocking seeing one witch after another just explode. This terrified the horses even more, and the archers had to let them go. But at least it was a stalemate.

Major Clutterbuck chose the moment well and fired his complete barrage of rockets. They were more successful than he or anyone else could believe. The first round took out more than half of the Valkyries. They fell to the ground, shocked, dead, or dying. The dying that fell within the British area were soon helped on their way. These Nordic maidens died just like anyone else.

The Musketeers learnt to target them as a single battalion. This improved their chances of knocking them out of the sky. The cannons fired, and the rockets delivered their death-blows. The Vikings were being pounded to death, and the Valkyries ceased to be anything more than an irritation.

A British victory was on the cards.

141
The Gods

Odin, 'It's not going well in Midgard.'

Thor, 'Who gave them the power of gunpowder?'

Mimir, 'It was a wizard from the future.'

Odin, 'Why did he do that?'

Mimir, 'Because they were under attack by a malevolent force called the Slimenest. They needed a way of beating them.'

Odin, 'But wasn't time wound back? They should have forgotten all about it.'

Mimir, 'That is true, but magicians can remember no matter what we or anyone else does with time. They still remember the previous timeline.'

Thor, 'So they still remembered how to make gunpowder.'

Odin, 'In that case, shouldn't we just kill every magician, do another time-reversal and start again.'

Mimir, 'If you did that, the magicians would just reappear.'

Thor, 'Then we kill them again.'

Mimir, 'We could, but there are always consequences. These time reversals never work out as we expect, and they are the cause of the magic loss.'

Loki, 'Magic loss?'

Mimir, 'You may have noticed that there is a lot less magic in Midgard than there used to be. There are fewer magicians, witches, Druids and Fay people. Magic is leaving the world. Every time manipulation is stripping Midgard of magic. It is our fault, and it will come back and bite us.'

Thor, 'If we don't do something, our Viking Army will simply be eliminated, and our plans for a Norse empire on Midgard will come to an end.'

Odin, 'I suggest that we intervene.'

Mimir, 'If you do that, other forces will be activated.'

Odin, 'What other forces?'

Mimir, 'I can't tell you, but there are always equal counter-balancing forces when the gods directly interfere. Those are the rules.'

Odin, 'Sod the rules, who is with me?'

Thor, Freya, Baldur, and Loki were up for it. They dressed for battle and crossed the Bifrost, the rainbow bridge between Asgard and Midgard.

142
The Battle of Hanley Swan Continues

The Vikings were hiding behind their shields and piles of dead bodies. They were confident that their gods would save them.

Commanders Squire and Mannering now realised that the cannons had served their purpose. It was time to use the archers. A few thousand arrows would make their mark.

Then everything changed again. Huge bolts of lightning shot out of the sky, killing hundreds of archers. If there were cover, the men would have found it.

The sky opened again, and five giant figures floated in mid-air: Thor, Freya, Baldur, Loki, and Odin. Odin was the largest of the figures and stood in the middle slightly in front of the others. He stamped his staff and spoke.'

Odin, 'Men of Midgard, listen to me. It is your destiny to become part of the great Norse empire that we are creating. I offer you the chance to surrender and join our cause. You will be treated well. You will have treasure and good times, women to fuck and the possibility of eternal life in Valhalla. What more could a warrior want?'

Thor, 'Listen to my wise father, the father of us all. Accept his offer or die.'

Thomas watched in astonishment.

The Fairy Queen, 'As I said, few of us will survive this day.'

Thomas, 'It is a tempting offer.'

The Fairy Queen, 'What world are you living in?'

Thomas, 'What do you mean?'

The Fairy Queen, 'You are the thickest magician that I have ever met.'

Thomas, 'Thank you.'

The Fairy Queen, 'Their offer means the end of freedom and free will. Those who don't comply will be eliminated. It means the end of literature, the arts, music, and love. Women will just be second-class sex-objects. We must fight on.'

Thomas, 'When you put it that way, we have no choice.'

Odin, 'Men of Midgard, what is your answer?'

No one answered. In many ways, no one was qualified to answer, but Major Clutterbuck just said, 'Full barrage.'

Every rocket battery fired, causing a quite impressive pyrotechnic display that got nowhere near the gods. Thor responded in kind. Not a single rocket battery or rocketeer survived the massive lightning bolts. Major Clutterbuck was a fried husk of a man that simply crumbled to dust. Thomas cried out in horror. It was the cry that alerted the counter-balancing forces.

Odin, 'You see what happened to that fool. Join us or die.'

Commander Mannering, 'Great Sir, there is no one here who has the authority to answer you.'

Odin, 'Bring me the elders here in an hour or you will die. I mean, what I say.'

Thor, 'Do you understand?'

Commander Mannering, 'We do.'

Thor, 'In the meantime, you will cease all hostilities.'

The British used the opportunity to take care of their wounded and remove the dead. Weapons were cleaned and prepared for reuse.

The Vikings used it as an opportunity to do a runner. They left the battleground and headed towards Guarlford. Major Abdilla moved his forces back to Great Malvern in case the Vikings turned towards the hills.

Commander Mannering ordered one of his aides to get the elders back here as soon as possible.

Commander Mannering, 'So, what did you make of that?'

Commander Squire, 'This always seems to happen. Just when we get the enemy trapped, something metaphysical happens.'

Commander Mannering, 'Are they really gods?'

Commander Squire, 'Who knows? I certainly have no intention of worshipping them.'

143
The Gods, Part Two

Odin, 'I think that went well.'

Mimir, 'You think so? They are not like your Norsemen. They will never worship you. They are not followers. Believe me.'

Odin, 'Nonsense. They will follow like everyone else, or they will die.'

Mimir, 'In that case, I fear they will die.'

Odin, 'Then so be it.'

Mimir, 'Is that what you want?'

Thor, 'We need new lands and young women for our men.'

Mimir, 'We are not short of land. We have the whole of Russia.'

Odin, 'But we want more.'

Mimir, 'But you are not going to have the men and women to populate these islands. If you don't occupy, you will not be able to retain them.'

Thor, 'We need women of child-bearing age for our men. With good northern seed, these islands will be brimming with youngsters.'

Mimir, 'That won't be true because you kill the girl babies at birth.'

Thor, 'They bring no honour.'

Mimir, 'But you obviously need them to grow a population. Instead, you feed them to the pigs.'

Odin, 'That is our way.'

Mimir, 'Then you will never have a steady growing population. Just think about it.'

Odin, 'We don't grow women. We steal them.'

Mimir, 'As your empire grows, who are you going to steal the women from?'

Thor, 'You think too much.'

Mimir, 'My job is to provide counsel. That is what I'm doing.'

Odin, 'Thank you for that, but we have our own plans.'

Mimir, 'What are you going to do?'

Odin, 'If they refuse our offer, we will kill them all.'

Mimir, 'Then?'

Thor, 'Then we have won.'

Freya, 'I think we should listen to Mimir.'

Odin, 'Keep out of this. It is men's talk.'

Freya, 'Fuck you. Listen to Mimir or suffer the consequences.'

Odin, 'I will listen to who I want.'

Freya, 'But you don't learn.'

Baldur, 'The hour is almost up.'

Loki, 'I'm looking forward to fucking a few of those British roses.'

Freya, 'Try to keep your cock in your pants. We need a plan.'

Odin. 'If they say no, then we kill them.'

Freya, 'Is that everyone in these islands?'

Odin, 'Of course not. Just the people in Malvern.'

Baldur, 'What about their armies in London and Oxford?'

Thor, 'We kill them as well?'

Freya, 'And the Fay?'

Odin, 'Some of them.'

Freya, 'I'm not taking any part in this nonsense.'

Odin, 'Please stay with us. We need your involvement.'

Freya, 'I will stay, but I'm not happy.'

Odin, 'Thank you.'

144
The Plot Thickens

Thomas, 'So what happens next?'.

The Fairy Queen, 'I think you know.'

Thomas, 'I honestly don't.'

The Fairy Queen, 'Well, the gods return, and the elders speak.'

Thomas, 'Then what happens?'

The Fairy Queen, 'The War of the Magics begins.'

Thomas, 'What does that mean.'

The Fairy Queen, 'You are all questions. Don't you have any answers?'

Thomas, 'I wish I did.'

The Fairy Queen, 'I've got to go and prepare myself. We are going to need all of the magic we can muster.'

Thomas, 'What should I do?'

The Fairy Queen, 'Whatever feels right.'

Thomas, 'What does that mean?'

The Fairy Queen, 'Questions, questions, questions. Feel what is needed and do what is right. That is all anyone can do.'

Thomas, 'I wish Robin was here. She would understand these things.'

The Fairy Queen, 'Goodbye. It might be my final goodbye as few of us will survive this night.'

Thomas, 'Please be careful.'

And in a twinkle, she was gone, and Thomas sat alone on the Beacon. Life just seemed like a paradox to him. What should he do? Where should he go? How come others knew what to do, and he didn't?

145
The Elders Arrive

The elders were literally dragged from their cells, thrown onto horseback and taken to the battleground. Little attempt had been made to respect their position and to be honest, none was deserved.

The remaining elders were marched into a tent with Commanders Mannering and Squire.

Commander Squire, 'So you are the so-called rulers of this land.'

Elder Three, 'How dare you talk to us like that?'

Commander Squire, 'You are the fuckers that got us into this mess. If I had my way, you would be hanging from a tree.'

Elder Three, 'If I had my way, your whole Army would be fed to the crows.'

Commander Squire hit him across the cheek.

Commander Squire, 'Listen here, you lump of turd, show some respect or that hanging won't be far away.'

Elder Eight, 'How can we help you?'

Commander Mannering, 'We had a visitation from the Asgardian gods. This is their offer ad verbatim:

"Men of Midgard, listen to me. It is your destiny to become part of the great Norse empire that we are creating. I offer you the chance to surrender and join our cause. You will be treated well. You will have treasure and good times, women to fuck and the possibility of eternal life in Valhalla. What more could a warrior want?"

'They have demanded to talk to you lot: the elders.'

Elder Eight, 'What do you want us to say?'

Commander Squire, 'What would you say given a free hand?'

Elder Eight, 'We would join the Norse empire. We have already had this offer in the past and were forced to accept it.'

Commander Squire, 'What do you mean?'

Elder Eight, 'Odin and Thor visited us with the same offer. When we weighed everything up, we decided that their offer was the best way forward for our people. It would probably save the most lives at the end of the day. We weren't happy with the terms, but our bargaining ability was poor, to say the least.'

Commander Mannering, 'So you are saying that the contents of the proclamation are effectively their terms.'

Elder Nine, 'Yes, that is the case. The part about us being dukes was their idea. We weren't really interested, which they couldn't understand, and some of us were already dukes. Most of us are beyond mere treasure. That has never really been our driver.'

Commander Squire, 'Let's look at the terms of the Proclamation, or should we call it the surrender terms?'

The proclamation notice was displayed on the table:

That Grand Britannica will become a formal member of the Viking Empire and will follow Viking laws and customs:

- That a Viking King will be appointed
- That the ten elders will be appointed as dukes with the nominated estates as per the agreement
- That the capital of the country will be London
- That the British Army and Navy will be dissolved
- That the Vikings will be responsible for the defence of the country
- That the Druids will have the province of Wales
- That witchcraft will be legalised
- That all magicians will be sentenced to death
- That all members of the Malander family will be treated as traitors and executed
- That all officers in the British Army and Navy will be treated as traitors and executed
- That all Fay creatures will be hunted down and executed
- That all property is now under the control of the king and his ducal supporters
- That all courts will be closed down
- That all Lord Protectors will be treated as traitors and executed
- That each port will be controlled by a Viking port- master.'

Elder Nine, 'I'm sure that some parts of it can be renegotiated.'

Commander Mannering, 'So what do we tell our Asgardian friends?'

Elder Nine, 'This is your problem now.'

Commander Mannering, 'They want to talk to you.'

Elder Nine, 'Our time has ended, which is probably a good thing. You are the new power in the land. Tell us what to say.'

Elder Three, 'I object.'

Elder Nine, 'Fuck off. What do you want me to say?'

Elder Three, 'It should be the Deputy Chief Elder who responds.'

Elder Nine, 'He turned out to be a female magician. From what I've ascertained, it was her that invited Odin and Thor to a meeting. It was never their idea. We have just been played like everyone else.'

146
The Gods Return

There was an almighty crack of thunder, and the gods reappeared.

Odin, 'Do you have the elders?'

Commander Mannering, 'I do.' The elders presented themselves.'

Odin, 'As the rulers of this island, what is your decision?'

Elder Nine, 'My Lord Odin, we request more time to respond. We need to consult with the Deputy Chief Elder before we give you our answer.'

Odin, 'That shouldn't be difficult.'

In front of them, Freya turned into the Deputy Chief Elder, then into Rachel and then back into Freya.

Elder Nine, 'This has been a total set-up.'

Odin, 'Indeed it has, but what is your decision?'

Elder Nine, 'Fuck you, we go down fighting you to the end.'

No one expected that. The other elders were shocked. The military were shocked, and even the gods were shocked. But then a quick lightning bolt ended his existence, and then, there was one less elder.

Odin, 'I regard that as a declaration of war.'

Lightning bolts came crashing down, and the entire British Army in Malvern ran for cover. Not that cover helped much. The gods started running amok, killing everything in sight. The Army tried to respond, but exposure meant death.

Then massive bolts of magical energy from the Fay rocked the gods. Whatever they were standing on literally shook. Odin had to lean on his staff to maintain his decorum, and Thor used his hammer to achieve some equilibrium. Fairy magic was used to close the Asgardian portal. There were loud cheers from the military. But it wasn't long before the gods were back.

Odin was fuming. He pointed his staff at the source of the fairy magic and used cosmic energy to kill thousands of fairies. It was particularly tragic as these were beings who were almost immortal. Fairykind never recovered from this disaster, but the Fairy Queen continued the onslaught. Thor's hammer was suspended in mid-air, a feat that no foe had ever achieved before. Both Loki and Baldur were temporarily blinded and had to retire. Odin called upon more gods to come forward and join the fight.

The British Army pursued the Vikings, picking off as many individuals as they could without exposing themselves. But then the gods turned seriously nasty: almost the entire woodland around Malvern was set on fire, packs of savage man-eating wolves were released, giant eagles attacked the Army in Great Malvern, and acid rain burnt any skin that it touched. Lightning bolts destroyed both men and buildings.

Thomas did his best, but in the scheme of things, it made little impression. The forces mounted against him and the Fay were just too great. He recognised Rachel's magic and focused on countering it. He was very impressed by the Fay contribution, but it was obvious that they were going to lose. It was a case of the moth fighting the light or children fighting the gods.

Thomas sat down on the Beacon, put his head between his hands and wondered what he could do. Then an old man sat down next to him. He recognised his presence but couldn't quite make out who he was.

Then a voice said, 'It is I.'

Then Thomas knew that it was him: his future self.

Thomas, 'Hello, Merlin.'

Merlin, 'Hello, Merlin. We are here to rescue you.'

Thomas, 'Who is we?'

147
Godly Peril

There was no doubt that Grand Britannica was being punished for its crimes. Odin's call to arms brought forward Sif, Tyr, Vidor, Hel, and Vali to assist in the murdering of the innocent. The gods now just killed anything that moved, whether British or Viking. They were on a merciless killing spree similar to one of their hunting expeditions.

The Elementi caused the gods quite a few problems with their power over the four elements. They put most of the fires out with water and earth. They sucked the air out of the god's bodies, but it didn't seem to harm them in any way. The Bansheei made so much noise that the gods couldn't communicate with each other. The Gremli caused the rainbow bridge to twist and turn. As far as the Fay were concerned, it was a fight to the death, and they were dying in huge numbers.

Giant fireballs smashed into Malvern. Razor-sharp icicles over ten foot long crashed from the sky. Hordes of savage creatures were let loose. Every conceivable nastiness was unleashed on Malvern. It was hell on Earth for the inhabitants but a great piece of fun for the gods. They hadn't been this active in years.

Thomas, 'Well, if the cavalry is coming, they better get here soon, or there will be nothing left to save.'

Merlin, 'Don't worry, they will be here shortly.'

Thomas, 'You heard about Robin.'

Merlin, 'She was my sister too.'

Thomas, 'Of course I forgot. How long did I take to get over it?'

Merlin, 'You never did.' And they hugged each other. Or rather, they hugged themselves.

Merlin, 'I have to warn you that things are going to get a bit weird.'

Thomas, 'They can't get any weirder.'

Merlin, 'Believe me, they will.' But this was another different Merlin.

Merlin, 'It will get so weird that your brain will find it hard to accept.'

But that was yet another Merlin.

Merlin, 'Hello Thomas.'

Merlin, 'Hi Thomas.'

Merlin, 'How are you doing?'

In the next hour, over two hundred Merlins arrived and were all sitting around the top of the Beacon.

Thomas, 'So who is the real Merlin?'

Merlin, 'We all are. We have come here from different times.'

Thomas, 'I don't understand.'

Merlin, 'Well, let's say that I'm today's Merlin. That one is yesterday's Merlin. The Merlin over there is the Merlin from last week. We are all the genuine article.'

Thomas, 'What happens if an earlier Merlin gets killed.'

Merlin, 'Don't worry about time paradoxes. Now I have to warn you things are going to get even weirder, but we need all the help we can get.'

148
More Weirdness

Having two hundred versions of you was pretty weird. In fact, it was so weird that it was impossible to comprehend. You suddenly realised that you were just another Merlin. Your own uniqueness was compromised, but it was hard to believe that they were you, especially as only the latest versions had the full memory set. They knew what was going to happen to you or rather their earlier selves.

One of the Merlins, and it was very hard to differentiate them, said that it was going to get weirder. That didn't seem possible until Lady Malander arrived. They ran to each other and kissed and hugged. Thomas was immediately embarrassed, but then he realised that his other selves knew everything. Then another Lady Malander arrived until there were nearly two hundred of them. There had been a lot of hugging and kissing.

This was followed by two hundred Bettys and even more hugs and kisses. Then came the greatest shock of all: Robin arrived. Thomas hugged her and sobbed and hugged her some more, but then another Robin arrived and then another. There were now eight hundred magical entities on the Beacon who had a job to do.

Lady Malander, Betty and Robin called for the help of the Angeli, and the call was accepted. Almost immediately, nearly ten thousand sword carrying angels appeared on the Beacon. The cavalry had arrived. To be fair, this had all been previously agreed upon.

But then the oldest of the Merlins, the one who had seen it all before, called for Alexander in the name of Arthur. Most of the Merlins had no idea what was going on, and who the hell was Arthur?

For the second time in Merlin's life, the hills quaked, and the beasts of great monstrosity were released. The giant white dragons who have slept for centuries under the Malvern Hills made their presence known. The army of eight hundred magicians, ten thousand angels and three dragons were ready to do battle with the Gods of Asgard.

149
Another Battle of Malvern

The Merlins wondered how you battle alien gods that appear in the sky. Are they in the atmosphere, or are they in a different dimension? You could possibly throw things at them, but could you arm-wrestle?

The Fay magic seemed to cause them distress, so it was possible to interact with them from Earth, but would it be better to go to their realm? While the Merlins were pontificating, the Dragons and the Angels attacked. They got fed up with the pontificating. There appeared to be some sort of rule that the level of pontificating increased in direct proportion to the number of Merlins involved.

Few entities could survive a full-on blast of fiery dragon breath. It wasn't just the intense heat but also the unique mixture of dangerous chemicals involved, including acids, corrosives, poisons, toxins, venom, and radioactive elements. But that was nothing compared to the power of the magic involved. It was intense, intimidating, and alarming. It was alarming because it was unpredictable. Magicians like to be in a position to counter magic. Here countering was difficult because the dragon just threw raw, unrefined magic at the victim. There was no structure or purpose, just potent magic.

Dragon magic wasn't good or evil. It wasn't black or white. It had a unique purity of its own. And, of course, it wasn't encountered that often. The Asgard Gods weren't sure what to do. They had a plethora of strange beasts in Yggdrasil but no dragons. They decided to run.

The dragons and the angels stormed through the dimensional gap onto Bifrost, the Rainbow Bridge. Heimdall stood firm guarding the passage. He used Gjallarhorn, his giant horn, to warn Asgard that they were being invaded.

Heimdall shouted in a deep manly voice, 'You shall not pass.'

Alexander, the White Dragon, quietly said, 'You will let us pass, or you will die.'

Heimdall, 'I have no fear of you. I have fought off the ice giants and Surtur, the fire demon.'

Alexander, 'I have warned you. Let us pass or die.'

Heimdall, 'Do your worst.'

And Alexander's worst was enough. One blast of breath melted Heimdall's famed armour. The second blast stripped him of all his flesh, and the third blast turned his skeleton to dust. Odin thought that Heimdall was invulnerable, but clearly, he was wrong.

The combined cabal of magicians, after some further pontifications, decided to follow the Dragons and Angels. The pontification was getting a bit silly as the Merlins couldn't agree with each other. Some of the Robins had to stop some of the Merlins fighting. Some of the Lady Malanders told them that they needed to focus on the enemy. Anyway, they arrived on Bifrost.

They found Odin trying to negotiate with Alexander with the angels nearby, screaming for blood. All of the Merlins had always thought that angels were nice fluffy things that espoused love and tranquillity. But if you think about it, they have swords, and there have been many battles in heaven. This lot were itching for a fight.

Now one of the first things a magician learns is that you don't negotiate with a dragon. They don't negotiate. They accept a mission, complete it, and return home. They are simple rules that dragons follow to the letter.

Alexander was tasked with destroying the Vikings. The only Vikings he could see were in front of him, and his patience was wearing thin. And it was time for bed.

150
Back on Earth

Commanders Mannering and Squire were rather disconcerted by things. Things like Nordic gods killing their men with lightning bolts. Things like the elders not being as villainous as first thought. Things like the Fay battling the gods. Things like Lady Malander coming back to life. Things like there being hundreds of Merlins. And the thing list just went on and on.

They managed to pull themselves together and then decided to kill every single Viking they could find. There would be no mercy, just death to the uncouth, barbaric bastards.

If nothing else, it would make them feel better. They had the men, the equipment, and the desire. Nothing would stop them. And then time was frozen. Nothing moved. Absolutely nothing. Everything was subject to the agreement.

151
The Deal

Alexander, the White Dragon, 'Prepare to die.'

Odin, 'I wish to negotiate.'

Alexander, 'Dragons don't negotiate. Prepare to die.'

Odin, 'Well, it is about time you did.'

Alexander puffed up his enormous belly and prepared a killing blast that would eliminate every Viking in sight and possibly a considerable number of the inhabitants of Asgard. He didn't see them as gods, just beings who were stopping him from sleeping.

Alexander, 'I have warned you.'

Hot steam was flooding from Alexander's nostrils. His patience that was already thin was getting thinner.

Merlin, 'So what does mighty Odin want to negotiate?'

Odin, 'Who are you? What right do you have to talk to a god?'

Merlin, 'I might be the only person who can stop Alexander from roasting you alive along with half of Asgard.'

Odin, 'I would like to propose a peace treaty. While that is going on, shall we freeze time to save any more pointless bloodshed?'

Merlin, 'You didn't seem so worried about bloodletting earlier.'

Odin, 'That was then, and this is now.'

Merlin, 'I agree to that.' And time was frozen. This caused a considerable drain on magic, but that wasn't the purpose.

Odin, 'So who are you?'

Merlin, 'We have met before.'

Odin, 'You are that stinking wizard who caused us so many problems. How come there are so many of you?'

Merlin, 'The more, the merrier.'

Odin, 'So is it merriment you are looking for?'

Merlin, 'No, I want to understand your negotiating position, or I will order Alexander to fry you, and our angels are itching to kill. This could be the end of Asgard.'

Odin, 'Asgard can't end.'

Merlin, 'Do you want to test that?'

Odin, 'You already know our terms.'

Merlin, 'You mean this:

- That a Viking King will be appointed
- That the ten elders will be appointed as dukes with the nominated estates as per the agreement
- That the capital of the country will be London
- That the British Army and Navy will be dissolved
- That the Vikings will be responsible for the defence of the country
- That the Druids will have the province of Wales
- That witchcraft will be legalised
- That all magicians will be sentenced to death
- That all members of the Malander family will be treated as traitors and executed
- That all officers in the British Army and Navy will be treated as traitors and executed
- That all Fay creatures will be hunted down and executed
- That all property is now under the control of the king and his ducal supporters
- That all courts will be closed down
- That all Lord Protectors will be treated as traitors and executed
- That each port will be controlled by a Viking port master.'

Odin, 'They are our minimum terms.'

Merlin, 'Alexander, you may proceed with the conflagration. Make sure you get that fat one first.' Not that Merlin could hide from his weight problem.

Odin, 'I understand. There is room for movement.'

Merlin, 'What do you suggest?'

Odin, 'We could divide the land up between us?'

Merlin, 'I can see where you are coming from.' And he handed over a map showing a suggested breakdown.

Odin, 'But how could you have known this?'

Merlin, 'One day, you will work it out. I propose the following, and you will accept:

- The lands in red are Viking lands: Danelaw
- The lands in brown and yellow are British
- The lands in grey are Celtic
- The Vikings will treat British subjects in their land with respect
- Any British person in Danelaw is entitled to move to Britain
- The Vikings will not invade any British or Celtic lands under threat of a Dragon attack
- The Vikings will help the British defend their lands against external invaders and vice versa
- Each area will manage its territory as it sees fit
- There will be no persecution of the Fay or the magicians
- Witchcraft will not be legalised
- Soldiers of each side will be given free passage home
- There will be regular meetings of a Council to resolve any issues.'

Odin thought about it and accepted it. In fact, he was quite thrilled by his negotiating success.

Merlin, 'You understand that we have the power to enforce it, but I would rather agree to a pact of goodwill.'

Odin, 'You have that pact.'

Merlin, 'Alexander, 'You have completed your mission.' And Alexander dissolved before their eyes, back to the land of nod.

Ten thousand angels winged their way back home.

The Merlins, Robins, Betties and Lady Malanders had a tour of Asgard. Some stayed. Freya made sure that she kept out of their way.

152
The Aftermath

Thomas and the oldest Merlin returned to the Beacon and sat down as before. It would be a couple of hours before Time started up again. Thomas, 'I have so many questions.'

Merlin, 'I suspect that I have so few answers.'

Thomas, 'Why did you give so much away?'

Merlin, 'You mean land?'

Thomas, 'Exactly.'

Merlin, 'I am you in the future. I know things. I know that the agreement we made was the agreement that was made. I was just following history.'

Thomas, 'But you could have changed it.'

Merlin, 'But we gained so much.'

Thomas, 'It doesn't seem that way.'

Merlin, 'We gained fresh blood. We gained mastery of the seas. We forged a great nation that would be respected throughout the world. We created the biggest empire the world has ever seen. We wrote great literature. We saved the world, and we had fun.

'It was the forging of the British and Viking spirits that did it.'

Thomas, 'I see, but what will the military think?'

Merlin, 'They won't like it at first, but this gives them and us peace. And believe me, we need that?'

Thomas, 'Will there be another war with the Vikings?'

Merlin, 'There will be some skirmishes over disputed land, but the Vikings will adopt our ways because they are the right ways. Eventually, we will become one nation.'

Thomas, 'I don't understand the appearance of the dragons. I was told that they only appear once for each Duke of the Malander family.'

Merlin, 'That is true.'

Thomas, 'So there must be another duke.'

Merlin, 'It would seem that way.'

Thomas, 'Is that all you are going to say?'

Merlin, 'Yes.'

Thomas, 'It was just fabulous seeing Robin, Betty, and Lady Malander.'

Merlin, 'Yes, but there are always consequences.'

Thomas, 'Like what?'

Merlin, 'You will find out soon enough.'

Thomas, 'Are all Merlins so enigmatic?'

He nodded and said, 'How come you still call yourself Thomas?'

They laughed.

Thomas, 'What do we say to the Fay?'

Merlin, 'About what?'

Thomas, 'They have given so much.'

Merlin, 'Their time has gone.'

Thomas, 'Is magic dying?'

Merlin, 'It's not dying, but it is leaving this world.'

Thomas, 'Where is it going?'

Merlin, 'I wish I knew. Anyway, I'm going now.'

Thomas, 'Who is going to explain everything to everybody?'

Merlin, 'When time starts again, they will know.'

153
The Aftermath, Part 2

Thomas was rather sad to see Merlin go, but then there had been far too many for his liking.

Then he was joined by an old friend.

Thomas, 'You made it.'

The Fairy Queen, 'I did, but so many of my family didn't.'

Thomas, 'I'm really sorry about that.'

The Fairy Queen, 'Don't be. They did their duty and did it well.'

Thomas, 'I was extremely impressed by the Fay's fighting ability and cleverness.'

The Fairy Queen, 'Yes, we were clever and brave and more or less ignored as I said we would be.'

Thomas, 'I fear that you are right.'

The Fairy Queen, 'Anyway, I've come to say goodbye.'

Thomas, 'Where are you going?'

The Fairy Queen, 'The brave amongst us are following the magic.'

Thomas, 'So where is that?'

The Fairy Queen, 'I wish I knew.'

Thomas, 'That does sound brave.'

The Fairy Queen, 'Thank you for being a friend. As humans go, you are not that bad.'

Thomas, 'Thank you, my Queen. That is a compliment, indeed.'

The End